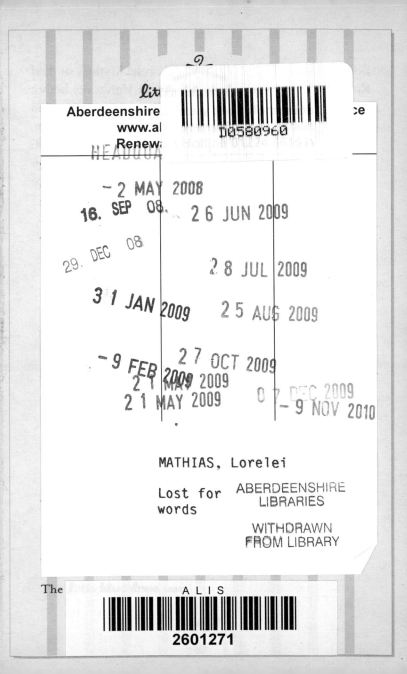

Born in Buckinghamshire in 1980, Lorelei Mathias studied English and Philosophy at Birmingham University before travelling and working abroad. She now lives in London where she has worked in both publishing and advertising. Her first novel, *Step on it, Cupid* was published in 2006 and she is also one of the contributing authors to *Common Ground* by 26, a collaborative group of people passionate about words.

Also by Lorelei Mathias

Step on it, Cupid
'Your Time Starts Now: Questioning What's Real
in David Lodge's Birmingham', in *Common Ground:
Around Britain in 30 Writers*, ed. John Simmons

Lost for Words

Lorelei Mathias

Typeset in TimesELB7 by Avon DataSet Ltd,
Bidford-on-Avon, Warwickshire

Printed and bound in Great Britain by Clays Ltd, St Ives plc

Headline's policy is to use papers that are natural, renewable, and
recyclable products and made from wood grown in sustainable forests. The
logging and manufacturing processes are expected to conform to the
environmental regulations of the country of origin.

HEADLINE PUBLISHING GROUP
A division of Hachette Livre UK Ltd
London

little
black
dress

Extract from *Fail Better* by Zadie Smith, first printed in the Guardian in
January 2007, and reprinted here with kind permission of A P Watt Ltd, on
behalf of Zadie Smith.

First published in Great Britain in 2007
by LITTLE BLACK DRESS
An imprint of HEADLINE PUBLISHING GROUP

First published in paperback in 2007
by LITTLE BLACK DRESS
An imprint of HEADLINE PUBLISHING GROUP

A LITTLE BLACK DRESS paperback
1

Cataloguing in Publication Data is available from the British Library

978 0 7553 3274 8

Prin   plc

Headl   e and
recyclable   rests. The
logging   to the

www.littleblackdressbooks.co.uk
www.headline.co.uk

To my mother, for all her lovely quirks

Contents

Contents

A Truth Universally Acknowledged

Paddington Press
Mercury Publishing Group Ltd.
10 Bishops Bridge Mews
London W2
editorial@paddingtonpress.com
www.paddingtonpress.com

Monday 12 June 2006

Dear Maggie,

Thank you so much for approaching Paddington Press with your manuscript, which I have read and enjoyed.

Initially, I couldn't put it down. I loved the concept, and I was gripped by the early exchange of emails between Gladys and George. From day one, when he successfully bid for her old Teasmade on eBay, through the weeks of online banter, until he finally plucked up the courage to ask her out for tea, I followed their ensuing romance with a keen eye. But I'm sorry to say that for me (and others may well disagree) this soon wore off. So much so that, by the time they married in Darjeeling, I felt the tension and energy had all but died, and I didn't feel I cared as much about the characters as I'd hoped to.

It might be that there's something missing. More bite? A quicker pace? Or is it that we've all just seen enough in the way of cyber-borne romance lately? Either way, in this increasingly cut-throat women's fiction marketplace, I'm sorry to say that we won't be able to find a slot for *Sold to the Highest Bidder: Sex and the eBay Generation*. That said, I do think your concept is an interesting one, and I wish you much luck with finding a suitable home for your work.

With the very best of wishes,

Daisy Allen
Editorial Assistant
Paddington Press

Rereading the letter one more time for good measure, she hit 'Control P'. She waited for the printer to make its beeping and clanking noises, and began tidying the already immaculate stationery on her desk. Then, having counted thirty seconds in her head, she walked over to the other side of the office. Picking up her tenth rejection letter of the day from the printer, she took her black Parker pen and made three small, elegant strokes across the page, before returning to her desk and adding the letter to the ever-increasing pile.

She smoothed back her ruler-straight strawberry-blonde hair and checked the clock: 11.38 a.m., Monday.

Hurrah. Halfway into her to-do list, and it wasn't even lunchtime. She picked up a red pen and ticked off tasks here and there. With glee, she remembered a job she'd completed before even adding it to the list. Looking behind her to check that none of her workmates were close enough to see, she took a glisteningly sharp HB pencil and quickly added the task to the end of the list. Then, picking up her red pen again, she drew a thick line through the newly added and already completed task, revelling in the satisfaction, although deep down she could hear a scathing voice in her head chanting, 'Daisy Allen, you really, really need to get out more.'

She jumped up as her phone buzzed with a text message. Maybe it was Miles, she tried not to think, as she picked up her new mobile and fought her way through the befuddling new technical functions to her inbox.

'Disaster. Total. Utter. No credit. Drop everything, ring me ASAP. Bx'

It was Belle – identifiable by her punchy, panicky style, rather than by her phone number. She was forever losing her phone and having to buy a replacement. It was 11.39 on Monday; what predicament could Daisy's sister possibly have managed to get herself into already? Looking around to check her boss Belinda was still in her Monday-morning catch-up, Daisy picked up her work phone and hit number one on her speed dial.

'What's happened this time?' she asked when Isabella Allen screeched hello. Daisy's sister was two and a half years older than her, but this made no difference to the fact that she was forever getting herself into pickles.

'It's horrendous. I've ruined everything. And it was going so, SO well!'

'Slow down. Deep breaths, my love. What's happened?'

'Do you remember last night, after my date with the curious George? How phenomenally well it went? How I simply couldn't wait to see him again and was literally counting the hours, thinking he could be The One?'

Daisy thought back to the night before. She'd been nursing a pot of Ben & Jerry's cookie dough, glued against her better judgement to the new series of *Lost*, and finding it to be both gripping and infuriating in equal measure. Belle had come bursting in, full of romantic anecdotes from her evening out with George: *the* enigmatic man of the moment whom she'd diligently been pursuing for as long as four days. A long time for Belle, who, unlike Daisy, became very easily restless when it came to men.

'I remember. Why, what's gone wrong? Have you met someone else already?'

'Worse. I've made a textual error that only the most sympathetic god of telecommunications could possibly fix. This morning, I was half asleep, lying in bed deciding which temp agency to ring and pester, when, instead, I thought I'd bash out a quick text to Hannah and tell her how amazing the date had been. So in my half-asleep state I wrote a message entirely unfit for male consumption . . . all about how unbelievably sexy George was, what lush eyes he has . . .' Belle paused for breath, as though the trauma of recounting her tale was becoming too much, '. . . how he'd been the perfect gentleman to me all night, and that I couldn't wait for us to spend more time together – I pretty much said I couldn't stop thinking about him, that . . . I wanted to have his babies.'

Daisy tried not to laugh. 'So? I don't quite see what the

problem is, love. What you've said is – reasonably – normal behaviour. Hannah's your friend, I'm sure she can take that kind of language from you. Can't she?'

'Well, yes, so you'd think. If only I hadn't been thinking about George when I sent it. You see – instead of actually sending this God-awful pervy text to Hannah, I actually fucked up. Royally. I was scrolling through my address book, saw George's pretty face in my head, and then instead of clicking Hannah, I went and sent it to George . . . he's the name right before hers in my phone, you see?! I mean . . . I may as well just go and become a circus freak now, be done with it – probably less painful in the long run.'

Daisy sighed. She could have seen this one coming. From Belle, this was entirely normal behaviour. Hardly a week went by when Belle wasn't ringing Daisy, in near hysterics, asking her to bail her out of another fine mess.

'Right. When was this?' Daisy said efficiently, getting to business.

'About two minutes ago. I've been sitting here in a state of shock since then, desperately trying to cancel the sending by pressing 'C' over and over, which apparently my phone is now completely immune to. Then I tried turning it off, throwing it across the room. Stamping on it. Nothing helped. I turned it back on, and there it was. Sitting smugly in my sent items, twiddling its thumbs, like it *knew* the trouble it had caused, and it *loved* it!' Belle stopped, hearing Daisy laugh.

'It's not funny,' Belle wailed, in between her sister's cruel cackles, 'Anyway, after catatonically staring at my phone for another whole minute, I decided to ring you. Dais – what the hell am I going to do? George will think I'm a psychotic freak! It's not fair! I really LIKE this one!'

'OK – there might still be time.' Daisy thought quickly. 'Have you thought about calling him? He could be away from his phone. He could be asleep. What work does he do again?' Daisy paused while she leafed through the logistics in her mind. 'He might've left his phone at home. Lost it. It could be out of battery, out of signal. There are just soooo many variables – any one of them could save your ass here. Deep breaths. Let's think positively'. We can fix this. Where does he live?'

'Oh, love you, Daisy chain. Where would I be without your logical brain? He – Oh, I don't know where he works! But he's a bouncer in the evenings, which means he could still be asleep. Hold on – maybe I could go round to his? He left me his card which has his home address on – somewhere in Dulwich, I think. But what if he's got the text already? He won't want to see me, he'll probably be on the phone to his lawyer, filing for a restraining order already . . .'

Daisy could hear the click-clock of her boss's three-inch heels on the wooden floor approaching the editorial department. 'B – I've got to go. But listen. Try his phone. If it's turned off, you're in with a chance. But! Don't do it from your mobile – do it from a payphone or something. Then peg it over there, try and get to his phone before he does.'

Just then Belinda appeared, a tower of manuscripts balancing precariously in her arms. She looked meaningfully at Daisy, just in time to allow Daisy's voice to change down a pitch. 'No, we don't have those in yet. Just typescripts at the moment. But I'll let you know when we have proofs, if you can give me your number and address?'

'Daisy! Don't go all Little Miss Efficient on me!'

shrieked Belle from the other end as Daisy wrote down these fictional details on to her notepad. Belle persisted squealing, 'Hon – can't you call him from your work phone for me? My nearest payphone's two miles away!'

'No, I'm afraid not. But thank you so much for your interest. I'll call you as soon as they're in. Best of luck with your article.'

As Daisy hung up the phone, Belinda eyed the receiver suspiciously. Daisy smiled saccharinely, and clicked on to her PC to check her already checked emails.

'Any messages for me?' Belinda asked.

Daisy shook her head. Belinda strode off towards her own very large corner office, dusted off the sign on her door marked Belinda Bancroft, Head of General Fiction, and closed the door firmly behind her. Daisy picked up her pen and straightened out her black-rimmed glasses. She looked at the ever-increasing piles of unread manuscripts, which seemed to grow in proportion to how many letters went out. She leaned over, grabbed a bunch of them, and began to read.

It never got any easier. Despite all her best attempts to be cold, hard and ruthless, Daisy couldn't help but find it terrifying, having this amount of responsibility and power over people's dreams. Although she loved being an editorial assistant, she still struggled with the rejection side of the job. There was always the same twinge of guilt that accompanied the ritualistic sealing of a 'No Thank You' envelope. Every day she spent crushing the hopes of budding authors, young and old, from all over the world, still it didn't seem to get any less disappointing – she always felt desperately sorry for the ones that got away – still wished she could publish them all.

Belinda's advice on the matter was simple. 'Oh, grow up, dear,' she'd barked on Daisy's second day, 'You can't go around being all oversensitive like that. You'll get tougher. You'll have to, if you're going to survive.'

But that was almost two and a half years ago. Daisy was still waiting for this much-fabled resilience to kick in. Maybe it just wasn't in her nature? Maybe it never would be. Much as she tried not to be, she'd always been something of a fragile, pathetic soul, perpetually teased by her peers for feeling sorry for the smallest of things. At school, for having to leave the room on the day of frog-dissection. On holiday, on the last day of her trip to Morocco, for giving her whole bag of shopping away to a beggar in Marrakesh. Belinda Bancroft, on the other hand, had a much thicker skin, after twenty-five years at the helm of the Paddington Press 'Just Say No' academy of publishing. Admittedly Paddington was just one meagre imprint of the Mercury Group Ltd., one of Britain's largest publishing conglomerates. But as one of the most senior women in the company, Belinda could happily make or break an author with one fell swoop of her pen, and felt no remorse when yet another batch of hopeful manuscripts went slushing towards the recycling area.

When she'd first arrived at the large revolving double doors of Mercury, fresh-faced and wide-eyed, her literature degree from Durham still wet on the page, Daisy hadn't realised how many soul-crushing letters she was going to have to write to budding authors. Worse, she'd never imagined quite how many budding authors in need of soul-crushing letters there really were out there. Despite having sent out twenty-three rejection letters this week alone (each of them a teeny bit different; she always tried to make them seem as un-template-like as possible), the pile of unread wannabe books still continued to grow with increasing speed. For every three letters she sent out, another five stacks of double-spaced, neatly typed manuscripts would come shooting into the vast post room at Mercury, itching to be read and to be deemed worthy of a publisher. 'Pick me, pick me,' she could hear them all weeping to themselves. Still, one of these days she hoped to discover something different. She hoped to stumble across some beautifully choreographed words – something unique and inspiring that she'd be able to put forward for consideration. In her darker moments, she'd go as far as imagining the moment itself. She'd be working late on her own, and she'd suddenly sit bolt upright like people on television when they're having nightmares, and she'd just know, with tingling certainty. This was something special. Until then, back in the real world – the world where people like Francis Slydewell from Clacton-on-Sea were convinced they'd written the world's first bestselling intergalactic chick-lit novel, told in the style of an alien's diary – until then, Daisy would keep on reading the slush pile, patiently sorting the mediocre from the diabolical.

'No, sorry, we don't do children's books . . . Yes, yes I know that's what we're called. But we're named after Paddington the PLACE, not Paddington THE BEAR. I know . . . yes . . . it *is* very confusing, isn't it? Yes . . . right . . . indeed, it might be silly, but it wasn't me who thought it up. Yes, I'll pass that on . . . thanks very much.' Daisy hung up the phone, resisting the urge to release a loud 'Arrrgghhh' kind of noise, and went back to compiling her third to-do list of the day.

'Some time later, Daisy felt a presence behind her.

'Excuse me.'

Daisy turned around to see the words FCUK staring right at her. Attached to these words were some stylish black oblong spectacles. Peering at her through these was a tall, slim brunette with a seasonable outbreak of freckles on her face. Daisy smiled, but no smile came in return. Instead, the girl declared grumpily, 'I've been sitting at this desk out in the hall for two hours, but no one's come to give me any more work,' she said, flapping a wad of A4 papers about in her hands. 'I mean, I've finished this odd little grid that Belinda gave me, so I don't know what else you want me to do . . .' she paused, before adding the immortal words, 'My time's not worth nothing, you know. I *have* got a master's degree from the London College of Printing.'

Daisy smiled apologetically at this classic yet understandable case of 'workie' frustration. 'I'm really sorry. It's just been manic this morning. I'll find you something meatier to do soon, I really will. Why don't you go on your lunch break now? Take as long as you like, and I'll have something prepared for you when you get back.'

The girl was unimpressed. 'Fine. But I have to say, I was much better treated at the last work experience I did.'

'Really. Thanks for letting me know. The canteen's on the first floor – do you need me to show you where it is?'

The girl shook her head. She wrapped her pink pashmina firmly around her, picked up Daisy's copy of *The Bookseller* magazine, and mooched sulkily away.

Daisy turned to face the window by her desk and looked out at the smoggy, unromantic vista of this particular corner of West London. She glanced at the sprawling, ugly bridge that was being constructed over the road, threatening to intrude further into her already soulless view. If only there was a touch of greenery to look out over, she lamented, then her working environment would be perfect. For the last two years, Belinda had maintained that she was allergic to plants and therefore couldn't possibly condone having any in the office. This, combined with Mercury's dilapidated air-conditioning system, left Daisy and Hermione – the older and relatively more glamorous assistant editor who worked with her – little in the way of non-stifling air to breathe. But she couldn't complain. She still woke up every morning feeling lucky to be able to come to work, loving what she did. Yucca or no Yucca, not many people could say that about their jobs, she reasoned.

Moments later Daisy clicked on to her PC to see if Miles had replied. She'd sent him a Chardonnay-enhanced email late on Friday afternoon, casually enquiring if he was back from LA. (By her own rough calculations, it had been six weeks, four days and three hours since he'd left, and he'd quite clearly said he was only going for five weeks.) But now, faced with nothing but a deafening silence, she was beginning to deeply regret having made the first move towards communication. Maybe he'd met someone else. Some curvy big-breasted Pamela Anderson clone. Or maybe he'd just finally decided that, once and for all, he really was bored with her. Either way, she knew Miles must *surely* be back by now. Especially if his computer was anything to go by – there had been a distinct lack of an 'Out of Office' auto-reply to her email – in itself a depressingly reliable indicator. Or, on the other hand, she considered with a new wave of optimism, perhaps he was just waiting until he was less busy? Saving himself for when he'd have time to write a nice, well-thought-out email, rather than a glib, rushed one. Yes, that was definitely the more likely option, she decided hopefully.

Anxiously checking her inbox a whole minute later for emails labelled Mmetcalfe@Agassociates.com, Daisy's heart sank. There was instead, a concise email from her friend Heidi, sent at exactly 11.59 a.m.: 'Girls. Am marvin. Can we go to lunch now – please? Park weather? Meet you down in the canteen in 3. Hxxx'

Half an hour later, Daisy was sitting out in the tiny park around the corner from their building with her good friend Heidi Black, who worked as a press officer in Mercury's publicity department. The pair were hunched together on the cramped little patch of lawn. Kew Gardens it wasn't, but since it was the only few square metres of greenery in this corner of West London, it was often surprisingly busy at lunch times. It was only June now, but as Daisy surveyed the sprawling crowds basking in the already hot sun, she wondered to herself how long it would be before they'd need to employ a 'one-in-one-out' policy to control the hordes of needy sunbathers.

Heidi, slumped on the lawn in a tailored purple summer dress, squinted her blue eyes at the unconvincing vegetable lasagne on her lap, and began picking at it gingerly. 'Already wishing I'd gone for the safe option,' she commented drily. 'I mean, you always know where you are with a spud and salad, don't you?' She laughed, then stopped, having spotted something in the distance. Daisy followed her gaze and saw their friend Amelie walking into the park. She was wondering around the little patch of lawn looking lost and flustered, her fizzy brown hair bobbing around her shoulders as she walked.

'Over here, Am!' shouted Heidi loudly. Amelie Holden walked over to them and sat down, fumbling with her red shoulder bag and multiple plastic carrier bags, arranging them around her in little heaps. Once seated, she began unwrapping her pick of the canteen cuisine – home-made vegetable korma. Opening the large grey polystyrene box, Amelie held up her plastic cutlery and got to work on her curry.

'How's the korma, Amelie?' asked Daisy moments later, smelling the spices wafting towards her.

'Mmmmnn . . . Doubtful. I've almost certainly made the wrong choice,' Amelie said, shovelling the food into her mouth regardless.

Although Amelie hadn't been working in her job in the marketing department for very long, she'd already caused quite a stir. She'd broken records for punctuality (or lack thereof) and also for her habit of unwittingly depositing her possessions in various places around the building. So far she'd mislaid her mobile phone in the building no less than eight times in the three months she'd been there. Daisy had been the first to discover one of Amelie's phones. She'd stumbled across it in the ladies' loo on the third floor, having heard it ringing from underneath an issue of *Campaign* magazine and a broken hairbrush. Being her usual, zealously helpful self, Daisy had decided to answer the phone. It turned out to be a husky Australian voice going by the name of Josh, who'd also been trying to locate Amelie since the day before. Having reunited Amelie with these items later that day, Daisy had felt compelled to take her under her wing. She saw a ditziness in her that reminded her of her sister Belle. Daisy wasn't sure why, but her whole life she'd gravitated towards dippy, scatty people; had felt the need to shepherd them in some way, sympathising with them and their unfortunate deficit of sensible, logical genes, of which she had an over-abundance.

Since this meeting, Daisy, Amelie and Heidi had become good friends; united by their hopes that one day, somehow, Mercury Publishing would start employing more men (ideally of the young, unmarried variety). For it was a truth universally acknowledged that the British publishing industry at large was insufferably understocked when it came to men. More worryingly, Mercury in par-ticular was notoriously biased towards women. Last time Daisy had checked, the ratio was at an industry record of 80 per cent women versus a dire 20 per cent men. Daisy and Heidi often reminded themselves, in times of drunken panic at launch parties, of the theory that most women meet their future spouses at their place of work. If this were true, it left them with Nige, the company's facilities manager – all three hundred pounds of him. Failing that, twice a week there was the opportunity to talk to Freddy Rhubarb, the after-hours security guard – notorious for his Jurassic dreadlocks and overtly sleazy behaviour. All other Mercury men, sadly, fell into one of three categories: a) gorgeous but married, b) friendly but gay, and c) charming but approaching octogenarianism. None of these were any good for Heidi and Daisy, who were in their late twenties and relentlessly discerning.

Amelie stood up abruptly, brushing some flecks of mud and leaves off her red summer dress. 'Um . . .' she began, 'the grass is a bit skankier than normal today – will would it be terrible if we sit on this manuscript?'

Amelie reached into a branded carrier bag with a big

red Mercury Publishing logo on it. She retrieved a couple of new manuscripts, hot off the press and loosely tied together with elastic bands that were threatening to ping at any point. Amelie grabbed a wad of pages from a book-in-progress entitled *The New History of Bus Shelters*, preparing to sit on them.

Daisy shook her head and said, 'Am, sweetie, you can't – that's someone's work. It's their livelihood . . .'

'Oh. No one will know, will they?' put in Heidi in defence. 'Actually, hon, have you got anything else I can sit on? My bum's getting a little dusty too – I'd hate to get grass stains on this new dress.'

'Sure – what have I got in here?' said Amelie, rifling through her bag, 'Oh, it's James Federot, another new crime writer we're launching. I'm meant to be coming up with a shout-line but I can't seem to get into it.' Amelie put the manuscript down on the grass, then ungracefully placed herself on top of it. 'I'll see if it works better as a seat – maybe that will give me some inspiration!'

Daisy was still shaking her head, shocked at their lack of respect for an author's work. 'Just as long as the author never sees you doing that, is all I can say.'

'It's fine, sweets – if it gets trashed we can just run off another printout,' offered Heidi, gathering up her wavy blond hair into a rough ponytail in an attempt to cool herself from the heat.

Daisy was about to say that this would then be a waste of paper and therefore damaging to the environment, but she held her breath, knowing they would move to an opposite corner of the park away from her if she did.

'So . . . how're both your love lives going?' asked Heidi,

whose love of gossip was far more evolved than her love of reading.

'Um, really good actually,' said Amelie. 'We're thinking of going away together soon.' Her blue eyes sparkled the way they always did when she got to talk about her current beau, whom she'd been seeing since her last job.

'Oh really? That'll be your first "mini-break", won't it?' gushed Heidi, who was very open about the fact that she was perpetually trapped in Bridget Jones's dialect.

'Where to?' enquired Daisy, traces of envy in her voice. 'I wish Miles and I were in a position to be going away together.' The truth was, they were on a mini-break of their own. Before Miles had left for LA, he'd vaguely requested some 'space', so he could work out what he wanted, leaving Daisy wondering where they were at, and in doubt over what kind of a future they had together – if any. 'Well, who knows,' she began, ever the optimist. 'Maybe when he gets back, things will be different . . . once he's had some time away.'

Heidi and Amelie locked eyes and exchanged knowing looks. 'I wouldn't get your hopes up, sweets,' Heidi said cynically. 'I'm sorry, but all those fuckwittish things he said about being afraid to be exclusive . . . to be honest, I can't believe you're actually waiting for him! That boy is so not good enough for you. If you ask me, you should just call it a day with him; use this time while he's away to just get him out of your system, once and for all.'

Daisy looked uncomfortable. 'But you don't know him like I do! I just keep hoping that this time away will make him realise, that he can't stay in that his can't-commit-won't commit state he's in for ever. And also, in fairness, he *has* just started a new job. He just needs some time to focus on that before he can decide what he wants with us.'

Amelie and Heidi were unimpressed. 'Hon, it sounds to me like he'll always be in that place of vague non-committalness,' said Heidi. 'Didn't he once say that thing about how he can't even dare to commit to a gym? That he'd rather just play the field, even on that one?'

'Um, possibly,' admitted Daisy reluctantly, 'OK, yes it's true. He once said to me that he didn't like the idea of tying himself down to one particular gym, in one particular area of the city. He was like, "London's so big . . . I'm always on the move, so I need to be able to go wherever the wind takes me – whether it's the Queen Mother in Victoria, or the Fitness First in Soho. I'd rather pay more each time than have to be tied down by one big membership fee somewhere . . ." ' she trailed off, smiling and embarrassed, when she saw the other girls laughing at her.

'Can't you see?' screeched Amelie, 'It's the perfect metaphor! He's giving himself a get-out clause! You know he was basically saying to you that he'll never, ever want to commit, don't you? Not to you, not to a treadmill, not to anyone! I mean, is he *really* worth holding out for?'

'Of course,' Daisy denounced firmly, 'you're just talking semantics anyway. It doesn't *matter* if he's still in hiding from the tyranny of labels. Which, by the way, is just society putting pressure on people,' she said, trying desperately to sound like she meant it and was actually a deeply nonconformist Jacobin who hated such conventions as these, and hadn't spent her whole life daydreaming of a white wedding, 2.4 children and a bungalow in the suburbs. 'Besides,' she went on, 'I know a different side to him that you've never experienced. And I know he cares about me, that's all that matters really.'

Heidi and Amelie looked at each other again, both privately counting the amount of times she'd said 'that's all that matters'.

Miles: the man of Daisy's dreams. A high-flying literary agent, working for one of London's most cut-throat agencies. Tall, handsome, educated at Cambridge, he'd ticked all of Daisy's little boxes the moment she met him at her first launch party two years ago. It had also been Miles's first party since he'd joined his new agency, having worked his way up as an editor before that. This, and various tiny coincidences, had all added up in Daisy's naive and overly romantic mind, to convince her that their meeting had been pre-ordained by the stars, and that he and she were simply fated to be together. Of course, in reality, it had been an incredibly slow process of getting together, while Miles broke up with his various ex-girlfriends, played the game and generally conveyed a slow, on-off interest in Daisy. All until finally six months, ago he'd been able to admit that they might officially be 'seeing one another'. But these were trifling details for Daisy, who adored the very ground he walked on. Since they first met, he'd become a kind of mentor figure for her, offering her support and guidance in her career whenever she needed it. As a result, it had been a long time before Daisy was able to properly fathom the true nature of their acquaintance – whether it was entirely professional or something more. Only when they started sleeping together did she begin to have an inkling.

Looking back over the last year, she knew she'd learned far more from Miles about publishing than she had from her own boss. But there was more to it than just a teacher/pupil dynamic; Daisy also liked to think that she knew

Miles's sensitive, caring side, beneath the suave, cool exterior he presented to everyone else. Equally, he liked to think of her as slightly naive and malleable, and in fundamental need of his help and wisdom. So in some senses, it was a good partnership.

'So,' Heidi said challengingly, 'did he reply to your email – that one you sent him on Friday?'

Daisy shook her head, 'No, but he's really busy . . . he'll only just have got back from LA. Besides, I'd forgotten, one of his authors has just come over from Belgium. Poor thing, he'll have been chasing him around town since then . . . he won't have had a moment to himself. No, he'll be in touch when he's ready.'

Later that night, having stayed at work late to finish some urgent title information sheets for Belinda, Daisy could feel her eyelids drooping. She clicked on to her emails one last time, and then shut down her computer. It was Monday, which could mean only one thing. Treadmills. Reluctantly, wearily, she forced herself up, grabbed her gym bag from under her desk, and set off towards the large council sports centre, which was just around the corner.

Some minutes later Daisy ambled up the slope in the gym towards the locker rooms. She swiped her card and pushed through the turnstile. Fighting her way through the overcrowded, noisy changing room, she slumped down on a bench. She thought about getting undressed. She imagined herself unpacking her bag. Doing warm-up exercises. Getting all sweaty, and even more hot and bothered than she felt already, after a whole day in the overheated editorial department at work. Then suddenly she realised, for what seemed like the first time in her

organised, routine-driven life, she just *could not* be
bothered. She admitted it to herself – the last thing she felt
like doing was jumping up and down on a sweaty treadmill
or cross-trainer, in front of all those scarily fit Lycra
junkies. No, today she just didn't have the energy. Besides,
she'd only joined the gym because she'd felt she *ought* to –
so she could be a fitter, healthier, more well-rounded
human being. It wasn't as though she *needed* to lose any
weight. On the contrary, and much to the fury of her
friends, Daisy had always had the appetite of a small bird,
and an elfin figure to match.

After a moment's deliberation, Daisy was off. She
grabbed her bag, stood up and marched out of the changing room, hoping no one would notice and be appalled at
her sloth-like behaviour. Hovering guiltily at the front
gates to the gym, Daisy thought about turning back, but
then remembered how much reading she had to get
through, and decided she'd get home to work on that
instead – a slightly lesser evil than forty minutes of cross-
training. She walked on, vowing to go again another day,
for twice as long.

As she walked towards the tube, Daisy thought about
why she could be feeling so low, and began scrolling
through her mental checklists. Work was great – tick. She
loved her social life – tick. Home life, fine – well, her
family weren't much to write home about but that was
another story in itself. So that just left her love life, which,
in honesty, probably wasn't going as well as it could be. She
hadn't wanted to admit this to the girls at lunch, especially
after they had always made their disapproval of him so
clear, but in truth she was getting tired of not knowing
where she stood with Miles. Before he'd gone away, she'd

loved seeing him – more than that, she'd craved seeing him; she could never have enough of him. But each time they did meet, it would always be the same – they'd never actually plan when they'd next be seeing each other. Miles would always just say casually, 'See ya then, beautiful. I'll be in touch.' Daisy had once made the mistake of sharing this with Amelie, who had promptly released one of her raucous shrieks of laughter. ' *"I'll be in touch"?*' she'd protested. 'Honestly, that's what your bank manager, or some high-powered potential employer says to you – right after they've interviewed you. I'm sorry, but that's so unromantic!'

Daisy had shrugged this off at the time, but with hindsight she had to admit, Amelie did seem to have a point. If you listened to the subtext of 'I'll be in touch', it did sound uncomfortably similar to the phrase 'Don't call us, we'll call you.'

Stepping out of the tube in Stockwell forty-five minutes later, Daisy began walking towards Union Road, where she lived with her sister in a ground-floor, converted council flat. Approaching her block of flats and grabbing her keys, she began dreaming of a long bubble bath, complete with her new luxurious Milk and Honey bath soak. She stepped into the narrow hallway of the flat, and felt her nose twitch in response to the surprising smell which greeted her. What was that, Daisy wondered. Was there a dead body somewhere, rotting slowly?

As she drifted further into the flat towards the kitchen, she saw that Belle's laid-back, bohemian lifestyle had taken its toll on the flat's cleanliness once again. She and her sister Belle had, for the early years of their childhood, lived in and out of many different motor caravans and council houses. Their parents had led a gypsy kind of life, and now lived largely out of the picture; away from their children in a commune on the west coast of Australia. As far as Daisy saw it, they were no longer her parents – just a distant memory of people who had once fed and clothed her (albeit mostly in ill-fitting hand-me-downs). If she thought hard, she could still picture in her mind the slime-green Volkswagen camper van that she'd lived in for most of her younger years, and the fluorescent mural her mother had painted on the side, with the help of a six-year-old Belle, artist-in-the-making. But she preferred not to think too hard about her childhood. Partly as her parents were no longer around and partly because, unlike Belle, she'd hated being different at school. She'd always tried to blend in unnoticed – rather difficult when every day you were dropped at the school gates in a smelly green caravan which huffed and puffed black smoke and then reliably broke down, setting off small explosive bangs as it pulled away again. Harry, they'd called it; Daisy had insisted upon giving it a human name while everyone else had been happy calling it the bogey – which essentially was what it was.

Belle had always been happy living in the shadow of their parents' carefree hippie existence, and her current lifestyle owed a considerable amount to their influence. Daisy, by contrast, couldn't wait to have her own children and give them the kind of stable, 'normal' childhood that she'd never had; even if that meant that Belle still sometimes told her off for being a narrow-minded snob.

Daisy looked around at the undone washing-up and the piles of laundry dotted around the kitchen; at the twister board that was laid out on the kitchen table – either acting as a temporary tablecloth, or something more recreational; she couldn't tell which. She wrestled with the mental Post-it notes that were scribbling themselves as she walked through the kitchen, passed the decaying washing-up into the living room; where she saw that perhaps she had been right – there actually did appear to be a dead body of some sort. Lying, stretched out on the living-room carpet, there was a half-naked man, his olive-skinned muscular physique sprawled all over the pink sofa. He lay with one arm in the air, his legs akimbo, clad only in some boxer shorts with little penguins on them. Only one word came to mind: Belle.

As though sensing her presence, Penguin Boxer Shorts opened his eyes, a broad smile leaking out.

Daisy smiled meekly in return. 'Hello. I'm Daisy,' she said nervously.

'Tyrone. Hi . . .' Tyrone stood up confidently, wiped his hand on his boxers, and held it out to Daisy.

'Hi, Tyrone. You're a friend of Belle's, I take it?' Daisy said, shaking his hand, as he nodded. 'Can I get you a cup of tea or anything?' she asked, praying that he'd say no and leave her to get to the bathroom for some much needed R & R.

Instead, the exact opposite. 'Oh – that would be wicked, thanks. Actually, I was just about to grab a quick shower. Only I've got to be at work in an hour.'

Daisy looked dumbfounded, as he added by way of an explanation, 'I'm a bouncer, you see. Do you have a towel?'

Daisy nodded slowly, forcing her most hospitable smile. 'Of course. Let me get you one. Milk and sugar?' she asked, bottling up her rage for when Belle chose to either reappear or phone her – although the latter was unlikely;

Belle was a disciple of the Pay as You Go school of never having credit. Daisy was just mulling this over, and studying Tyrone's shorts in wonder, when she heard a key in the lock.

Moments later, Belle was in the living room, looking ruffled and rosy, and holding hands with an extremely tall man of similar build and dark good looks to Tyrone.

'Daisy, hello! I see you've already met Roney . . . Great! And' – she said, looking adoringly up at the man by her side – 'Daisy, this is George.'

Rejection

Date: Monday 12 June 2006 19.50
Sender: Mmetcalfe@Agassociates.com
To: Daisy.Allen@paddingtonpress.com
Subject:

Hello – Hi, how goes it? Sorry not to reply sooner, been manic with Gerard all weekend – he's over here from Belgium. Hope all's good. I'll call you soon. Best, M x x x

'So?' asked Heidi sternly, having just finished reading this aloud, slowly and carefully to an audience of Amelie and Daisy.

'I don't see what the big deal is,' continued Heidi. 'It's a straight, run-of-the-mill email. Aloof, even.' She passed the crumpled piece of A4 paper back to an even more crumpled Daisy.

'But, look!' protested Daisy in response to her friend's noises of pessimism, and gesturing to the end of the three-line email. 'Look, progress! He's never, ever, put three kisses before. Always a reserved one, or on special occasions, two. This is surely a breakthrough, no? Maybe it means he's broken through to the other side – maybe he's ready to enter a new phase with us? Maybe this time apart has had a good effect on him!' Daisy looked earnestly up at Amelie and Heidi, who looked back down at her with genuine concern. It was the following day, and the three girls were in the park eating lunch and helping Daisy try to dissect the latest instalment in her romantic saga.

'Sweetness. You need to get out more,' said Heidi sternly, 'Honestly. You simply *cannot* be counting e-kisses. It's *pathetic*! And anyway, did he call you yet?'

Seeing Daisy shake her head, Heidi added, 'See – it's just a throwaway comment, isn't it?'

'You know, she's absolutely right,' agreed Amelie. 'This obsessive email analysis has absolutely GOT to stop. From now on, you read his emails, you reply to them, and you delete them. Job done. OK?'

Daisy looked mortified. 'But! You don't understand! I'm an editor! Well. OK, not quite. All right, I'm an editorial assistant. But you see that makes it my job to analyse words. To look between the lines for meanings, you know, get involved with the text . . . do you know what I mean? I'm NOT insane, I'm just conscientious!'

Seeing she was fighting a losing battle, Daisy slowly trailed off. 'I'm sorry – I know it's really sad. But it's sort of an occupational hazard. I get attached to his emails because they're his words – his thoughts – and, I don't know, I just love well-put-together words.' Seeing Heidi and Amelie's expressions of concern and disbelief respectively, she changed tack. 'OK, I know, I should stop being such a sentimental moron about everything. But I just really like him, a lot, more than any guy I've ever liked . . .'

Amelie put her arm on Daisy's shoulder and stroked her light red hair. 'I know, lovely. But these words aren't well put together, or anything. They're not even significant – especially when you consider that he's not seen you in weeks! And also, *who* says 'best' apart from when they're being businesslike and formal? It's kind of cold, don't you think? Anyway, love, I really think you shouldn't put all your eggs in this one basket. At least until he starts acting less complacent about where you stand with each other, I think you should be looking for what else is out there.'

'Yeah, like maybe at this launch party tonight,' chipped in Heidi excitedly. 'You know – I've seen the guest list – there's a fair few D-listers going; maybe your ideal husband will be one of them? You never know . . .'

Daisy looked unimpressed. 'I don't want to meet any other guys. Plus, I meant to tell you, I can't go tonight – I have a hot date with a treadmill. Don't look like that at me! You know as well as I do – the D-listers won't turn up, and it will be just the same old lot of us playing hunt-the-canapé. Face it, Heidi, there won't be any nice or available men – we work in publishing, for the love of God!'

Back at her desk a few hours later, Daisy was crafting the perfect email response to Miles. She'd written three different drafts, each taking a very different tack, and each of them carefully designed to sound carefree, aloof and spur-of-the moment. Deep down, she knew the girls had a point; that she needed to step back from it all and stop obsessing about him *quite* so much. The trouble was, she still couldn't shake the thought that she and Miles, when you stripped away all the other consequential details, were quite simply meant to be together. He was just so lovely.

And charming. And so on her level. Like the time when they'd been watching that Trevor Griffiths play, and both cried at exactly the same point. Like the way, just like her, he'd worked in the editorial department of a large publishing house straight after university; before he moved on into agenting. And like the way that they'd both grown up in small commuter towns only a rounders ball away from one another, and had ended up going to high schools in uncannily similar areas in Suffolk, accessible only via similar school buses. Had they travelled on the same buses of a morning? This she had always wondered, but never managed to retrieve from Miles, who was relatively less interested in this bit of trivia than she was. Either way, she still couldn't ignore all these similarities – surely somehow they must be significant in some way? If not, what else *was* there? If we don't have fate, Daisy often wondered, what *do* we have?

Empowered by her own rhetoric, Daisy decided she had too much work to do to waste any more time fretting about the consequences of each email. Reluctantly, she picked one – the second aloofest of them all, and clicked send.

Hey Miles,
Thanks for your email. Don't worry, I've been hectic all weekend too. Hope it went swimmingly with Gerard; I meant to tell you that I completely adored his book. Maybe see you soon, Dx

As she watched it fire off into the ether, Workie Number Two was clearing her throat nearby.

'Hi. Hi, Daisy – I'm Siobhanna – we met this morning?'

Daisy looked up as Siobhanna was fluffing up her bushy dark brown hair, causing her bangles and gypsy earrings to jangle together noisily in time with the rhythm of her gum-chewing.

'Yes, I remember,' said Daisy, smiling. 'Hi, how's it going? Can I help?'

'Well, no one's given me anything to do. I've been here for three days now, and so far all I've done is stuff envelopes. And ... well ... I've got a first from Sussex, you know. I *am* capable of something slightly more demanding.'

Listening to the girl, Daisy wondered briefly whether or not she was living in a *Groundhog Day* tribute world. She looked down at the piles of undone jobs reclining on her desk. She considered which of them she could explain how to do in a few minutes, and realised that most of them would actually take far longer to explain than it would take to do the job herself. She didn't really have time to explain that to the workie, so instead she just said, 'I'm sorry, Siobhanna, I'll try and find you something to do in a minute. For now ... um, all I've got is these rejection letters. You can send these out, if that's OK?'

Siobhanna looked down with disdain at the big pile of white A6 envelopes, and at the tower of rejection letters perched next to them, then looked back at Daisy. 'Fine. I'll get on with these,' and she sauntered away.

Some thirty minutes later, she was back at Daisy's desk.

'Hi, Daisy. Sorry. I've finished all the work you've given me. So ... Is there any slush pile stuff you want me to attack? I mean, I know most of it's probably toilet paper, but I'd be happy to relieve you of the burden, if you like. Honestly, I don't mind. You never know, I might end up discovering the next Harry Potter!'

Daisy was almost giddy. This girl was a towering inferno of confidence. Daisy had to suppress a smile as she leaned over towards her window sill to grab a wodge of manuscripts. 'Here you go. If you could write me a two-page report on each of them, that'd be fab. Thanks.'

'Great,' Siobhanna said, clearly delighted, and went to turn away. But then quickly she swung back round to face Daisy. She spoke slowly, as though confiding in her new-found comrade, 'You know, I've been here a good week or so. I was in the marketing department before this, and I did a bit of publicity too . . . I reckon I'm more than capable of a job – so if you see any going, you will let me know, won't you? Or maybe you're about to be promoted? I could have your job, then? In fact,' she added, looking around, 'I've been told the pay's shocking in publishing, particularly bad in editorial . . . d'you mind me asking how much you're on?'

Daisy masked her surprise with a smile and said sagely, 'Well, let's just say I'll be paying off my student loan for a very, very long time. Anyway, I'm afraid I've got lots to do. But give me a shout if you need any help.' And she turned away, slightly unnerved by this girl, and began to wonder why she wasn't more pushy herself sometimes.

'DAAAAAAAAAIIIISSSSSSSSYYY!'

That was why. She just happened to have one of the most tyrannical, manipulative bosses imaginable. In all of her part-time jobs, she'd never met anyone quite like Belinda. She was only around the corner from Daisy, but instead of walking around to see if she was free, or even calling her on the phone, Belinda always preferred to holler across the quiet, library-like editorial department, at the top of her voice. Day to day, Belinda's communication methods ranged from the more muted, slow chanting of Daisy's name, to a more thunderous impatient roar, with a subtext of 'Drop everything now please, this is urgent'. In Daisy's experience, this most recent holler fell into the latter category.

'Yes?' Daisy called back, jumping to her feet and heading round the corner to Belinda's large air-conditioned office.

'Hello, darling. Sit down. My goodness, I haven't *stopped* today! I've been on the go since 6 a.m. – I simply must have a break or I shall wear myself out! Anyway. Thought we could have a quick catch-up. Is everything alright with you?' she fired at Daisy. Only Belinda could make a potentially warm, well-intentioned question sound snappy and aggressive.

Daisy nodded hastily, 'Yep, fine. No probs. I've almost done the stuff for the six-monthly presentations. And I've finished all those title sheets you needed.'

'Good. Good. And you've sourced those new readers and translators yet? And, you're on track with everything that we need so far for the next sales conference?'

'Um, no, not quite yet. But it's all next on my list.' Daisy angled her red and black notebook towards her boss so she could see her neatly drawn tasks.

'Right, well. You'd best action them all soon,' she said self-importantly, placing a stress on the word 'action'. 'Be sure to CC me into any of your chasing emails if that helps push people along. Especially those slugs in Marketing. Lord only knows *what* they actually do all day. That's all for now I think? Oh, except that I'd murder a smoked salmon bagel, darling . . . but only if you're going out anyway, that is. Please don't just go on my account.'

Daisy had been here before. It was almost 4 p.m., and she didn't need to go out. But experience had taught her to say that she was going out anyway, even when she wasn't. Belinda also knew this. It was just one of the many games they played. 'Fine – no probs,' said Daisy, 'I've got to pop out anyway. Thanks,' and she got up to leave, just as Belinda remembered something.

'Oh – that's right – I meant to say. Hermione's booked a new workie to come in next week, and she's just realised she now hasn't got time to look after them. You wouldn't mind another one to shepherd for a week or so, would you?'

Daisy's heart sank. A third overzealous newly grad to look after and find jobs for. 'No – not at all. Lots of jobs I can give them,' she lied.

'Great. I'll have Hermione liaise with you. Can you minute that? They'll be in next Monday.'

Returning from bagel-shopping some twenty minutes later, Daisy felt her stomach lurch. There, waiting in her inbox, a Reply From Miles. And what was this? A lunch invitation? What kind of a lunch, she wondered, her fingers almost shaking as she clicked on it hastily.

Date: Tuesday 13 June 2006 16.20
Sender: Mmetcalfe@Agassociates.com
To: Daisy.Allen@paddingtonpress.com
Subject: lastminute lunch

Apologies for the lack of notice. Will Belinda manage a lunch on Friday with Gerard and I? G's only just become free, and he's very keen to speak with Belinda

face to face while he's over here. And, as you know,
he's only here for this weekend before he shoots back
home. Let me know, asap if you could. Will understand
if it's too tight.

Best, M

He'd done it again. Somehow, quite unwittingly, he'd
managed to raise her hopes and then cut them right down
again, leaving her feeling idiotic and wretched. She tried
not to overreact – this was clearly just a case of the fuzzy
line between business and personal, and of once again
being unsure of exactly which side things fell into. But
then she thought, in a throwing-her-toys-out-of-the-pram
kind of way, why didn't he at least invite her to come along
too? Hmmph. She'd done a heap of work on Gerard's book,
ever since the manuscript had first been delivered. More
to the point, though, why was he being so aloof again, and
giving no mention of her own email to him?

Recalling Heidi's advice from earlier, and suppressing
the urgent need inside her to call Amelie over and have
her formally deconstruct his email, she decided to brush
this off and to try, once again, to be less obsessive and
oversensitive. She checked Belinda's calendar, and quickly
bashed her own curt, short reply that yes, Belinda would
love to make the lunch – would the River Café suit?

Minutes later, Daisy had buried her head in the slush
pile – the absolute best form of escaping from recalcitrant
yet gorgeous males. Soon she began to forget Miles, to
blank out his soft brown hair; to block out his deep brown
eyes, and instead focus on the half-formed novels on her
desk. Opening up the first one on her pile, she read about
Manuel, who told in his poignant cover letter how he'd

given up a gargantuan salary and high-powered job on the board of a financial company in Madrid, in favour of two years spent in a writers' retreat, sweating over his masterpiece in dedicated isolation – 'please find enclosed – no pressure!' She read about a zealously committed fifty-year-old from Hayes named Mirella Browne, who told of how she'd taken her children out of private school, remortgaged their house, and effectively sacrificed her whole family's well-being, to fund her dream. Reading a few pages of the ensuing novels, it was only minutes before she felt the rejection templates appearing in her mind, against all her will – would it be a 'this isn't quite right for our list', or was it more on the side of a 'we just don't have a slot for it at this time'?

As she leafed through all the prospective novels, she found once again that the most harrowing submissions were those from the writers who had written not one book, and not two, but whole tomes of work. The ones who had created elaborate, complex universes, furnishing them with newfangled political systems, whole intricate new vocabularies; spanning six generations and altogether comprising a whole trilogy of work that sadly, heart-breakingly, somehow just wasn't readable. Daisy sighed and wished she could give them all a deal. After all, she always asked herself, who was she to judge them? She was just a twenty-six-year-old girl from Southwold who loved to read; what did she know? Who had granted her the power to make or break their destiny?

American Psycho: The Literary Years

'Now, before I tell you what this one is about, I have to say, hand on heart, that this is hands down, any form of hyperbole aside, the absolute BEST THING I'VE READ ALL YEAR. Ever since that book – you know – the one about the dead dog and the fork? What was it called? You know, with the little boy who kept imagining the little red cars.'

Daisy looked knowingly across the meeting table at Heidi, who smiled back. A speech like this one was a regular occurrence from Belinda, head buyer of fiction at Paddington. Every other week, she was just finishing 'the best book she'd ever read'.

'He wasn't imagining them. The cars were real,' Heidi said under her breath, but Belinda Bancroft went on talking unawares, her dark brown eyes addressing the brightly lit meeting room that was stuffed full with Mercury's weary-looking marketing and publicity contingent. It was Friday's weekly launch meeting which Belinda insisted on hosting first thing at 9 a.m., much to the dismay of the people in the room, a large proportion of whom seemed to be either nursing hangovers of some genre – from a launch party the night before; either that or simply wishing they were elsewhere, pursuing more pressing tasks. Daisy herself was slowly tuning out, compiling a mental checklist of what jobs she was going to give to Workie Number III when she arrived the following Monday.

Holding her Advanced Title Information sheet up in the air, Belinda launched into her pitch for why *A Dog's Dinner* was going to be this year's one-way ticket to Richard and Judy heaven.

'So', she was saying minutes later, 'the bad news is, we've paid an extortionate amount of money for this – truth be told we've gone way over budget. But, the good news is, we did manage to wrestle it away from the other big houses, so we've got to do ALL we can with this to make it work. I'm talking massive billboard twenty-six-sheet tube campaigns, snappy, funny shout-lines with a nice big fat pun . . . full-page ads in *The Bookseller* and *Publishing News* . . . everyone needs to know we're making a song and dance about this . . .'

Belinda acquired a dreamy look in her eye as she continued, as though her speech was as motivational and galvanising as they came. 'I'm thinking front of store, huge point-of-sale material, three for twos and BOGOF bins in Smiths and Books etc. . . . And we'll need a huge publicity blitz: serialisation in a broadsheet, full magazine and national press review coverage . . . Oh, and anything else out of the ordinary that we can think of. Stunts. Ambient whatever-you-call-its. Sampling. Dressing up. Anything that works. We really need to push the boat out with this one. Think outside of every box . . . push every single envelope there is . . . look to the blue sky, and all of that. Oh, and what are those things called – viruses?'

Amelie burst out laughing uncontrollably. 'Virals. You mean a viral campaign? Yep, we can have a go at that.' Amelie chuckled as she wrote something down on her pad.

Belinda looked around at the throng of nodding, caffeine-deficient faces. She glanced at her watch. 'Codswallop, is that the time? I've got to pick up Gordon from the orthodontist's in Surrey, so I'll need to get going . . . But if anyone needs a manuscript, give Daisy a bell and she'll copy you one when they arrive next week.' She looked around the room, then at Ronald Morley-Green, the Marketing and Publicity Director. He looked back at Belinda and, glad to have his authority restored, said, 'Fine, well, if no one's got any AOB we can call that the end of the meeting.'

Everyone looked faintly relieved, pushed in their chairs, and prepared to leave. Daisy walked out of the meeting room. En route back to her desk, suddenly something clicked. The River Café. Miles. What was all this talk of the orthodontist's and Surrey? Daisy rushed into Belinda's office, just in time to see her gathering her bags and preparing to leave.

'B – have you forgotten your lunch with Gerard and his agent? The table's booked for 12.30. How on earth will you get there in time from Surrey?'

Belinda's face fell. 'Oh rats. I've ballsed up entirely and completely. I forgot to write it down in my paper diary again. It's just Gordon's braces need refitting, he's been up all night having tantrums, so I can't reschedule . . .' she ran a hand through her half-head of highlights. 'Bugger, you know what, maybe you having control of my electronic calendar's not enough – from now on, I give you permission to write in here too,' she said breezily, passing Daisy her diary and leaving the office.

'Um, OK,' said Daisy, flummoxed. 'But, that doesn't solve the immediate problem. The lunch? I can't just cancel Miles and Gerard – that will look very bad, surely?'

'No, you're right. That won't do at all,' she said, as though this had just occurred to her. 'Well, there's no way around it. You'll have to go instead. Just make sure you get a receipt? You *do* have enough in your account to pay the bill, I take it? I mean – I know we pay you a pittance?'

Daisy was speechless. A Lunch With Miles, after she'd not seen him for six whole weeks. With no prior warning! This was terrible news. She'd had no time to prepare herself – no time for facials, manicures – not to mention the shambolic outfit she had on; her sloppy hair, her mismatched jewellery, all heaped together this morning with a raging hangover that had taken precedence over her usually immaculate coordinational faculties. She'd no heels either, having foolishly voted for a 'comfort' day. In real terms this meant that, since Miles had only ever seen her in heels, today in his eyes she would have all the majestic height of a dwarf. No, this was very, very bad news.

'Daisy?' Belinda was staring impatiently at her. 'What's the matter with you? Why aren't you responding to what I'm saying? That will be OK, won't it?'

'What, sorry? Yes, fine. No worries,' Daisy stumbled, her heart rate slowing down as she realised she might be able to fit in an emergency-style consultation with Heidi, who was widely considered to be Mercury's most well-turned-out, skilfully coordinated lady.

'Great. Thanks,' Belinda said, walking away down the

corridor. Then, retracing her steps slightly, she added in a more hushed tone, 'Just tell Gerard that I'm extremely, extremely sorry that you made this unfortunate mix-up over the dates, and that I'll call him later.' Two air kisses dispatched, and she was gone, leaving Daisy staring after her in astonishment. Wanting to scream after her boss, 'it was *your* fault, not mine', but instead smiling merrily. Miles. Metcalfe. In the same room as her.

Nanoseconds later she was on the phone. 'Heidi, can you come quick? It's an emergency.'

Daisy pulled the cab door shut behind her and adjusted the strappy three-inch heels which Heidi had lent her. Admittedly, they were about one and a half sizes too small, but at least the same couldn't be said about Daisy now that she was wearing them. At least 'Where did your legs go?' wouldn't be the first thing on Miles's mind when he saw her for the first time in six weeks.

She looked out on to the river, admired the classically London vista of sparkling thick brown water peppered with people's rubbish, and then looked back towards the restaurant where she was confronted with an altogether more arresting sight. Miles. Lovely Miles. Sporting a freshly topped-up Californian tan, and a mop of dark brown hair tinged with sunlight, he was guiding 'The Slickest Name in Crime' – otherwise known as Gerard Bogaert – to his seat. Bogaert was a Belgian author of theirs who had just had his fifth crime novel published by Paddington, to much critical acclaim.

While Miles was looking as handsome and debonair as ever, Daisy was desperately trying to restrain all her bubbling-over feelings of jealousy, lust, anticipation and insecurity over whether they still had any kind of relationship left to salvage. Strapping a smile to her face, she affected as professional an appearance as possible as she walked over to the restaurant and joined him at his al fresco table.

'Daisy! How are you!' he held out his arms and kissed her on both cheeks. Her stomach did an Olympic display of somersaults as she took in how pleased he seemed to see her.

'Hello! Good to see you, too. Let's just say the Californian sun agrees with you.' She smiled shyly and looked away. 'Hello, Gerard! How are you? Have you had a nice trip so far?'

'Oh yes, very pleasant thank you. Almost enough to make up for the six hours I spent waiting at the airport out there, followed by no less than four hours waiting at this end for the bloody baggage handlers to handle my baggage . . .'

Seeing that Gerard's infamous curmudgeonly side was seeping through already, Daisy smiled and nodded while she took her seat.

'Now, shall we order wine,' Miles said, taking charge. 'Red, or white? Daisy, what are you in the mood for? Shall I order a nice Sauvignon?'

'Yes, please. Or whatever Gerard fancies. I'll just have the one glass though.'

A half-hour and two bottles later, Ronald Morley-Green appeared at their table to join them. Soon they were engrossed in a conversation about the Edinburgh Book Festival, and how this year's was going to be the biggest one yet. Daisy's contribution to the discussion was scant – Belinda having never allowed her to attend.

'Oh, let me make a note of that,' Miles said in response to Gerard's mention of an author reading that he simply had to catch. Miles reached into his inside jacket pocket. He pulled out what Daisy had always taken to be one of his most treasured possessions – a black, A6-size Moleskine notebook. Miles smoothed back his sleek dark brown hair, and opened the notebook at a fresh page. His eyes narrowed with concentration as he jotted down the details into it. Then he looked up at Ronald and Gerard, and paused – apparently in a quandary over whether to say something or not. Catching Gerard's eye, he began, 'Here's my new moleskine – picked it up in LA. How do you like it?'

'Mmmn, it's not bad,' cut in Ronald. 'I see you've gone for uniform black like everyone else. Mine's a nice deep brown, actually.' Then, making sure Gerard was watching, Ronald delved into his jacket pocket and retrieved his own. 'It's even got an extra-big expandable inner pocket,' he said smugly, revealing the notebook's pocket, which was gaping open, stuffed with extra jottings. 'But,' Ronald said with concern, looking curiously from Miles to his notebook, 'I see that yours doesn't have the diary pages running all the way through it?'

'No, I don't like the idea of that,' Miles pontificated. 'Call me a purist, but I think the true Moleskine should only be for thinking, ideas, jottings – not for organising one's schedules, no?' he looked at Gerard, the Writer, and therefore official Moleskine Specialist, for approval on this matter.

Daisy was bemused. Why wasn't she in any way interested in this conversation? She looked for support to Gerard, but she saw with regret that he, too, was reaching into his pocket. Gerard smiled as he pulled out a large, pristine navy blue Moleskine. Miles and Ronald gasped in astonishment.

'My moleskine . . .' said Gerard with attempted humility, opening it out to reveal a host of flaps and detachable elements, 'is actually a new, slightly bigger model. It's called a Cahier Moleskine. Here, you've got the heavy duty cardboard cover – as standard – with a special black and buff stitching on the spine, see? And here, look – the last sixteen sheets are detachable. See?' Gerard demonstrated, salesman-style, as he spoke. 'And here's some graph paper in this section, some plain pages here, and . . . here, look, there's even an extra, extra-wide pocket for loose notes. Great, no?'

Daisy groaned inwardly and had to suppress a Niagaran tide of laughter at what came next. Gerard, with no trace of irony, leaned in and inhaled the centre of the open book – as though invigorated by the musty, leathery aroma. The men nodded mutely, in a state of awe. Eventually, Miles broke the silence. 'Wow. That really is the Daddy of Moleskines.'

Daisy said nothing, but couldn't help thinking how oddly reminiscent this was of the business card scene from *American Psycho*. She was just amusing herself quietly with this thought when Miles interrupted her by turning his two interrogative brown eyes on to her. 'Daisy, you don't have a Moleskine of your own?'

'Um, no. I just tend to write notes into my phone these days.' Daisy slammed her mouth shut, sensing a hushed, hostile reaction around the table. Clearly, she'd said something sacrilegious – a naive remark which contravened the very heart of the literary publishing tradition.

'But, but surely there's not enough space in most phones for what we creative types need to say?' said Miles, perplexed. Daisy searched his eyes to see if he was being ironic – her heart sank when she realised he wasn't. Miles went on with a sparkle in his eye, 'You know, the Moleskine has a heritage, it symbolises the great ideas of the great thinkers of our century – and the last one.'

Daisy said nothing, but part of her was quietly reeling from his suggestion that he was more creative than she was – and also that he could happily refer to himself in the third person as a 'great thinker' like that. Ronald also appeared to have noticed this, and asked pointedly, 'So, Miles, you dabble yourself, do you? I didn't realise – want me to see if I can pull some strings and get you a deal?'

A shadow crossed Miles's face. 'Good lord, no. I don't write. I just read . . . and champion proper writers. You can't do both. Very, very few agents make writers, everyone knows that.'

Daisy smiled at him knowingly. She knew that Miles had a secret burning ambition to write. He'd told her once over a drunken dinner that he was just biding his time, just slowly getting to know the industry before he was ready to bring out his own Great Novel. Daisy looked at Miles. She watched him sip his last glass of wine, and decided that, despite all of his occasional tendencies towards arrogance, he was still gorgeous. And she knew that, beneath all this, he had a more vulnerable side – he just didn't like to show it very often. Staring at him across the lunch table, the noisy conversations of the others fell mute as their eyes met; and for a wee small moment it was just the two of them sitting there.

'Anyway,' she said, snapping out of her reverie, 'that's

surely all there is to say about notebooks – how about we talk about something else. Dessert, anyone?' She took four menus from a passing waiter and handed them around.

'Now Daisy, that's *no* way to talk about the Moleskine,' Miles continued, meanwhile playfully knocking Daisy's foot under the table. She smiled back at him, inwardly hoping no one else could see the obvious sparks that were flying off in all directions in front of them.

'It truly is an institution, Daisy,' Miles went on, clearly having memorised the blurb on the back. 'A tradition started by the legends of Picasso, Hemingway and Chatwin. It symbolises man's great reservoir of ideas and feelings through time. The spontaneity of thought, the spark of genius – it's all here, in these blank pages.' Miles smiled, then in all seriousness, bent his face into the book and inhaled its scent, just as Gerard had done earlier.

Daisy stifled a laugh. She didn't quite understand this extreme level of passion for something which was, let's face it, just a little notebook. Part of her knew that Miles was being deathly patronising to her in front of all these people – perhaps he was even trying to show her up as ill-informed. But it made no difference. She still felt her stomach swell with butterflies from being this close to him. Soon – she kept thinking – their lunch would be over. Soon she would be back at work, and the not-knowing would kick in again. She stared at him, willing him to read her mind. She wanted to ask, 'When are we going to see each other again? Are we still on a mini-break? What's going on?' Words failing her, she felt her foot extend itself under the table, reach out and nudge his foot flirtatiously. Miles flinched and he turned to her, his eyes shining. Checking that Gerard and Ronald were both deeply immersed in the dessert menu, Miles narrowed his eyes, gave a flirtatious grin, and nudged her back. Daisy smiled, feeling elated but also praying to herself that Ronald and Gerard were none the wiser.

An hour later, Daisy found herself saying, despite herself, 'Well, it's almost half three.' She looked at the others, and could feel the white wine making her slur. 'I know it's Friday and everything, but I guess we should be getting back.' She suppressed the tide of hiccups which were threatening to break out at any point, and asked a passing waiter for the bill.

Eventually, their cabs arrived and they got ready to go. Ronald, who seemed in a hurry to get back to work, quickly said his farewells. He stepped into a cab, burping to himself and adjusting his skewed brown glasses. Miles called farewell to Ronald, and then leaned in to kiss Daisy on the cheek. As she felt his skin brush against her, she felt the need to say something, to stop him from going. But the small remnant of her that wasn't swaying with alcohol remembered she needed to act professionally, so instead, 'Thanks for coming. Lovely to see you,' passed her lips. She kissed Gerard goodbye and watched him get into his cab. Miles, holding the door open for Gerard, looked back at Daisy, hovered for a second, and then leaned back towards her. 'You look amazing,' he whispered in her ear, then shook her hand. Daisy smiled back, and as she pulled her hand away, she could feel a small piece of paper buried between her fingers. She said nothing, merely looked down and squeezed it tight between her fingers lest anyone else should see. Miles climbed into his cab, and Daisy waved them both away before stepping into her own. As Ronald leaned forward to explain the convoluted

Paddington address to the cabbie, Daisy hastily opened up her crumpled fingers to reveal what was inside. Her heart in her throat, she saw that it was one of Miles's pages, torn from his precious Moleskine, bearing a message scrawled in spider-print handwriting: *'Tonight. Come over to mine as soon as you can. I'll cook. I'd love to catch up with you, beautiful. It's been too long. Mx'*

Hobbling in Heels

Turning into Union Road, Daisy limped the final leg of the journey up towards the flat. Holding her two strappy shoes in one hand and her handbag in the other, she hopped her way to the front door. Delving into her bag, she fished around for much longer than usual before eventually finding her keys and turning them in the lock. Breathing a sigh of relief at the welcoming view of the front hall, she cast her shoes and bag aside, peeled off her cardigan, and dived headfirst on to the sofa, in a most un-Daisy-like way. She closed her eyes and fell instantly asleep, fully clothed.

Two hours later, Belle kicked off her red strappy shoes at the corner of Union Road, and hopped all the way to number 42. Fishing for her Wonderwoman keyring, she flung open the door to the ground-floor flat, threw her bags down next to Daisy's, and headed straight for the living room. She had intended to nose-dive on to the sofa but was shocked to see her usually so pristine sister there, reclining, sloth-like, in the middle of the afternoon. Belle, perplexed and surprised, stood staring at her snoozing sister. Daisy was usually the pinnacle of tidiness, and at this time on a Sunday could normally be relied upon to be cleaning behind the sofa or sifting through laundry. Usually so anally tidy and immaculately dressed, she seemed somehow now to be wearing the same outfit she had left the house in on Friday morning.

Elder stared at Younger. Belle was itching to talk – she had questions – so many questions. As though she was somehow sensing Belle's stares, Daisy's eyes flung open. She looked confusedly at her elder sister, whom she had not seen for almost a week since that first encounter with Jerome and George.

'Well, hello,' whispered Daisy, hoarsely.

'Hello, dirty stop-out . . . So, what have you been up to?' Belle took up a place on the sofa next to Daisy, shoving her into a more upright position.

'Oh, my head,' Daisy exclaimed, feeling an extreme head-rush and a swooshing, room-spinning sensation as she sat up. Then, 'Oh dear GOD! My FEET!' she shouted even louder, remembering that her toes were utterly throbbing with pain after having been compressed into a microscopic space for the last two nights and days. She looked down at her feet with trepidation, and examined the purple colouring and unpleasant clusters of blisters populating her usually pristine toes.

'How the bollocks did your feet get like that?' Belle shrieked. Daisy shook her head as if to indicate what a long story it was, and Belle went to make a pot of tea.

An hour later, they were up to speed on their weekends. Belle told Daisy how she'd spent the last week in and out of George's house, and was now totally besotted with him. As it happened, she'd gone round to his house on the Monday to try and prevent her own textual apocalyse.

Much to her luck and utter disbelief, he'd not yet turned his phone on that day. Again to her luck, by the time she'd got to his place and was standing on his doorstep like a lost puppy in the rain, he'd felt compelled to invite her in. Belle had gone straight for his phone while he was in the bathroom, turned it on and quickly deleted the message. Then, George returning from the bathroom, one thing had led to another, and soon she'd completely forgotten why she was there. By the time it occurred to George to ask why she was there, she was in a euphoric, being-tickled state, and had no qualms about telling him about what she'd done after all.

Rubbing her blisters, Daisy opened up to Belle. She told her all about the impromptu lunch, and then about how Miles had charmed her into going round to his later that night. She'd gone round there as soon as possible after work, after which they'd shared what was from then on going to be referred to as the Most Romantic Weekend Ever. They'd spent all Saturday at the Tate Modern being wonderfully cultural and sophisticated, followed by a walk along the Thames and a surprise supper at the Oxo Tower restaurant. By the time Sunday morning had come around, Daisy was convinced that she and Miles had entered the Next Phase in their relationship. Although they hadn't talked about any of this yet – every time Daisy had broached the subject in conversation, he'd silenced her with a kiss – still a part of her could just *tell* from the look in his eyes that he still felt something; that they were back on. And, although she hated having gone without clean clothes for the duration, she couldn't wait to tell Amelie and Heidi the next day, and refute their suspicions that Miles was just a player. No – he was definitely keen.

Home-made-eggs-Benedict-with-smoked-salmon-breakfast in bed, followed by an hour of Thai massage, kind of keen.

Daisy curled up on the sofa, remembering how all morning they'd lain in bed together, drinking coffee and reading manuscripts. He'd read aloud the opening of a new book by a young female author he was thinking of taking on, and in turn Daisy had showed him sections of a new historical novel she was helping edit for the first time – he'd been full of inspiring, thoughtful comments as usual. Daisy had nodded in awe while he ran his hand up and down her leg and told her the story of how proofreading marks had first come about. Then he'd moved the pages aside, draped his arm around her, and, before long, the manuscript was in pieces all over the floor while they kissed and quickly forgot all about the important difference between an M-dash and an N-dash. Back on the sofa hours later, Daisy felt a twinge in her stomach thinking about him again. She took the last sip of her tea, and suddenly remembered something.

'But hold on, what did he actually say about the whole text message thing in the end?' she said, turning to Belle.

'What text message?'

Heading up Bishops Bridge Road the next day, Daisy had to consciously restrain herself from actual, full-blown, Little Bo Peep levels of skipping along. She was singing to herself, the sun was shining for the first time in days, and the usually pathetic-looking flowers outside the Mercury building were today out in full force. Even the smog in the sky seemed lighter and fluffier than usual. As she arrived at her floor she had to deploy all her energy and restraint not to go running up to Belinda and kiss her on the cheek, by way of a thank-you for Friday's lunch mishap. But, not wanting to arouse suspicion, instead she dispatched a more reserved 'Yes, it-was-very-pleasant, thank-you-for-asking' reponse.

First things first, arriving at her desk she bashed out a victorious, bordering-on-smug email to Heidi and Amelie. Seconds after clicking send, there was a call from Maggie on reception. 'Your workie's here already,' she said.

Daisy groaned. She'd completely forgotten about the imminent arrival of Workie Number Three. 'OK then, please send them up. I'll meet them by the lift, thanks.'

Waiting by the third-floor lift moments later, Daisy began to examine her nails. Definite manicure needed after the weekend, she noted. And maybe a pedicure at the same time, she thought, remembering her throbbing purple feet. She was just deciding where she could go to get this done and thinking, 'hang the expense, life is fabulous and wonderful again', when the lift opened. She peered in and scanned the lift for a 21-year-old Sloaney-looking girl. Seeing no such person inside the lift, she popped her head back out. She was just about to descend the stairs down to reception when the person who *was* in the lift suddenly spoke up. In an almost-whisper, he said, 'Um, hello.' He shifted his feet about, and added, with a little more volume, 'Are you, by any chance, Daisy?'

Daisy looked around her in surprise, wondering who this slightly awkward red-faced man could be looking for. 'Um, yes. I am.' Then it clicked. 'Oh, I'm sorry. You're not here to do work experience, are you?'

He nodded, and brushed a flop of shaggy dark blond hair out of his eye. 'Yes, that's right.'

'Sorry, How funny, I could swear Hermione told me you were a girl called Ellie,' Daisy said – uncharacteristically tactless for her.

The man flushed slightly and looked down, pretending to give himself the once over. 'Nope – last time I checked I was definitely a bloke.'

Laughing, Daisy added quickly, 'Sorry. Forgive my rudeness. Of course you are.'

He held out his hand. 'My real name's Elliot, by the way. But you can call me Ellie, if that works for you . . .' he trailed off.

'Well hi, Ellie,' she said, shaking his hand and laughing. 'No really – you wouldn't believe how rare it is to have men here of any sort – so if in doubt, we usually assume any newcomer is female. Sort of a rule of thumb now. Silly really, I know.' Daisy stopped, aware of her excessive verbosity, and also that they had yet to move away from the lift.

'Anyway, I'm Daisy – oh, but you know that too. Sorry!' she laughed, struck by how convoluted and difficult the act of speaking seemed to be today. 'Apologies – I'm not totally with it at the moment. If you want to come with me, I'll show you round.'

Elliot smiled, releasing a current of tiny crinkles across his forehead. He looked at Daisy, his eyes reflecting a wisdom that suggested he might be a good few years older than the workies she was used to shepherding. Daisy smiled back, and led Elliot through the old and rickety door marked Editorial, which quickly and loudly slammed shut behind them.

They strolled into the open-plan, dimly lit room past all the heads buried deep in manuscripts and musty concentration. 'Now, Ellie,' Daisy said, gesturing to a cluttered desk in front of them, piled high with dusty book-proofs and weathered catalogues, 'Here's where you'll be sitting this week. It's Charlotte's, well, Lottie's desk – she's a senior editor but she's away on her summer hols now. If you want to dump your stuff, then I'll take you round to meet everyone?'

Elliot smiled, and stood still awkwardly. Daisy waited for him to fuss over a coat and bag, but all he did was place a brown paper bag on to the desk, slightly ashamedly. Daisy was staring into space. Elliot cleared his throat and stared at her quizzically. Daisy snapped awake and laughed awkwardly, 'Oh, right, you're a boy. Boys don't have lots of bags and things, do they? Sorry – I'm being imbecilic today. I'll be normal again tomorrow, I promise. Right, then.'

'Heavy weekend?' Elliot asked, with a knowing grin.

'Yes. Something like that.'

Some hours later, Daisy was showing Elliot where the Jiffy bags lived and explaining, with lucid detail, how to do mail-outs.

'OK, no probs. So, no more than six books in this size of bag, yes?' Elliot asked, smiling, apparently not alarmed by the tedium of the day's work ahead of him.

'Yep, that's the stuff. And just one of each jacket, ATI, and blad – I mean sampler, to everyone on the list. Just give me a shout if you need anything else, OK? I'm going to go for lunch now. Feel free to go whenever you like. There's a canteen downstairs, if your stomach's feeling resilient.'

Elliot grinned shyly, and gestured to his brown paper bag on the desk. 'No, you're all right. I've brought my own today,' then he added, looking embarrassed, 'Money's stupidly tight at the moment. I've just got back from travelling – I've been away three years . . .'

'Really? That sounds brave,' said Daisy, who had always found the idea of backpacking and living in a shack somewhere, being bitten by snakes and savaged by mosquitoes, rather an unappealing one. 'So whereabouts did you go?'

'Bits of Africa, Asia, and all round Europe. It's hard to believe this time last month I was driving round Europe in a battered orange combie . . .'

Daisy watched as Elliot looked dreamily off into the distance, wide-eyed and whimsical at the memory of his backpacking days. She examined his unshaven, shaggy looks, and smiled. As she wandered off to meet the girls, she couldn't help thinking that, once George was past his sell-by-date, this new workie – endearingly scruffy and friendly – would make the most perfect match for Belle.

'This is incredible. What *do* they put in this stuff ?' Amelie exclaimed two days later, picking at the lunch in her lap, which today comprised a grey polystyrene box overflowing with a mixed vegetable casserole of some description. Once again the weather was unseasonably hot for June, forcing most of the girls in the building (i.e., most of the building) to flee the stuffy Mercury offices for the park, to bask in the sweltering sunshine.

'It's hard to tell,' commented Daisy, leaning in to examine the lunch in Amelie's box. 'But I will say this – it reminds me very much of what was on offer yesterday, but in an earlier incarnation. Yes that was it – ratatouille – now it looks like they've mixed it up together with the remnants of an old salad, and called it something else? Ick . . .'

Daisy turned to face her own box of food, a simple mixed salad. 'To be honest, I'm not sure about today's salady concoction either – I mean, look – they've put bits of apricot, with potato, basil leaves, tuna, and, what's this? These are definitely baked beans. I mean, I know there's being experimental, but this is surely taking it too far?'

Heidi looked smugly at both their meals, bit into her Pret no-bread sandwich and smiled, 'Never mind that, girls. There's something of the utmost significance which we need to discuss. Have you—'

At that moment, Elliot came walking into the gardens. Breaking into silence, Heidi looked across the lawn to the other side of the park. She watched him sit down on a bench. She stared as he opened up the brown paper bag on his lap, bit into a sandwich, and began to read from a crumpled, dog-eared copy of Martin Amis's *The Rachel Papers*.

'So – *that*'s what I needed to talk to you about,' Heidi said quietly. Leaning in closer to the girls, she whispered, 'Have you *seen*?'

Amelie looked up. Her blue eyes zoomed in on Elliot and she studied him as though he were a rare specimen in a petri dish. 'Yes – I think I've seen it wandering about the building.'

'Of course you have,' said Daisy. '*He* is my workie. Lovely chap he is,' she said flippantly. 'Very helpful – gets on with whatever I give him, without *ever* complaining of being bored. He's even started entering the blurbs for the next issue of the *Buyer's Guide* – can you believe that? Out of choice? Who *does* that?'

'Never mind the fact that he's *diligent*, Daisy!' scolded Heidi, 'Has the fact that he's completely *stunning* somehow escaped your attention? Do you not see? This is a break-through for publishing! The very idea that a non-freaky, presumably heterosexual male, *without* scales all over his body, and with no visible warts, would want to work here? This is an amazing thing for the industry! I'm serious. I think we should call the Society of Young Publishers immediately and have them make an announcement.'

Heidi stopped talking a moment and watched Elliot in wonderment. Silent, she studied the way he took his final bite of sandwich, then brushed the crumbs away from his lap, before settling in to read his book. She shook her head, marvelling at him as though he were a rare bird looking out over the precipice of extinction.

Daisy stared at Heidi doubtfully and rolled her eyes, 'You really think he's that nice?'

'Absolutely,' put in Amelie. 'He's got that whole messy, unshaven thing going on. Lovely. And he's got a great tan too.'

Daisy shook her head. 'That's because he's been slumming it on a beach for the last three years. Sorry – I mean, he's been exploring the world. Anyway, this is silly, us sitting gawking at him like this. Why don't I just invite him over to join us?'

Heidi's face stretched into a broad smile as Daisy stood up and waved Elliot over. Minutes later, they were all chatting together – Daisy trying in vain to protect Elliot from Heidi's viper-like questions, and attempting to keep the conversation civilised and educational for Elliot.

Daisy gestured to his book. 'Are you enjoying this?' she asked inquisitively. 'I've not read that one yet. Now *The Information* – that's amazing. I really think it's his best one . . .'

'I know!' agreed Elliot enthusiastically, 'I LOVE that book. It's *so* funny, I nearly wet myself the first time I read it – it's probably my favourite book actually – well, it's at least in my top five.'

'Me too,' agreed Daisy, feeling that perhaps the 'wetting himself' comment might have been just a little too much detail. 'Um, how about *London Fields*?'

'No, not got to that yet – although I really should do – I've just moved into Hackney, too, so it's my neck of the woods. Well, not for long. I'm sleeping on a friend's sofa until I've saved enough to rent somewhere.' He smiled. 'Hence the reason I'm doing about three different jobs at the moment!'

'Three? How *do* you manage?' asked Heidi, leaning in closer towards him, her face contorted with how very impressed she was. 'So where else do you work?'

Elliot looked mildly embarrassed at being asked to dissect his own levels of impoverishment, but nevertheless, he began to share. 'Well, first up, there's there's this lovely work experience here – which is, as you know, unpaid. Then, two nights a week I work in a pub in Soho. And, if I'm really unlucky, the charity call centre will ring me and get me to put in a few hours begging old ladies to send in their money – I hate doing that – I tell you, there're few things in this world more soul-destroying.'

Daisy laughed, 'Poor you! What else? Or surely that's enough for one man?' she said.

'So you'd think, but if you saw my overdraft you'd see why. The rest of the time I do the worst job in the history of mankind.' Seeing that the girls were hanging off his words, eager to hear more, he went on, 'I do evenings and weekends in a rather hideous place called What's Under My Skin?'

The girls burst into mild hysteria, and Heidi exclaimed, 'What on earth is that? Are you a stripper of some sort?' a flirtatious look in her eye hinting that she was hoping he'd answer in the affirmative.

Elliot's cheeks flushed momentarily but he struggled through it, 'Christ, no! It's an exhibition. You know – you'll have read about it. The one with all the dead bodies that have been dipped in acetone? They're dehydrated and then put in a vacuum filled with silicone polymer, dyed all manner of colours, filled with liquid silicone rubber, and then left to solidify into a state where they can be permanently displayed, so people can learn about the human body until long after the human race itself has passed away?'

The girls were entirely lost and confused.

'No? Well, I tell you this for free – after the novelty's worn off, you soon realise it's just a glorified morgue. And a *very* smelly one at that.'

Daisy laughed. 'It sounds horrific. And completely unethical. I mean, did the bodies sign a form before they died? Did they know they'd be used?'

'Well, apparently they've signed a contract of some sort before corking it – apparently lots of them volunteer enthusiastically for it! I could be wrong, but that's just what I've heard. Oh, and get this – they always display all the bodies holding tennis rackets and basketballs, in these lifelike sporty positions, so you have to double-take to tell if they're still alive or not!'

'Gross!' Amelie pushed her polystyrene lunch away from her, 'I'm suddenly not feeling very hungry.'

'No, me neither,' said Heidi, frowning. 'Actually, it's time we headed back in. But we really should do this again soon,' she said, smiling pointedly at Elliot.

And so they headed back, each of them trying to block out the mental images of football-playing corpses – all the while Elliot looking woeful that he'd taken his anecdote too far. In defence, he added quietly, 'Well, I guess the upside is it's really educational for people – and important for medical research, and all that stuff.'

Daisy smiled at him sympathetically as they walked up the stairs back to their floor. 'I promise to try and get you some lunch vouchers, OK? And if you're lucky, maybe even some travel expenses – then hopefully we can get you out of that awful, dreadful place!'

Elliot winked at her by way of a thank-you, and they walked back towards their desks.

Hours later, Daisy was still feeling guilty about Elliot having to take so many jobs. She got up and walked over to him. 'You know – you can take as many books as you want while you're here. Really, please help yourself to as many as you like!'

'Oh, bless you,' Elliot said humbly, 'I'll be fine. It's just that I was just stupid enough to max out all my credit cards on the last leg of my travels . . . plus I've got a student loan backlog from uni. I mean, it's all my fault, so please don't feel sorry for me.'

'OK – I promise to try. But it's just in my nature to feel sorry for people, unfortunately – even when they don't want me to. It's a problem, but I'm dealing with it. Would you like me to make you a cup of tea or coffee?'

'Christ, no. You go sit back down and do some work. *I'm* meant to be the skivvy round here, not you!' he said, giving her a nudge before going in search of tea for the department.

Moments later, Hermione, the assistant editor, emerged

from her office and headed toward the communal printer to collect some work. 'He's lovely, that one, isn't he?' she commented quietly to Daisy as she breezed past, nail file in hand.

'Certainly is. Ellie's quite the friendliest workie we've had for a while!' Daisy joked, reminding Hermione of the confusion that had occurred when they first all met Elliot.

'Shame he's only here for the week, isn't it?' Hermione added, running her fingers through her sleek dark hair and smoothing out the non-existent tangles. She was beautiful, Hermione, but beautiful in a preened kind of way. Daisy always got the sense that, when Hermione waved goodbye on a Friday afternoon, she then spent the *entire* weekend working on her appearance, so that when she arrived on a Monday she could look even more excessively well-coordinated and chic. Clearly, her year in a Swiss finishing school hadn't been for nothing.

'Really, why's he not staying longer?' Daisy enquired casually, suppressing the tide of unkind and judgemental thoughts.

'Can't afford it, I guess,' Hermione conjectured, leaning against the printer and getting to work on her nails.

'Oh, right,' Daisy said, feeling guilty again, just as Elliot returned with a tray of tea. His hand wobbled slightly while he walked, and the tray looked for a second like it might topple – the fear of which was painfully present in Elliot's eyes, as was the relief when he safely delivered it to his desk without any spillages.

'There we go. And, no tea overboard either.' He smiled, and handed the tea around to an array of gratitude.

'So, Daisy, what's next today? What jobs do you need me to do?'

Daisy drank a sip of tea and thought for a moment. 'Well. You've done most of the mail-outs that need doing this week. There're a couple more, but you can do them tomorrow. So, I suggest you attack some of the slush pile today. That's over here, by my window sill. Follow me.'

Elliot's eyes widened as Daisy lead him over to the ever-growing pile of manuscripts, big and small. They stood by the pile for a moment, and Elliot's expression appeared to change. Staring at the tower of potential bestsellers as though it were a hallowed tower containing rare and precious jewels, his face grew pensive. While Daisy began rifling through the pile, splitting it into sections, Elliot was struck still.

'Wow,' he managed. 'Is it true that the first Harry Potter manuscript was first discovered here? By some unpaid workie like me?'

'Well yes, according to publishing folklore, it was found on a slush-pile. But not this one; the Bloomsbury one. Yeah, they really struck gold there, lucky buggers. Although I'm not sure whatever happened to the clever workie that first dug it out . . . last I heard she was working in Wimpy. But that sort of thing's very rare indeed. So I wouldn't hold your breath. It's mostly . . . um, how shall I put it . . . not very good.'

With that, Daisy stuck her hand into the pile, rum-maged about with all the concentration of a plumber examining a cistern, and eventually held out a handful for Elliot to take. He bit his nails, smiled, and then cleared his throat. 'Right. That sounds great. I mean, fine. Thanks,' and he grabbed the pile with both arms, then carried it over to his desk.

As they stood by his desk, Daisy began explaining the

drill. 'So, it's pretty simple. I trust your judgement. If you see something you think has potential, then just leave it out for me. But it's most likely that you won't. You're sure to smell the 'no's' within the first few paras. Once you see them, just put them all in a pile, and then I'll send you all the different templates.'

'Templates? You mean, there're lots of different ways of saying no?' Elliot enquired.

Daisy's face fell. 'I'm afraid so – many of them very well rehearsed. It's a shame, I know. But at least we have a policy of trying to sound as polite and as human as possible. Bottom line is, we're helping to crush people's dreams here. Well, not quite on the level of Simon Cowell, but it sometimes feels like we're of the same ilk. Personally, I find that the best way to ease the guilt is just to be as nice and as personal as possible.'

Daisy fished around for some old letters and handed them to Elliot. 'Here're a few of mine you can read to give you an idea. I always try to make each letter refer back to the writing they've submitted – that way they know you've actually read their work, too. Oh, and be as diplomatic as possible; even if it's horse manure, just be nice about why it's horse manure – you know?'

Elliot was staring at Daisy, clinging to her every sentence as though her words were those of a fascinating, illuminating gospel.

Daisy studied Elliot with mild concern. 'Is that OK? Am I overloading you? Just say if I am.'

'No, no. Thank you. This is fine. Really.'

'Great. And, after that, I'd like to get you writing a few reports too, if you do find some in there that you like. It's simple really – just two pages with a synopsis, and your opinion of it. But you can ask me more about that when you get to it.'

'Sounds great. Thanks. Right, best be getting on,' Elliot said, then walked back to make a start on the rejections, a look of anxious excitement in his eyes.

Daisy smiled and went to sit down. Doing her best to remain nonchalant, she clicked casually on to her email to see if Miles had been in touch yet. Nothing. Sunday was three days ago – was she therefore technically allowed to email him yet? She picked up the phone to check out The Rules with Heidi, who usually knew best in these situations.

Paddington Press
Mercury Publishing Group Ltd.
10 Bishops Bridge Mews
London W2
editorial@paddingtonpress.com
www.paddingtonpress.com
Wednesday 21 June 2006

Dear Jon,

Thank you very much for approaching Paddington Press with your manuscript, which I have read and enjoyed. I must say I found Hephzibah to be a particularly intriguing creation.

Although I found her portrayal of life on a desert island growing up under the guidance of circus freaks and wild boars to be both compelling and fascinating, I'm sorry to say that by the end of the journey I didn't feel quite as sympathetic about her plight as I had initially hoped.

It might be that there's something missing, or even too much of something. Fewer characters? Fewer hatches? Or is it that we've all just seen enough desert-island spin-offs lately? Either way, in this increasingly cut-throat men's fiction marketplace, I'm sorry to say that we won't be able to find a slot for *Wherever I Lay my Sombrero*. That said, I do think your voice is a unique one, and I wish you a great deal of luck with finding a suitable home for your work.

With the very best of wishes,

Elliot Thornton, on behalf of Daisy Allen
Paddington Press

When is Lunch a Lunch?

'**B**ugger, arse – sorry.' Elliot mouthed across the office to Daisy as he snuck through the door into Editorial and tiptoed over to his desk. It was five past ten and he'd been hoping to slip in unnoticed. Luckily Daisy was the only person in so far. Elliot dumped down his bag, switched on his PC, and gruffly combed through his mottled tufts of hair with his fingers.

Daisy walked over to his desk, smiling breezily. 'Hey, that's OK, really – no need to feel bad. It's not as if we're paying you!'

Elliot delved into his bag, which was bursting at the seams with various uniforms and odd-job paraphernalia. He began sifting through it while he spoke, and Daisy spotted a black baseball cap that had, 'What's Under My Skin?' emblazoned across it, poking out of his bag. A blue badge with 'Can I help you please, my name is Elliurt' fell to the floor. As he bent down to pick it up, the top half of a green 'Pledge your support now' T-shirt began to fall out of the side of the bag. He fumbled around, gathering these items together. 'Thanks . . . I mean . . . sorry – really – I had to go into the call centre at 6 a.m. this morning. They had a fund-raising emergency.'

Daisy laughed. 'Who could possibly want to donate money for charity at that ungodly hour?'

'Oh, we're phoning abroad now – times are desperate. Turns out there's a whole bunch of generous people overseas. Much more chance with them than us tight-arsed Brits. Anyway, jeez – I've got to leave that job! It's just soul-destroying – even more so than the exhibition work. The scripts they make you read out! Oh, and it turns out the supervisors are all dictators. You'd expect them to all be warm, altruistic fluffy people. But oh no, they're right slave-drivers. If you don't meet your targets for that morning, they give you hell. Smile and Dial!'

Suddenly he stopped, aware of how long he'd been ranting for, and looked sheepishly at Daisy, to find her laughing. 'Sorry. That's their catchphrase they make you say. Sick, isn't it? Anyway, it's too tedious to talk about. Sorry I'm late,' he stopped, finally, and stood up. 'Can I get you a coffee?'

'That would be lovely. White with one,' fired Belinda as she strode in through the swinging doors. She smiled at Elliot, dispensed a self-important 'Daisy' before marching off to her office, exhaling speed and efficiency.

Daisy shook her head. 'I'm fine, thanks. Trying to cut down on caffeine anyway. It's terrible for you, you know,' she said, surprising herself at how motherly she sounded, as she went back to tending to the slush pile.

Hours later, Hermione sauntered in, also apparently trying to conceal her own extreme lateness. She was dressed in what seemed to be last night's clothes – short black Biba smock dress, purple leggings and black sequinned Kurt Geiger wedges. Her dark brown hair was marginally less immaculate than normal, and seemed to be glistening with the stray remnants of glitter spray from the night before.

'What. A. Night,' Hermione smirked at Daisy as she glided past her desk and self-importantly threw her handbag on to the small meeting table in the centre of the room. 'Christ. That's the absolute last time I accept an invite for one of Dad's club opening dos – they're a riot! Far too much free Cristal ... Anyway, ohmigod! I was literally standing THIS CLOSE to Christian Slater! Not sure what he was doing there, but I tell you what – his reputation's not for nothing, you know; he was almost certainly trying it on with me ...'

Daisy smiled, nodded, and opened up her email. In the background, Hermione was diving into more graphic detail about her night dancing with A-listers, and talking about how so-and-so was most definitely as anorexic as the papers said, but Daisy didn't hear a word of it. There, in the foreground, she saw with uncontrollable elation, was an email from Miles. Finally. The subject read 'Late lunch?' With trepidation, she clicked on to the email, just as Elliot turned up at her desk.

Not wanting to be rude, Daisy looked up and said hurriedly, 'Oh, no, sweets. I didn't want one.'

'Oh – I know. I just wanted to ask you something.'

'Hi – sure, what is it?' she said, itching to get back to Miles. She looked up briefly at Elliot, then, while he began talking, she felt her eyes drifting quite beyond all her control back towards the email. Her eyes quickly scanned the content for whether it was a goodie or a baddie. Looking at the second paragraph first, she saw it was a goodie – it ended with the words: 'let me know and I'll book us a table now'.

'Daisy? Did you hear any of that?' Elliot smiled. 'You really are a workaholic. You know, you *can* tear yourself from the screen to have a conversation – I'm sure Belinda would allow that, occasionally,' he joked.

Daisy wrenched her eyes from the screen and looked distractedly up at Elliot. 'Sorry. How completely rude of me. Sorry, lovely, what were you saying?'

'I said I wanted to take you out to lunch as it's my last day – sort of by way of thanks for this week.' He shifted about nervously, his eyes darting around the room. 'Um – it's just – I've learned a whole ton of stuff this week, and I've really enjoyed it. It's a shame I've got to leave, really. Sooooo . . . if you're not busy, that is, I'd like to treat you.'

Daisy quickly scanned the rest of Miles's email and looked up sympathetically towards Elliot. 'Oh hon, that's really very sweet of you to offer. But I'm afraid I've got plans this lunch,' she said, turning back to her screen, 'sorry.'

Elliot looked down at his feet, 'Sure, no problem.'

'But hey – you should definitely keep in touch. If any jobs come up, you'll be the first to know!' Daisy smiled at him, then turned back to Miles.

Just as she did, Hermione's voice shrilled out across the office floor.

'I've got nothing on this lunch, Elliot! D'you want to go to Wagamama with me? My treat?' She came out of her office. 'Lord knows, I need some carbs to soak up the alcohol pumping round my veins at the moment.'

Elliot looked around to see Hermione holding out

her right arm out towards him, every chance that she was still drunk.

'Well – that sounds great,' he said and smiled. Hermione's arm was still extended. Elliot stared at her for a while before realising that she intended him to take her hand. He obliged her and, securing it, Hermione frogmarched him away, towards her twin goals of carbs and a much-needed hair of the dog.

Before long Daisy was heavily involved in her emails again, feeling the butterflies return to her stomach. Was this a Lunch, or a *Lunch*? she wondered, as she ran to the ladies toilet to apply some emergency make-up.

Definitely a *lunch*, Daisy decided, an hour into the meal, as she stared at Miles and thought for the forty-eighth time that day how lovely his smile was. His was the kind of smile that you just could not turn away from, even if you tried. If you saw it coming, you might not be aware of it, but you'd suddenly have to stop what you were doing and watch it all. The whole thing, from start to finish, in full-blown Technicolour, until it passed. Only then could normal life resume. She'd never noticed this before, but really, when Miles Metcalfe delivered one of his smiles, it was like someone pressing a pause button on the whole world. That said, Daisy knew she had to learn to be more resistant to things like that. She also knew that she definitely ought to hold this information back for now – his head definitely didn't need to get any bigger.

'Mmmm. Right, I see,' Miles said, scratching his head. While they were waiting for their dessert, he was looking over some passages of a crime novel, which she was co-editing with Hermione. He indicated the area on the page with the most red ink. 'See this bit you've circled here. You were right to question it. I can see what the author's trying to do, but it doesn't work,' he said, in his usual tone, brimming with wisdom. 'I'd cut that whole section, if I were you – it's a total red herring, but in a bad way.'

Daisy nodded eagerly as he went on, thumbing through the pages. 'And you see this bit here? I'd get him to just write that in the third person, otherwise it's a bit clunky. Switching narrative modes sporadically is rarely successful – you stand to lose a lot by gambling with modes like that.'

'Right you are,' Daisy said, marvelling at his eloquence, and looking into his eyes. His eyelashes were so long and thick, she'd often seriously wondered whether he wore mascara. She'd once made the mistake of asking him, and he'd flushed the colour of her hair with embarrassment. Proof that yes, he definitely had a soft side in there somewhere. Maybe now was the time to tap into it a little.

'So – I was thinking – it's been a while now, you know,' she began.

'What has?' he said, offering her some of his orange sorbet dessert.

'I mean . . . oh, no – no, thanks. I'm allergic to orange, I'm sure I've told you that before? Anyway, I mean, it's been a while – like – almost six months now, ish, since we've been, well, seeing each other . . .'

Miles looked uncomfortable.

'And I was just thinking – that's nice, isn't it?'

'Yes.'

Daisy looked expectant. She'd been hoping for more than monosyllables. But in return, Miles simply looked defensive.

'Like I said before I went away,' he began, patiently,

'let's take things one step at a time . . . you know, neither of us wants anything too serious at the moment, do we?'

'Oh no – not yet, of course,' said Daisy, nodding so vigorously that even she almost believed herself.

'So, tell me about the gossip at Mercury,' he said, back in agenting mode. 'Is Belinda still carrying on with what's-'is-face?'

'Miles! Sometimes I wonder whether you are, in fact, female! No, I think that's all blown over now,' Daisy said, smiling gingerly as Miles took her hand in his and squeezed it affectionately.

Some two hours later, Daisy stumbled into the lift, staring at her watch in shame and disbelief. A quarter to four? She'd never been this late back from lunch. As soon as the lift doors to the third floor opened, she ran out and flung open the clunky editorial door. She raced over to her desk. Looking over to Elliot's desk, she saw with surprise that it was empty; his jacket and bag gone from the chair. Then she remembered – he'd asked to leave early today for an emergency exhibition shift. She hadn't meant to be out so long with Miles – but then he just seemed to have a way with her. Of smiling that infectious smile of his, of subtly refilling her wine glass, and of looking at her in that effort-lessly piercing way. And as a result, out went her normally so rigid sense of time-keeping. She felt doubly guilty now – first for rejecting Elliot's invitation, and now this; not even bothering to come back and say goodbye on his last day. He'd been the best workie she'd ever had, and she'd barely even thanked him! She'd email him as soon as possible to apologise for her bad form. Or at least she would, if he'd left his email. Rats. She had no way of getting in touch with him! Mentally chastising herself over her uncouth behaviour, which was so unlike her, she tried to console herself with the fact that this was all down to Miles, and the fact that Lunch With Miles II had been a fabulously romantic event once again. Well, all except for that whole 'taking things one step at a time' business, but not wanting to spoil her mood, she buried this thought for now.

Sitting at her desk, her hands clasping the throbbing patch on her forehead in an attempt to balance out the swaying brought on by the fourth glass of rosé, she soon became aware of a newly erected mountain of manuscripts on her desk, towering intimidatingly above her. And, on top of that, there was a handwritten note, scrawled on torn Moleskine paper and nestling upon the top of the manuscript tower. Rather like a fairy on a Christmas tree, she thought, in her much-too-much-rosé-kind of way.

'Gosh!' she exclaimed aloud when she spotted who it was from. 'Hurrah for Elliot.' Then, with a frightened gasp, she looked around her to check if anyone had heard. She was all-too-often bullied for the times when Enid Blyton terminology fell inexplicably from her mouth unchecked. Swaying slightly, Daisy read the note and was relieved.

Daisy, here's the latest batch of slush. This is as far as I got to, I'm afraid – so still a fair bit to get through. Sorry I had to dash (those charmless corpses wait for no man). Thanks for everything. I owe you one – if you ever need any other help, in any way, don't hesitate to call. E. [07311] 444 025, or elliotthornton@yahoo.co.uk

Such a shame to see him go. She was going to miss having him around. What a relief that he'd left his details, though. Fighting off her drunken lethargy, she emailed him to say thanks for everything, best of luck, keep in touch – all the usual clichés which came to mind. She vowed there and then to keep in touch with him properly, and to try, in her own small way, to help him into the industry.

Signal Failure

The next few days flew by in a busy midsummer haze. Over the weekend that had followed, Daisy was falling a little more in love with Miles, while Belle was falling a lot out of love with George. Miles was away on business, so in his absence Daisy spent a quiet weekend sleeping off the week's hangover and pottering in her flat – baking, tidying, ensuring that her fingers and toes got their much-needed manicure and pedicure, and all the while reminiscing about her lunch with Miles. Late on the Sunday, Belle had reappeared, having been at George's most of the weekend. Daisy could see from Belle's sunken expression as she strolled in that sure enough, George had just expired from Belle's stringent Use-By date. In her defence, Belle did always try and fight it, but if her history was anything to go by, very few men ever made it past her two-week mark.

'Itchy feet again already?' Daisy asked, raising the kettle in the air in a questioning way towards Belle.

'Yes – and yes again. I really need tea,' Belle said as she sloped through to the living room and draped herself across the sofa, switching on the television and idly yo-

yoing through episodes of *Friends*. 'Seen it, seen it, seen it, ooh – might not have seen!' She grabbed a cushion and curled up with it. 'So, how was your weekend? Looking forward to work tomorrow?'

Daisy dropped two tea bags into the two matching mugs which she'd spent the previous evening bleaching out. She looked deep inside the mugs and admired her handiwork in removing the tea stains, and wondered with increasing alarm why things like that gave her so much pleasure. Was she ill, she wondered? Old before her time? Suppressing these chilling thoughts she shouted a reply to Belle in the living room, 'Um, well, not really ... Dull Charlotte's still away so I've got all her work to do. And since my really nice, helpful workie left, I've suddenly got tons more to do than I realised. I wish he'd come back!'

'Oh!' Belle was saying to herself on the sofa, barely listening to Daisy. 'There was something amazing I had to tell you. What was it? Damn it, it's gone! I had it!'

Daisy poured boiling water into the mugs, not listening to her sister either. 'You know what, actually, if only he was still working with us – I reckon he'd really be your type, this guy. Elliot was his name ... thoroughly nice bloke. Messy, skanky-looking hippie type, all chiselled, stubbly – right up your street ... Belle, are you even listening?' she called through to the living room, where Belle had just leapt into the air, sending her cushion flying.

'*That* was it!' She ran into the kitchen, almost colliding with Daisy and almost sending the boiling tea flying.

Daisy calmly returned the mugs to the kitchen table. '*What* was it?'

'The thing I had to tell you! *The* best news. The Bedford – the pub down in Balham – it's started that open mike night again – well, it's more of a jam night – where randoms just get up on stage and make music together – you know, total strangers, all with different talents, jamming together!'

Daisy's face creased with confusion, 'Sounds dreadful to me – do people *pay* to go and see it?'

'No! Anyway, you're wrong. It sounds amazing! I've got to go! And you, lady, are coming with me! It's time I got spotted. I've been on the shelf too long . . .' she trailed off, and launched into the chorus of one of her favourite songs that she'd written.

Belle's music career had been on a back-burner for some time now, while her waitressing career took centre stage. She'd been made manager of the local café round the corner from them, which was fine for a few weeks, until she realised that accepting a promotion in a job like that was basically like saying she'd given up on her music altogether. It was actually George who'd been able to convince her to give her singing another go. Two years ago, she'd been so close to a record deal that she could smell it, but it had fallen through at the last minute. But now, having quit the waitressing job on impulse, she was itching to get out there again. Bella Allen was back with a vengeance – so she announced to an inwardly fretful Daisy.

'The only trouble is, I'll have to change my name, now that Lily Allen's all popular now. I don't want people getting me confused with her. Or worse, thinking we're related. What do you think? How about . . . Bella Black?'

'Ick. It sounds like Cilla Black!'

The girls burst into laughter as they arranged cushions and made themselves comfortable in front of the television.

'Anyway, never mind that. Have you thought about how you'll make your next rent cheque?' Daisy asked, unable to mask her concern.

'Shhhhh . . . this is the really funny bit!'

Two days later, Daisy was stirring an almost completely cold cup of tea, and staring straight ahead of her at the weathered book poster, which was tacked up on the wall in front of her desk. Where to start, she wondered. So much to do, yet she still didn't seem to be able to get into gear. Now that her most Efficient Elf Ever had been gone for over a week, there suddenly seemed to be so much more work to do than normal. She was just about to go in search of fresh tea, when a little envelope popped up on her screen.

Date: Tuesday 27 June 2006 19.08
Sender: elliottthornton@yahoo.co.uk
To: DaisyAllen@paddingtonpress.com
Subject: Thanks and please

Hey Daisy

Thanks for your email. Great to hear from you . . .
Well, life's OK – just going from crap job, to slightly less crap job, to Oh God, please let me die job. Under My Skin rocks though – I've made up a new fun game, you should come and partake sometime soon. Call centre is still unbearable. I was there yesterday, and was seriously tempted to chew my fingers off, just to break up the monotony of the day. How's Belinda? Has she stopped the 'toilet ban during work hours' yet?!

Anyway – am just getting back on the old applying for jobs wagon. Which means at least 15 begging letters and spec CVs a day. So . . . you being the well-connected editorial princess that you are, I wondered if I could poach you for any contacts. Emails, phone numbers, addresses . . . you know, so my stalking campaign can really get off the ground. Also, I've been through my CV and added the gargantuan experience gained at Paddington, but I'd be infinitely grateful if you wouldn't mind looking through it and giving me your advice on it? I've still got things like boy scouts on there (my mum forced me to go when I was a wee sprog) – I should take that off, right? Undoubtedly. Trouble is, that doesn't leave me with much in the way of hobbies. Aside from reading and writing. Is it too much to include breathing in 'other skills'? Any ideas humbly received.

God, sorry, just read this back and it's official – I'm alarmingly dull.

Anyway, herewith attached, my CV. Let me know if it works – have tried to attach it three times and file keeps enigmatically disappearing. Hotmail and 'Ozzie's Internet Bar' aren't a happy combo. If you can bear it, I'll attach some of my cover letters another time. But I'm going to have to go now as it's horrendously hot in here, and the man with cauliflower ears who has been staring at me with a manic look in his eyes for the last half-hour is making a beeline for me. Right, I'm going to stop waffling nonsense and go.

I'd say 'let's meet up for a coffee' sometime, but I can't foreseeably see (sense?) when I'll next have any spare time. I'll let you know in a week or so when I'm a little calmer though.

Hope all's well, and thanks again,

Elliot

Chuckling to herself, Daisy began browsing through Elliot's CV. She *loved* looking at other people's CVs – it gave her a strangely guilty feeling of pleasure, as though she was being terribly nosy, even though it was actually allowed. She looked at Elliot's birth date and was surprised to see that he was actually only a year older than she was. She'd had him down as much older – but that could just be on account of his stubbly, worldly-wise expression. She read on, discovering with a slight sense of awe that despite his humble, self-deprecating exterior, he was actually alarmingly accomplished for his age. Not only did he have a first from St Andrews, but at secondary school he'd been one of those infuriating clever kids that got pushed up a year, so as not to be 'slowed down by his peers'. Not only that, but he also spoke three languages fluently, and had been an intern at Random House Publishers in Sydney only eighteen months ago. Suddenly feeling like a hopeless underachiever, Daisy made a few notes on his CV, and began to type out a quick reply.

Soon it was gone eight o'clock, and everyone else had left, except for Hermione, who was pottering in her small office next to Belinda's. Hermione, it seemed, was doing her usual trick of appearing to work very late, but in reality using her desk as a base for all kinds of personal activities.

Hermione didn't know it, but when her door was slightly ajar, Daisy could hear every last word of Hermione's phone conversations. It really wasn't in her nature to listen but after a while, eavesdropping became an unavoidable reality. She tried as hard as she could not to hear all about Hermione's ex-boyfriend and his yacht on the Mediterranean. She tried desperately not to hear all about the offer Hermione was putting in for the flat in Clapham, and how the last one fell through and this had better not happen again, please, Daddy. And in vain, she tried not to see the sailing holidays which were being so diligently researched on lastminute.com, which would surface one by one on the communal printer as Daisy went over to collect her own immaculate Excel grids which so eloquently narrated all of next year's publishing schedules. Most of all, Daisy tried not to notice the speculative job letters which came spurting out on to the printer tray addressed to all manner of other publishers – Penguin, Macmillan, Virgin, Bloomsbury and Random House. Of course Daisy didn't mind that Hermione was doing all these things – Daisy was Office Skivvy; she knew her place. But, she began hoping, if those letters were anything to go by, maybe there was a light at the end of the tunnel? Maybe one day, she'd get to rise out of this eternal state of assistant-dom which had plagued her for the last few years. The Mercury recruitment motto, it was a known fact, was simple: 'everybody stay where you are'. The policy, for as long as Daisy, Heidi and their other friends had been there, was that you stayed in your current position, unless anyone moved. Even if you were amazing at your job, you stayed there for a year, for five years, until someone above you in the food chain either expired, gave it all up to go and be an investment banker or, worse, jumped ship to a rival publisher. This was also a real shame for someone like Elliot, who was clearly talented, but unable to find a way into the industry. Or was it just the fact he'd left the phrase 'keen member of the Boy Scout Association 1987–89' on his CV all this time, which would surely be enough to make most employers run for the hills?

'If you're just going to stare into space daydreaming, sweetie, you may as well go home and do it there – don't you think?'

Daisy jumped. Looking up, she saw that Hermione was staring down at her, clutching the wads of paper in her arms. Daisy hovered. She'd meant to email Miles to find out whether he was back from his business trip yet. But catching Hermione's pained expression, and noticing that she clearly wanted to make her phone calls in peace, Daisy nodded, grabbed her handbag and holdall full of manuscripts and stood up. 'Sure thing. Night, then.'

'Night, poppet,' Hermione said saccharinely. 'Oh – and you didn't see anything on the printer just then, did you?'

'Me? No, not at all. I've just been sitting here, staring into space, like you said. Time to take myself to bed, I'm shattered.'

She walked away, catching Hermione's look of relief out of the corner of her eye.

Half an hour later, Daisy was waiting on a crowded, sweaty platform at Embankment. She saw with dismay that the Northern Line had picked today to break out into its weekly rash of signal failure. Eventually, after much delay and tantrum-like behaviour from a frustrated South London contingent, a rusty, graffiti-adorned tube train finally pulled in. Waiting for the sea of eager commuters to thin out, Daisy prepared herself for battle. She took a deep breath. She clambered on to the crowded tube car, clutching her wad of A4 manuscripts close to her chest as everyone else pushed and shoved their way aboard, most of them awash with got-to-get-a-seat-anxiety. Fortunately, Daisy had spotted her target early and, reaching it, gleefully sat down. She sighed with colossal relief and began leafing through her latest batch of submissions, hoping they'd all be good at taking her mind off Miles. She considered which one would grab her attention first. She thumbed through the pile of photocopied pages despondently. She knew already how they'd be – the usual collection of badly written, ill-thought-out meanderings, dotted with clichés and implausible characters. In fairness, the senior editors did get to read the better stuff – the stuff that came from agents and had therefore already been filtered out to some extent. It was Daisy's job to read everything else out of politeness. Leafing through the wads of loose bundles, she suddenly felt herself lose grip of some of the papers. Before she could stop them, three or four thick clusters of manuscript pages went shooting out in different directions all over the tube carriage floor. Her face flushing instantly red, Daisy apologised to the throng of irritable faces looking down at her.

'But you've got a seat,' she could hear them thinking scathingly, 'you jammy princess, while we're all standing. And yet, you can't even keep a grip on all your belongings. Sort yourself out, woman,' they all taunted in her overactive imagination. 'Sorry,' Daisy mouthed as she fumbled about awkwardly in amongst their feet and bags, to try and gather together the stray pages. 'So very, very sorry.'

Fortunately, there was a man fumbling around on the

floor with her. She looked across to see a kind-faced man with thinning dark brown hair who, quite incongruously, seemed to be trying to help her. After a moment's grappling on the floor, he passed her a wodge of papers. 'Don't worry about it – here you go,' he said, placing the pages in her hand with a smile.

Daisy grinned excessively at him and stammered, 'Thank you . . . so much.'

Sitting back down on her seat, her cheeks hot with shame, she looked back down at the bundle of papers and noticed that there now seemed to be one title page which stood out more prominently than the others. Raking together all the other submissional detritus, Daisy stowed them safely in her bag, but kept this one small bundle of neatly typed pages aside. Daisy looked up to thank the man again for his help, but he was nowhere to be seen; he must have just left the train at Waterloo, the last stop, she presumed. It had all happened so quickly. She hadn't even noticed him go, and now felt slightly bemused by the whole thing. She looked back down at the thin sheaf of pages in her lap, casually stapled together. Unlike all the others, there was no covering letter of any sort accompanying these chapters. No heartfelt plea about why this was such a good book. No sales points. No ill-conceived marketing ideas. No unwieldy potted biography. None of that; just a simple title page, which read in tiny, modest letters, *Duende Dawn* by Will Marwood.

Daisy straightened herself up, forgot all about the other passengers and their seat-envy, and began to read. She smiled. An odd first line, but intriguing nonetheless, she decided and read on. She read through the opening pages, which told of one Edward Bean, a quirky, slightly neurotic man in his mid twenties. One page in, Daisy became oblivious to everything around her – even to the muffled announcers over the intercom bringing tidings of further signal failure and delays.

She read on, learning more about Edward. He was an aspiring artist, based in London, and had a job doing grudge work in an independent art gallery in Islington. In this piece, the prologue, he was talking about how things could all have been very different if it weren't for life's little complications. Daisy quickly felt herself warming to the author's style, and before long she arrived at the closing paragraph of Chapter One. With a smile on her face, she read on at hyperspeed into the next.

But then she saw with trepidation that the author – who was showing a good deal of promise so far – was now about to experiment with the much-maligned literary technique known as the flashback; widely considered in most publishing circles to signify Death To All Pace and Authorial Tension. Nevertheless, Daisy read on without looking up, hoping Will would have it in him to prove them wrong. In a flash, the setting changed. Edward, in preparation for an exhibition he was giving in the autumn, had taken a three-month sabbatical, in the hope of gathering inspiration and producing some paintings. From his mould-ridden flat in Finsbury Park, the book travelled across the continent to southern Spain. Over the next chapter, the book began again in the romantic world of orange blossom, tapas bars and horse droppings.

As Daisy read on, Edward was finding his feet in Seville, wandering about in the relentlessly sweltering heat, gathering sketches in his notebook whenever something caught his eye. Then, at the first pangs of hunger, he began searching for the perfect tapas bar. Eventually he found one, went straight to the bar and made some bumbling, stammering attempts at ordering. After a while it was clear he wasn't going to get anywhere, on account of his non-existent Spanish vocabulary – other than *venga*, which meant 'hurry up' and now seemed faintly ironic. Edward was just about to give up, having only managed to order several types of potatoes, when a woman next to him asked, in perfect English, if he would he like any help. He was about to turn to her and compliment her on her fine English accent, when he stopped mid-sentence. Of all the bars in all the world . . .

Daisy took a deep breath. As she went to turn the page into Chapter three, she felt her stomach lurch.

'All changeplease. Thisistheendoftheline. Morden-station. Allchangeplease.'

Daisy looked around her in horror. This was unthink-able. How had this happened? How had she managed to travel all the way past Stockwell and into deepest, darkest Morden, without even noticing? She'd never once missed her stop, not for anything!

She gathered up her pages and hurriedly stepped off the train. She walked up the stairs and over the open foot-bridge towards the northbound platforms, then descended into hordes of flustered, weary faces, and a sign: '*Severe delays northbound on both branches. Customers advised to seek alternative transport.*'

She sighed and leaned against the white breeze-block wall. How annoying! She hugged herself from the cold thinking how bizarre it was to be trapped in Morden (or Mordor, as Belle always liked to call it), the most far-flung, stop on what was officially known as the worst line in the

Underground network. So, not just the end of the line, but the end of the Misery Line? So, you might say, this was the metaphorical equivalent of reaching the outermost limit, the lowest echelons of gloom? Sighing, Daisy decided she didn't have the strength left in her for negotiating South London buses, and would rather settle in for the long wait until the trains recovered themselves. She wrapped her summer jacket around her tightly, pulled out Will's final chapter, and sat down on the bench. Even though it was now the last week in June, here in Morden it felt more like autumn – with its own cooler climate, distinct from the sunny smog of London proper. Feeling the thickness of the remaining pages of Will's book, and lamenting that there wasn't more left to read, Daisy turned reluctantly to the third and final chapter of the sample.

While Daisy was trying in vain to blank out the despondent noises of the commuting community around her, Edward was trying in vain to get over the shock of seeing Lauren Harper standing next to him – Lauren, the girl from the gallery, the one he kept seeing around back in London but had never dared speak to. After some time, Edward was finally able to speak, and gratefully accepted her offer of help, before asking her to join him. She admitted she'd seen him around before too, but she didn't know where. Before long they were clinking glasses, getting to know each other over calamares and patatas bravas, and marvelling at the smallness of the world.

Around Daisy, the speakers began to announce the rebirth of the northbound trains. Her ears pricked up and she felt people moving to the opposite platform, where the first train was almost ready to depart. But she remained frozen in her seat. She was determined to get to the end before going anywhere. As she read through the final pages and her eyes landed on the final few paragraphs, a strange feeling swept over her. Edward was telling Lauren in garrulous detail all about what it had been like growing up in France, in a farmhouse in the Dordogne, when suddenly he stopped, realising that he had no idea where Lauren was from herself. Abruptly, he demanded to know where she'd grown up as a child. Lauren shrugged, flapped her hands in the air dismissively, and said, 'Oh – you probably won't have heard of it. It's a small, uninspiring little place near Wimbledon, right out, about as far-flung as you can get, at the end of the Northern Line'.

Daisy read on, feeling a slight wooziness as Edward demanded to know the name and Lauren replied, 'Morden.'

Sofas and Serendipity

Daisy was in early. She raced out of the lift, clasping a tower of books under one arm and a frothy chai latte in the other. People sent casual 'hellos' in her direction as she raced through the corridors, but mostly they didn't reach her – all she could think about was getting to her desk.

She logged on at hyperspeed, watching her computer load up, impatiently tapping the mouse as if to speed it along. She straightened out the title page with the email address on it, and opened up her email. This time she didn't even glance at the contents of her inbox; instead, she sped straight into compose new mail, her fingers bashing the keys impatiently.

Date: Wednesday 28 June 2006 08.17
Sender: DaisyAllen@paddingtonpress.com
To: justwilliam26@hotmail.co.uk
Subject: DUENDE DAWN

Dear William

Thank you very much for sending us your manuscript

for DUENDE DAWN. I very much enjoyed reading this material, and think there might be something here. Would you be able to send me over the rest of the novel, together with a synopsis of some sort (just 1–2 pages summarising the plot)?

Then perhaps we might meet, and you can tell me a bit about yourself, and how you came to write it etc.?

I look forward to hearing from you.

Thanks, and all best wishes,

Daisy Allen,
Editorial, Paddington Press

Daisy clicked 'send', and then stared at her outbox, watching the email disappear. She started to imagine what would happen next in the book. Hours later, she'd made feeble attempts to get on with her work, but her eyes kept wandering back to her screen, to her inbox. It was almost as though watching it would make him reply sooner. As though starting another task of some sort would slow the email down. Or, somehow the email would know that she wasn't there, watching its arrival, and it would get an attack of shyness, and crawl back away from her inbox. She tried to get on with the many other tasks that desperately needed her attention, but something kept pulling her back. She knew she was being slightly hysterical, but she couldn't bear the thought of a reply coming and her not being there to receive it the very moment it arrived. She kept wondering, what would happen next in the book.

What was this author like? How old was he?

'Daisy! Daisy, are you listening to me?'

'What, sorry, who?' Daisy looked up to find Belinda staring at her anxiously.

'I *said*, I'm just off for a coffee with Ron, so take any calls for me – I'm expecting an important call from Germany. And photocopy this for me and distribute it to everyone on the list,' she barked, throwing the pile of pages down, before mooching thanklessly away.

'Right, yes, of course,' Daisy said firmly, trying to propel herself into action. She looked down at the papers in her hand and tried to focus. She had so much work to do it was almost getting out of control. And yet, it all seemed to be in Dutch to her today – every task she started she didn't seem able to finish. Ever since reading the extract last night in Morden she'd not been able to get this book, nor this Will Marwood figure, out of her head. Who was he? Where was he from? Scotland? Seville? Morden?

At lunch, she tried to take her mind off the still non-existent reply from Will, and tuned into the girls' gossip in the canteen. Now that the heatwave of early June had been and gone, it was raining heavily outside and the girls were huddled together round a booth, sharing a large plate of home-made pizza. This week was 'Italy Week' in the Mercury Café. Maybe next week the promotion would be Spain, Daisy hoped, but didn't say.

'Mmmmm,' exclaimed Amelie. 'This is surely the best grub I've ever tasted here. Chapter Ten is going up in the world!' Chapter Ten was Mercury's café – so called because it corresponded to their street number in Bishops Bridge Mews.

'I know – it's really good. What do you think, Dazey one?'

The girls looked at Daisy, who was staring into space, prodding her food with her fork in slow motion, a vacant look in her eyes.

'Oh, God, what is it now? What's Miles done this time? Sweets, why are you looking even *less* focused on reality than normal?' asked Amelie.

'Oh, it's nothing. It's not Miles. He's fine. Well, I guess. Actually – it's just this submission I've had. I can't seem to get it out of my head, that's all. I think it might really be worth something.'

'Don't be a cretin,' scoffed Heidi, 'there's never anything worth anything on the slush pile. You said so yourself. All the other editors get the good stuff before you. Are you sure you didn't imagine it?'

'I'm quite sure. It's weird – I don't know much about it. There was no covering letter, no synopsis – it wasn't even that well presented compared to the others. But I read the first four chapters last night, and I'm telling you . . . I'm just really intrigued by it . . .'

'Really, what happens?' asked Heidi, suddenly more interested.

'I'll tell you more about it soon. But last night, the oddest thing happened.' Daisy began a rapid narration of how she'd ended up in Morden by mistake. She paused for breath. 'I mean, this is *me*! I've *never* missed my stop! Not for anything! And there I am, suddenly in the centre of the town where the heroine of the book just happens to be from! I mean, talk about blurring the line between fiction and reality! How weird is that!' she said, in her best don't-you-dare-disagree-with-me voice.

'Well, it is sort of creepy I guess,' said Amelie.

'No, it's not,' said Heidi forcefully, 'it's just a coincidence – it doesn't mean anything – surely you can see that, love? You and your love affair with serendipity . . .'

'Well, yes, but I don't know . . . it just kind of weirded me out,' Daisy stopped, trying to find the right words, 'and, I know this sounds ridiculous, but now I just feel oddly connected to this piece of writing – as though it was some kind of sign or something. Which is really rather silly of me, I know . . .'

Heidi and Amelie laughed and – as was so often the custom at these lunch meetings of theirs – looked at Daisy with concern. 'Yes – yes, it is rather stupid, Daisy dearest,' put in Heidi in her best attempt at sensitivity.

'I also can't help wondering now . . . was there something funny about the man on the train who helped me? Like, I mean, is there any chance that he *gave* me the manuscript? It's just, this book is just so, so different to everything else I normally dig up on the slush pile!'

'Now that really *is* ridiculous, you ditzy girl,' scoffed Heidi, 'What do you mean? This man, he just carries it around, all the time, in case he bumps into ditzy editorial assistants?'

'Yeah, right,' Amelie put in sarcastically, 'I expect he just rides up and down the Northern Line, on overcrowded tube carriages all day long, just in case . . .'

Daisy frowned, feeling crestfallen that her friends weren't as excited as her. 'Well, I'm just holding my breath for him to email me back with the rest of it. And, for him to tell me a bit about himself – until then, I just keep wondering what he'll be like; how old he is, and all that stuff.'

'Daisy honey, you're sounding like a bit of a mentalist again. Why can't you just see things as they are? Why are you always taking these one-way trips into la-la land?'

Daisy felt hurt. 'Well – I *was* going to tell you what it's about, but I'm not going to now. I think I'd rather keep it as my little secret . . .' she said half teasingly, with a look of mock protest. 'Anyway, you guys can finish this bit of pizza, I'm done. I've got to get back . . .' and she slipped away to go and catch up with her emails.

Back at her desk, she saw with elation that it had finally come! But there was nothing attached.

Date: Wednesday 28 June 2006 13.10
Sender: justwilliam26@hotmail.co.uk
To: Daisy.Allen@paddingtonpress.com
Subject: **Re: DUENDE DAWN**

Dear Daisy

Thank you very much for your email. I'm delighted that you enjoyed reading my work, and I'm sorry it comes to such an abrupt end at the moment.

I would love nothing more than to send you the rest of my novel. Unfortunately, though, I'm still in the process of writing it. I do have a few more chapters written, but they're presently in a very crude form, and need quite a bit of attention. Once I've edited those sufficiently, I'll happily send them over to you. As for the rest, I'll get my head down and get on with it as soon as I can. I do have it all planned out, so it should take me a matter of weeks, months . . . Would that be OK?

If there's any problem, then please don't hesitate to get in touch. Would you like me to send you it in dribs and drabs, or all in one go when I'm done? I'm not sure how these things normally work.

Hope that's OK. Thank you very much again,

William

Daisy thought for a moment. What would Hermione or Belinda do in this sort of situation, with an incomplete script? She meditated on this for a while, until she was interrupted by the sound of yelling from the direction of Belinda's office.

'What do you mean, it was down on the order form? No, it quite simply wasn't! That's what I've been trying to explain to you for the last twenty minutes! I. Ordered. A. Matching. White. Set. Of. Leather. Sofas. And that, quite frankly, isn't what you and your cavalcade of monkeys have delivered to me! Not only did they turn up two hours later than was indicated by their vague promise of "any time between 6 a.m. and 12 p.m.", BUT they've also delivered the wrong thing!' Belinda paused for breath. 'What do you mean, that's what the computer says?'

Pause.

'GGRRRRHHHHH!!!' I give up!' With that, there was the noise of Belinda slamming down the phone. Then the sound of her bashing in a new number, and proceeding to narrate the entire contents of the previous conversation to her husband, a harassed headmaster of their local grammar school in Walton-on-Thames. 'Lawrence? Lawrence! I've had nothing but trouble from those sofa people again! Will you speak to them please and sort this mess out?'

Daisy went back to her email. Rather than asking Hermione or Belinda for advice, she decided on following her instincts.

Date: Wednesday 28 June 2006 13 : 38
Sender: Daisy.Allen@paddingtonpress.com
To: justwilliam26@hotmail.co.uk
Subject: **Re: Re: DUENDE DAWN**

Dear William

Thank you for your email. That *is* a shame – I was really looking forward to seeing what happens next. But don't worry, it's no problem for us, we'll happily wait until you're ready.

Yes please, do drip-feed me with the new stuff as soon as it's done. I'm really intrigued by the story already – and at the risk of giving you a big head, I think the way you handle the flashbacks, and the change in setting is very impressive.

Obviously this is still extremely early days, and this is just my humble opinion talking at the moment, but I have to say I really liked what I have read.

There's no pressure – please just get on with writing the rest when you can. Things are so busy here at the moment, I think it would take a while before I could pin down my boss long enough to get her to read it anyway. If, in the meantime, you would like to meet up for a coffee, then do let me know.

That's all for now. I shall eagerly await the next instalment . . .

All best wishes

Daisy

Daisy sat staring at the screen, anxious for a reply. When none came, she began to reason that perhaps the last exchange needed no further comment. She began to think about when to tell Belinda about all this. But the more she thought about it, the more demonic a prospect that became in her mind. Quickly, she decided it would be far more sensible to put this off until another time. Yes, best to wait until she'd read the rest, and she was really sure of it. She sat watching her screen a little while longer, until the growing din coming from Belinda's office became too much to bear, and she got up to see whether she could be of any help. The closer she got to the office, the more afraid she became.

'Hello! At last! I tell you, if I have to listen to "Greensleeves" a minute longer, I swear that someone there is going to get very hurt! Now, can I speak to your supervisor? Oh, and please . . . NoooooooooO!!!!!'

Daisy backed away from the door, recoiling in fear. Walking back to her desk, she decided that the best thing to do in this instance would be to keep well away. She could hear her phone ringing, and sprinted back just in time to catch a phone call from reception.

'Hello?'

'Hello, it's Maggie. Guess who's got flowers?!'

Daisy thought for a moment. 'Belinda? Really? Who are they from?'

'No, silly – you! Come see, they're beautiful!'

Daisy had never been sent flowers before. She ran down the stairs two at a time, and bounded up to Maggie on the large reception desk. 'Wow!'

'They're lovely! They're lilies,' gushed Maggie, pointing out the obvious. 'Look, they've even got little daisies in them – how thoughtful!

'Wow – yes, they are,' Daisy managed.

'Who are they from?' asked Maggie, smiling the big, maternal grin she reserved for her favourite Mercury girls.

Daisy looked at the label. 'Wow,' Daisy said a third time, genuinely shocked. The note read *I'm back from NY. Meet me for lunch tomorrow? M.'* This must surely be a good sign, she thought.

'They're from my boyfriend. He's never sent me flowers before!'

Once Maggie had made sufficient cooing noises, Daisy clutched the flowers to her chest and headed upstairs, a huge smile on her face. After raiding the third-floor kitchen for a vase, she trimmed the stalks and arranged the flowers neatly on her shelf. She desperately wanted to phone Miles, but thought better of it, and decided that a more detached text with just the one kiss would suffice for now.

'Thank you for the lovely flowers! So sweet!
Cu tomorrow for lunch, Dx'

A reply from Will eventually came, but not until the next day, just before lunchtime.

Date: Thursday 29 June 2006 13.00
Sender: justwilliam26@hotmail.co.uk
To: Daisy.Allen@paddingtonpress.com
Subject: Re: Re: Re: DUENDE DAWN

Dear Daisy

Thanks for that. Big relief. I'll aim to have two more chapters with you within a week. After that, I've managed to move things around work-wise so that I'll have a bit more time on my hands to motor on with the rest of it. I'll keep you posted.

Thanks again, and have a good afternoon,
Will

Date: Thursday 29 June 2006 13.10
Sender: Daisy.Allen@paddingtonpress.com
To: justwilliam38@hotmail.co.uk
Subject: Re: Re: Re: Re: DUENDE DAWN

Will,

Excellent, thanks very much indeed. Where do you work when you're not writing, then? Or is that a bit of a nosy question!?

Daisy

When Will came back a minute later with an aloof 'Oh, it's too much of a long story to go into now . . .' Daisy began to worry that maybe she *had* been a bit inappropriate. Had she unwittingly crossed a line as far as 'new author' care and etiquette was concerned? And maybe it was a stupid thing to say in the first place? She couldn't help it – she was just dying to get beyond the surface of his formal emails, to know more about this author who had nothing to pin him down in terms of age, nationality, even gender. For all she knew, this could be a woman pretending to be a guy – all she had to go on was this elliptical email address. Be patient, Daisy, she told herself. Stop obsessing – we'll all find out soon enough. She looked at her watch and remembered. Miles. Lunch. Five minutes ago . . . how bizarre to forget! Grabbing her bag, she jumped down the stairs two at a time and, without stopping to check her make-up, she ran out the building to the tiny underground restaurant around the corner where they usually met.

Miles was standing outside the restaurant dressed in a smart blue shirt, loosely unbuttoned at the top. He was fiddling with his mobile, mid-text, when Daisy came bounding up to him and threw her arms around him. He quickly snapped shut his mobile and threw on a smile. 'Hello, gorgeous lady!'

'Sorry I'm late! I don't know what happened – things are crazily busy at the moment.'

'I didn't even notice; don't worry. Shall we?' and he held out his arm, resting one hand lightly on her back in that protective way that she loved, and led her into the restaurant.

'So, how was your trip?'

'Good, good,' said Miles, guiding them to their seats. 'So did you like your roses?'

Daisy was confused. 'Roses? You mean lilies? Yes! They were gorgeous, thank you so much again!' she exclaimed as they took their seats. 'And the little daisies with them – so thoughtful of you!'

Miles looked mildly embarrassed. 'Oh, it was nothing,' he said, before thrusting a menu in Daisy's face, and then hiding behind his own. As they started to look through their menus, Daisy began to tell Miles how excited she was about Will's book. 'It's just great. It reminds me a little of Laurie Lee's *As I Walked Out One Midsummer Morning* – you know, the same wide-eyed sense of adventure, and the exotic Spanish setting . . .' She broke off and looked to Miles for approval.

'I wouldn't know, I've never read that one. I'll never get time to, either, the amount I've got to read in my new job . . . it's even worse than being an editor!'

Daisy continued her story with enthusiasm, despite Miles's distinct lack of any. 'So anyway, it's about this guy who works in an art gallery in Angel, and he keeps on seeing this girl around – she sometimes comes into the gallery, as she's an artist's assistant, and he's always noticing her from afar . . .'

Daisy spoke at hyperspeed, without stopping for breath. 'Anyway, there's all this stuff about how she never, ever, notices him, doesn't really know he exists, while he just keeps seeing her randomly. On tube trains, in the library, in shops and that. And he starts becoming fascinated with her – but to the point where he's a bit too scared to say anything to her. He's kind of your shy, neurotic type, you know, very charming but it's not his style to chat up random women. So instead they just live and move in separate circles – very nearly crossing paths but not quite . . . and before long he realises he's falling for her, but from afar . . . which is sort of weirding him out a bit. Anyway, it's all just really well portrayed, I think, and then he goes to—'

'Yes, beautiful, it sounds great.' Miles looked mildly impatient. 'Are we ready to order?'

If Daisy felt shot down by his indifference, she didn't show it. She shrugged it off and said through forced smiles, 'Uhmm, I'll have the risotto. Oh – and you know the best bit?'

Miles looked up, disinterest written into every crease of his forehead. Daisy went on regardless, 'The great thing is, no one else has read any of it yet! So it's still my baby! Isn't that just so exciting?'

This time Miles didn't even respond. Just smiled, almost a hint of condescension in his eyes. As the waiter came and took their order, Daisy couldn't help feeling a little hurt by Miles's reaction. She was always so supportive of him and his ventures, and whenever he took on new clients. But then, she supposed, men were a different breed, weren't they? Maybe that was all it was.

An hour later, as they were waiting for the bill, Daisy's phone vibrated. 'Oh – sorry – I'd better get that, it's Belinda . . .'

Miles smiled as if to say go ahead, and picked up his own phone to resume texting.

'Are you busy? What are you doing?' barked Belinda down the phone.

'Oh – hello. Sorry, Belinda, I've just been having lunch with my b— with Miles, Metcalfe . . . But we've just got the bill . . .'

Daisy trailed off, seeing that Miles was gradually losing all the colour in his cheeks. She felt her stomach flicker with nerves, and began wondering what could be wrong with him. 'Anyway, it's fine, Belinda, I'll be back in five mins, I'll come straight back – do you need a bagel picking up?'

'No that's fine – just get back soon.' And Belinda rang off.

'Sweetie, what's wrong? Is your food going down the wrong way?' Daisy said, placing her hand on Miles's.

'Um, no. It's nothing. It's fine.' He shrugged, staring at Daisy with concern, with the look of a schoolboy who'd been caught red-handed.

'What is it? You can tell me,' Daisy said as they stood up to leave.

Miles shook his head, placed his hand on her back and guided her out of the restaurant. 'No it's fine, really.' He hovered, as though deciding whether to say something.

'Um. No, it's just something you said back there. About – being out to lunch . . .'

'Yes?'

'. . . Out to lunch – with me – as though I'm your boyfriend, or something.'

She felt her heart sink. 'Right.'

'Daisy,' he said, taking her hand, and standing with her by the restaurant. Daisy looked around nervously, hoping no one from Mercury would see them.

'Please don't take this the wrong way. I like you a lot – I think you're the cat's pyjamas, Daisy, really I do. I'm just not quite ready for other people to know that yet. It's just so, so hard to make your way in agenting. And I'm relatively new to it all, so I need to be 110 per cent focussed. I don't have time for any other commitments. Least of all, to a girl who works at Mercury. If anyone found out, it could be hugely frowned upon. I'm sorry – I just don't want to jeopardise anything to do with my career at the moment. Does that sound totally selfish?'

Daisy said nothing. She was concentrating very hard on trying to look composed, aloof and non-traumatised by this news.

'I'm sorry if it does,' he went on, 'but I really just hate saying those words "boyfriend" and "girlfriend" to people. It makes me feel I've signed a contract, you know? I admit it, it's my problem – I'm sorry. Shit, I don't want to stop seeing you, though! I really, really like you! I think you're so, so special, Daisy.' He put his arm around her, and brushed some strands of hair out of her left eye. Daisy remained silent while she concentrated hard on looking calm and unaffected.

'Are you OK with this? I don't want to hurt you – and by the way, it doesn't mean that I want to see anyone else, either. But, please can we keep on seeing each other, and just keep it as our secret for now? Look, I'm asking you to trust me. You know me better than anyone else. I'm not saying things won't change in the future – you just need to give me a bit more time before we . . . go public, as it were.'

Daisy stared into Miles's eyes and watched him perform another of his iridescent smiles. How did I end up here? she wondered. How could she, a self-confessed control freak who hated disorder of any kind, have ended up in this insecure, undefined mishmash of a relationship, with no discernible label of any kind? And, as if that wasn't bad enough, it was now all to be kept a secret!

But then, things with Miles had been ambivalent from

the word go. It was just this kind of ambiguity that reminded her of the night they'd first met. They'd been at an uber-glamorous launch party for a book Daisy could now barely even recall the name of. Miles had been working the room, and she'd had fleeting, intermittent conversations with him throughout the evening. She'd watched his chiselled face and dark brown head of hair towering above the crowds, as he weaved his way among the canapés and all the other girls at the party. Each time he came back for another snippet of conversation and a bite of canapé, he would leave her with some eloquent, thoughtful response to one of her questions about eligibility for literary prizes or some such topic, and she would feel her cheeks growing hotter and hotter with every exchange. But, as she'd made it her business to find out that night, rumour had it that Miles Metcalfe had a long-term girlfriend. No one had ever seen her out in public, but according to publishing folklore, a girlfriend he undoubtedly had. So, Daisy priding herself as a person of strong morals, had thought nothing of this attention, and busied herself with chatting to her colleagues from Mercury for the rest of the evening.

Which was why when, at the end of the night, Miles came to bid Daisy goodbye, and out of nowhere planted a light kiss on her mouth, Daisy had been more than a little thrown. It was two years ago since then, almost to the day, but she could still taste the bewilderment on her lips. She'd looked up at him as if to say – oh – did we cross some sort of line there? But Miles was just smiling breezily as ever and said, 'Call me any time, if you ever want any advice about the Samuel Johnson Prize, or any other prize for that matter . . . and do give my regards to Belinda.'

And that had been that.

Until the next day, when she still hadn't been able to get that weird, nondescript kiss out of her head. It wasn't quite enough to qualify as a romantic kiss – really, it was just a peck. Plus, the all-important detail: he had a girlfriend. But on the lips? Surely that was just a little beyond friendly?

And that was the day the endless ambiguity had first begun. She'd begun to wonder whether he might call her sometime, to follow things up. She'd begun to think, *do* men just kiss girls lightly on the mouth, even when they're just friends – or business colleagues even? Especially when they're supposed to have girlfriends? What exactly were the rules here?

'It's actually just one of life's unsolved mysteries,' Heidi had informed Daisy at the time over G and Ts in the local pub, the Black bird. 'Men have been kissing girls on the lips, but not in a snoggy way, for years – and no one's ever been able to confirm, scientifically or otherwise, why it sometimes happens, and indeed why it never seems to bind them to anything. There's not much we can do about it.'

'Yes – but – what do *you* think he meant by it?' Daisy had enquired, like a budding trainee on a relationships apprenticeship.

'Well, it sounds to me like he wants to get in your knickers,' Heidi had said, frank as ever.

'Really?' Daisy was hopeful, then mindful of her morals. 'Oh – but nothing else? And what about his girlfriend?'

'Well, you see, there's the rub. The girlfriend's presence – however far in the background – says to me that this guy doesn't want anything else. He's just messing around, seeing how far he can push it. I've not met him many times, but I'm getting a definite player vibe off him. Yes, I'd stay well away, if I were you . . .'

But despite this, when Miles had got in touch and asked her out for lunch, Daisy hadn't been able to resist. They'd met up for coffee a couple of times, and he'd opened up to her a lot about his own fears and aspirations – immediately presenting her with a softer side apparently divorced from his public self. Daisy was smitten straight away – for her there was every chance it had been love at first sight.

Suddenly, landing back on the street outside the restaurant with a thud, Daisy could see Miles staring at her quizzically, a concerned guilt in his eyes. She said nothing. She could hear her phone buzzing. 'Shit – that will be Belinda. I'd better go,' and she started to walk away.

'Daisy!' he called after her. 'What about this weekend? Are we still getting together? Are you still going to cook me dinner, like you said?'

'I'll see you later, Miles. Thanks for lunch.' And she headed back into work, to an office filled with a grumpy Belinda and approximately three thousand musty paperbacks, all in chaotic clusters around the editorial department. As Daisy looked around her, perusing the precarious, Jenga-like towers of dusty book-proofs and battered hardbacks, the phrase 'bomb-site' came into her head, followed closely by the fear of what was coming next. Her heart sank as Belinda fulfilled this realisation.

'*There* you are! I'm having a clear-out and I need your help. Right. See these books? I don't want any of them here. They're doing my HEAD in! I'll never get time to read them – not even if I retire TODAY! Can you deal with them?'

Mugs R Us

Ahhh, possibly this one, she thought, giving it another nudge. No, still too hard. She picked up yet another one. Nope. Way too mushy. She studied her tenth avocado and sighed. It was Saturday morning, and she had a feeling she was going to be here hours. She felt ridiculous, standing on tiptoe, leaning over the organic broccoli and stretching with all her might so that she could reach the highest, hopefully-at-their-optimum-ripeness avocados which were apparently hiding from the less conscientious shoppers, right at the back of the tray. And yet, she couldn't leave without one. Her famous chicken and avocado salad just wouldn't work without two perfectly ripe avocados. And that would leave her romantic dinner for two for Miles left completely wanting, which wouldn't do at all.

Daisy looked around her and became aware of the lady at the nearest checkout – a round, bespectacled lady with a mousy bob – who was staring back at her in amusement. I know what she's thinking, thought Daisy. Anal, obsessive freak, no doubt being a mug and cooking for your boyfriend who still won't admit he's your boyfriend. As if cooking him a lovely three-course meal is going to be the clincher. The thing that makes him change his mind. Well, it might sound muggish, but I'm going to give it a try, she thought defiantly. Sadly, when Daisy Allen decided to attempt something, especially a recipe, it had to be perfect – or it just wasn't worth doing. That was just the way things were.

Daisy gave it one last try, stretched out her right arm and reached up high to grab one. She gave it a gentle squeeze and thought, yes, that will have to do. Then she grabbed a second one. Victory, she thought, as she reclaimed her full-to-bursting shopping basket and strolled over to Smug CheckOut Lady.

Three hours later, Daisy was laying up her masterpiece when she got the call. Not hearing her phone ring, on account of Belle's very own Saturday evening 'X Factor' antics blasting out in the background, it went through to her voicemail. Returning to the kitchen a few minutes later, she felt a punch in the stomach. 'I'm really sorry, sweet-cheeks,' went the message, 'I've got to go to an author dinner at the last minute – I tried calling you earlier. Frances Harbour's over from the States; she's insisted on taking us to the Ivy . . . I just couldn't say no. I'm sorry . . . um, come for dinner at mine instead tomorrow? I'll get something in . . . Hope you haven't gone to too much trouble. I'll call you later . . .'

'Belle!' she yelled out over her sister's deafening and mind-numbing singing practice exercises.

'La-La-La-LA-LA-LA-la, La-La-La-LA-LA-LA-la,' went the warm-up, which Daisy knew all too well.

'Belle!!!'

'Yai-Yai-Yai-YAI-YAI-yai—Yes? What?' Belle came into

the kitchen, letting out a slightly huffy noise at being interrupted. 'What's up, hon?'

'Oh, nothing. It's just – don't worry about ordering pizza for yourself. I've got plenty enough for two here now.'

'Marvellous! Thanks! Much healthier than pizza, too!' Then Belle's happy face clouded over. 'Why, weren't you doing all this for Miles? He *hasn't* stood you up?'

' "Stood me up" 's a bit strong,' she said calmly, 'he's got to work. But it's fine, really, I'm not bothered. We can have some sisterly time. You, me, the warm-up exercises. What else *is* there on a Saturday night?' And Daisy laughed, feeling slightly better.

'God – I remember when we used to go out! Do you remember, when I had an actual *income*, and you didn't have Miles eating up your time?' Belle dipped her finger into Daisy's huge bowl of exquisitely prepared salad, and licked her finger. 'Come on, what say you eat this, and then we go out?'

Belle was getting excited, formulating a plan as she ran around helping Daisy pour out the wine. 'Yes – I'll call up some of the girls and see what they're doing. Not seen Miriam and Ruby in ages – yes, let's have a night out. Then you won't be able to stay in and get sad. Actually, you've no choice in the matter, OK?'

Daisy smiled. Belle was right; it was probably better than staying in and deciding what she was going to do about Miles. No, putting off that decision for a bit longer would definitely be best. As it happened, he didn't call that night. He didn't call for the rest of the weekend. And, although Daisy had had an enjoyable enough time, she'd also quite sadly devoted a large proportion of it to the activity known as Trying Not to Think About Miles, and trying to avoid looking at her phone every ten minutes. Finally, by Sunday afternoon, she picked up her phone, turned it off, and threw it across the room for good measure.

'Right. I'm entering a new phase,' she announced, turning to Belle on the sofa, her lips clown-shaped with remnants of Ben and Jerry's Fair Trade Vanilla ice cream. 'No more moping. No more thinking about him. Am now going to play it cool. Will forget seeing him as my boyfriend, the object of my future, my plan for life – and instead just see him casually, when it suits me. None of this being all hung up and emotional and downright PATHETIC. It's not getting me anywhere, is it? And I'm losing all my self-respect!'

Belle smiled and clapped her hands, 'Hurrah! Yes, this is all very positive indeed. No more cooking him nice meals, no more doing sweet, loving things for him. No more emailing him, and definitely no more literary criticism of his text messages. Just go out when you want, and see how it goes. I mean, listen . . .' Belle took a blob of ice cream to her mouth and licked her lips. 'Sweetie, I'm going to say something now, and I don't think you're going to like it very much.' Daisy's face clouded over with tension.

'Right. From everything you've ever told me about you guys, and I've got a *lot* of material to work with here . . . I think that with Miles, you're falling in love – not with him, but with a projected ideal that you yourself have created. From his emails, from his incandescent, ever-so-charming manner, from all the things that you, in your head, have decided you want from a man, and have assumed that he's able to give you. It seems to me that you're not in love with Miles the man. You're in love with the *idea* of Miles; with all the things that you've built him up to be.'

Daisy frowned. 'I never said I was in love with him,' she argued, missing the point. 'But besides, how would you know? You've never even been in love yourself, have you?'

'Well, no.' Belle grinned. 'Except for little Timmy Jessop. But he was eleven, and I only liked him because he was the best at kiss-chase. So no, I don't suppose I don't know what it feels like yet. Listen, Daisy, I might be wrong about Miles, but that's just the sense I get, from all you've told me.'

Daisy shook her head. 'No. You're wrong. You just don't know Miles like I do. I wish you and the girls would just understand – there is a good side to him, honestly. Anyway, can we *please* stop talking about this now?'

'Absolutely,' Belle said, visibly relieved. 'I'm bored to tears with it. I was just talking about it as I thought you wanted me to! But seriously, hon, it does sound like he's cooled off a little lately – so you really should do the same. See if things warm up again. If they don't, then it's his loss.'

And that – according to Belle, who pressed 'play' on the movie they were about to watch about street fighting in Tokyo – was that.

A Light at the End of the Tunnel

Date: Monday 3 July 2006 22.15
Sender: Daisy.Allen@paddingtonpress.com
To: justwilliam26@hotmail.co.uk
Subject: Re: Next chapter, DUENDE DAWN

Dear Will

Thanks so much for sending me this next passage, which I think follows on directly where the other left off? I read it as soon as it arrived, and thoroughly enjoyed it. In fact, I've just looked at my watch and can't believe it – you've made me miss the gym again. So the fact that I'm still grossly unfit and lard-ridden is now entirely all your fault. Hurrah. (Sorry – probably a bit too much information.)

Anyway. I have only a few major issues which I list below, but I'll send over a more detailed edit once Belinda's involved – it's a bit early for that at this stage (she heads up the imprint). My thoughts so far:

- To start with, I think you need to make it clearer from the outset why Lauren and Ed have never spoken before. They've both been working in the same building, at the art gallery in Angel, right? I know you touch on this earlier, but I think for the sake of not alienating the less astute readers, you need to make this more apparent. Why did she never speak to him before? Is it because the artist she's working for is slightly possessive of her attention – did he see her as his muse, perhaps? Or something maybe less obvious.

- Think you can afford to tone down the Lonely Planet bits here and there. I mean, did you do a research trip? Great, but the reader won't care – they don't want too much Sevillian history rammed down their throat. You might want to drop a few details here and there.

- A quick note on style. Occasionally (and please don't take this the wrong way) I think you have a tendency to reach for a more commonplace phrase when a more vibrant one would do better. Like where you say 'she shrewdly observed', I think it would work better if you thought of a less hackneyed way of describing the way she looked at him? Don't always take the easy way out, or use stock phrases. Instead, make sure you're writing naturally, like yourself.

- Sometimes you're in danger of slipping into a more journalistic mode, and that doesn't suit the rest of

the narrative. Switching narrative modes sporadically is rarely successful.

- Also, there are a few instances where you say 'one'
  instead of 'I', and you risk sounding pompous and
  unnatural here.

- Generally, question some of your descriptive
  passages – e.g., opening to Chapter five – cut out
  any excess adjectives. Make sure every word
  needs to be there, really question why it's there,
  and cut out anything too generic. Apply some
  rigour to these passages, and you might find your
  prose comes out sharper. The reason I say all of this
  is that I think you have a brilliant story to tell, and
  you really have an accomplished style. I think your
  writing, with a little light pruning, has big potential.
  And most of all, the voice is great, and is already
  very well established.

That's all, so far. Let me know if anything doesn't make
sense, or if you want to discuss any of these points.
And do give me a call any time if you need to.

Hope you're very well, and thanks for getting this to
me so fast.

D

Daisy looked down and read through the new section
again. The more she read of Will's book, the more
intoxicated she could feel herself becoming – with the

language, the vivid imagery, and the warmth of the characters. Almost a week had passed in the calendar of the book now, over which time Ed and Lauren had been growing closer and closer. So Daisy was surprised when, in the next chapter, Lauren casually dropped in the newsflash that she would be leaving for New York in only a few days, to start a work placement at the MOMA art gallery. While Ed seemed to want to dwell on this melancholy detail, that their affair now had a sudden time limit imposed upon it, Lauren insisted that they shouldn't waste a second of their remaining time together. Impulsively, she took Ed's hand and dragged him through the streets to a small theatre in the Barrio Santa Cruz, announcing that he was about to see 'the finest flamenco in all of Andalusia'.

As Daisy read on, the pages jumped out at her with colourful descriptions – the dancing, the vibrant, sexy costumes, and the never-ending sangria. It was here that Ed first experienced the notion of 'duende'. In Lauren's words, 'The true flamenco artist needs an abundance of one thing, and one thing only. They call it the duende – the spirit – of being able to captivate an audience.' This was also the first Daisy had ever heard of 'duende', but already she was wondering whether it was confined to the arena of dance, or whether it could exist in other art forms, such as literature.

Right away, Ed was captivated too, and began taking copious pictures and movies on his camera, under the premise that he would paint them later, for his exhibition. After a little too much in the way of snapping and clicking, Lauren became agitated and told him off for trying to experience life through a lens; instead of seeing it first-hand. After a period of mock-bickering, a strange, playful bet emerged, in line with what Daisy had been wondering only minutes before. To prove a point, that painters can and should be able to paint from their memory alone, Lauren issued a challenge; that Ed, 'the Artist', should try and capture the concept of duende on his canvas. Playfully, she demanded that he paint one flamenco dancer in particular; indicating the tall, striking brunette in a red polka-dot dress who was centre stage, raising her leg and her castanets high in the air.

Daisy smiled and looked at her watch. She turned to the last few pages, where the rules were being outlined. First, that Ed would have to do all this without his camera, using only the mind's eye and his own memory. And second, that he would have until the end of summer to complete it. Ed was more than a little dubious, as was Daisy. But the bet had been agreed, and the terms negotiated. If Ed painted a terrible painting, he would win, and Lauren would be proved wrong. Or, if he managed to paint a great picture, which truly conveyed the spirit of flamenco, then Lauren would buy him dinner in a restaurant of his choosing. They shook on the bet, and Ed was beginning to talk about where they would meet up again, when Lauren interrupted him with a kiss . . .

'Hello?' came a voice, making Daisy jump.

'Yes? Hello?' she looked around her, sensing lights being turned off all around her. She saw that Freddy Rhubarb, the after-hours security guard, was standing in front of her, thumbing through his matted dreadlocks. He was standing a little too close for comfort. She could smell the pepperoni pizza on his breath.

'Sorry. Can I just send this email quickly and shut down? I had no idea how late it had got. Sorry.'

Freddy smiled. 'No problem, love, just take as long as you need to.'

Daisy smiled gratefully, scanned through her email to Will, and clicked 'send'. She looked at her watch. It was 10.30 p.m. She'd been sitting in the same position, glued to her screen, reading and editing, for over three hours. She shut down her computer. Feeling racked with guilt yet again, she removed her gym clothes from her bag, buried them deep under her desk, and left.

The next day, Daisy was staring with intense concentration at cars. She was trying to make up words out of the letters on the number plates in the staff car park – toying with the idea of writing a haiku out of the words. But after a while she ran out of vowels and got bored. She gave up and turned away from the window to face the weekly publishing meeting, just as Belinda was getting into her stride discussing the budget for the next publishing cycle. The majority of Paddington Press editorial were scattered all over the large meeting room, most of them counting the minutes until lunchtime. As Belinda left the room to make a phone call that simply couldn't wait, Ronald Morley-Green began to speak, in an attempt to fill the awkward silence that was ensuing.

'So, you won't believe what I dreamed last night,' he began, 'I dreamed the zip on my bag was slightly broken.' He looked around the room. No one was really listening, only a few were even looking at him, but still he went on, unfazed, 'And the thing was, this morning I saw the bag, and – it's no longer broken!'

Daisy and Amelie tried to suppress their laughter. But then, apparently feeling sorry that no one was listening to her boss and his predictably dull anecdote, Amelie spoke up, offering a compassionate, 'Wow – that's intriguing. Which zip, exactly? Maybe I'll be able to fix it? I'm quite good with zips, you know.'

Ronald, amazed to have an audience – even an audience of one – smiled gratefully. Then he turned to her and explained carefully, 'No, but don't you see – it turned out *not* to be broken all along. I'd dreamed the whole thing after all.'

The door swung open, revealing Belinda, who immediately readjourned the meeting. For once, Daisy and Amelie sighed with relief at her reappearance.

As they left the room half an hour later, Daisy could overhear Ronald confiding in Amelie: 'But of course, the next thing was, I dreamed that the glass that I keep forgetting to take downstairs was still on the top of my cupboard.'

'Have you ever thought of going to a dream analyst?' Amelie asked, with only a hint of sarcasm.

'No!' said Ronald, as though this was a suggestion of immense genius. 'Do you know one?'

'Yes. But I think he'd just tell you that you need to get out more.'

Ronald looked sunken. As the girls walked past him and then began descending the staircase to the outside world, Heidi started to lament Elliot's departure for the third time that week.

'I just miss him, that's all,' she said en route to the park.

As they crossed the road, Heidi went on, 'I mean, it's so boring now there's no office eye candy any more. For a moment there, it was like working in a different industry. One with men in it. I mean, this reminds me of when I was little. When I was at boarding school, and we all used to wish that our parents had let us go to the mixed school – so we'd be able to interact with *boys*. Instead, we'd be doing ballroom dancing and midnight feasts with girls. So dull!' she broke off, disappearing momentarily into her own reverie. 'But Oh! Elliot was so . . . he was like . . . I don't know, like a light, at the end of the tunnel . . .'

The girls sat down on the grass and got involved with their home-made sandwiches. Once a week, they each made a pact to take part in BYO day – just to give their stomachs a well-deserved day off from the canteen cuisine.

'He's more than just a pretty face, you know,' Daisy pointed out, straightening out her crumpled salami sandwich in readiness for eating, 'He's also very clever. He did psychology at St Andrews, you know.'

Heidi was mid sage-nod when her eyes lit up with a sudden flash of inspiration, 'I know – aren't there any jobs going here that he can apply for?' she asked excitedly. 'It's just, I feel like we had a real connection, you know?'

Daisy laughed. 'But you hardly spoke to him! And no, there aren't any jobs going here that I know of. Besides, I think he's getting quite a lot of offers elsewhere, from the sound of things . . .'

'What do you mean? Offers from whom?' Heidi was intrigued.

'Well, we've been in touch a few times. He emailed me to ask for some advice for a job he was applying for. And now, he's become kind of like, my project.'

Heidi was in bits. 'Your WHAT?'

'Well, I like to call it my "Project-find-Elliot-a-nice-editorial-job-somewhere". I mean, we've been emailing quite a bit since he left, that's all. I've reworked his CV and covering letter for him, that sort of thing . . . we're friends,' she added lamely.

Heidi's was the face of someone who had just uncovered layers upon layers of betrayal and deception. 'I'll give you *reworking* his covering letter!' she said, somehow managing to lace this sentence with innuendo, 'Why didn't you *tell* me?'

Daisy laughed, and protested, 'There was nothing to tell you! You can have his email address if you really want.'

Heidi's face found its colour again. 'And his phone number?'

'Well, I don't know. Is that . . . ethical?'

Amelie, having been silently attacking her ham salad roll, began to laugh, 'Oh, you're so overly conscientious, Daisy. It'll be fine!' Amelie laughed, 'I mean, it's not as though little Elliot's going to have the guts to get in touch with the lovely Heidi all by himself now, is it?' Amelie toyed with her last bit of roll before adding, 'I suggest you hand over the number, and let Heidi work her magic!'

Daisy smiled hesitantly. 'Do you really like him? Still?' Daisy was sceptical. If there was such a condition as ADD (Attention to Dating Disorder), then Heidi was certainly fickle enough to be diagnosed with it. Her attention span from man to man was sometimes even shorter than Belle's. But in fairness, this time she did appear to have her heart set on Elliot.

'OK, then. Here it is.' Daisy opened up her mobile, and reluctantly scrolled through to Elliot's number. She read it aloud to Heidi, who tapped it into her phone, sandwiching Elliot in between Eddy, Eric and Fred and Frankie. Heidi scrolled through them, a dubious expression on her face. 'Really ought to cull a few of these – I can barely remember who some of them are – I certainly don't remember ever meeting anyone called Eric ... does anyone else?' she wondered aloud, Amelie and Daisy smiling with their eyes at each other.

'Actually, Heidi, thinking about it, you might have to compete slightly with Hermione – I know she took a shine to him,' Daisy cautioned.

Heidi's eyes narrowed. 'That is soooo not fair!' she whimpered, 'she's got a wardrobe budget threefold bigger than mine. Still, I can but *try*, I suppose ...'

Daisy laughed. 'Of course you can – and you're a much nicer person, too. If that helps.' Suddenly Daisy caught sight of the time on her phone. 'Shit. I've got to go!' And she stood up, grabbed her shoulder bag and cropped grey cardigan, noticing the girls staring at each other in surprise.

'What's the rush?' Amelie was curious.

Daisy was reluctant to say, 'Well. It's just my emails from Will – they only ever seem to come at about this time every day. I haven't figured out why yet – all I know is that I want to be there the second when they arrive. In case there's anything new to read!' She headed off towards Mercury Towers, the girls shaking their head in befuddled amusement.

A few minutes later, Daisy was stunned to discover an ornately wrapped box of chocolates sitting at on her desk. Posh, Belgian chocolate oranges, with a huge bow and a sparkly label. Rejoice! Another present! Quickly, she turned it over to reveal, '*To D, from M*'. No kiss, no personal message, and certainly no heartfelt apology for the no-show at the weekend. Daisy couldn't help feeling mildly disappointed. This was the second gift from Miles in as many weeks, and yet she felt surprisingly unswayed by all this attention. But it wasn't long before Daisy's more rational side woke up and she began to feel guilty for thinking such ungrateful thoughts. Even if the note was a little lacking in warmth, and even if she was allergic to orange, it was still always nice to receive chocolates. And manners were manners, she thought, bashing out a quick thank-you email. No sooner had it gone, than she was suddenly far more interested in the shiny new envelope which had simultaneously popped up on her screen.

Sleepwalking

Date: Tuesday 4 July 2006 13.24
Sender: justwilliam26@hotmail.co.uk
To: Daisy.Allen@paddingtonpress.com
Subject: Re: Next chapter, DUENDE DAWN

Dear Daisy

Many thanks for all your comments. I've taken them all on board. There are just a couple of things I'm still unsure about.

You said about giving them both more of a romantic history – I see what you mean here, but if you agree, I was thinking of adding a few more flashbacks. Back to when they're both working at the gallery – that sort of thing, and showing hints of their wider circumstances before they got to Seville . . . Or do you think that might be to the detriment of the pace?

Re. what you said about it being research-heavy – I

take your comment, but I was under the impression that these bits gave it a bit more depth . . .?

And the pruning – yes – I see what you mean. Over-description is a perennial habit of mine. But I'll keep a keen eye on it.

Anyway, I'm glad you're enjoying it. I'm sorry it's taking so long. Thanks for your comments, and for reading it so fast.

Will

Date: Tuesday 4 July 2006 13.41
Sender: Daisy.Allen@paddingtonpress.com
To: justwilliam26@hotmail.co.uk
Subject: Re: Next chapter, DUENDE DAWN

Thanks for all that, and yes, sure, W. you're totally right, the research does add depth etc.

I wasn't suggesting strip it all out. It's just that you should make sure that it's the story, and most importantly, the characters, that you're leading with. All I mean is, soften it a little – you don't want your writing to come off as research-heavy. McEwan's *Saturday* was an brilliant book, but some people had a go at him for over-filling it with medical background . . . totally different novel, obviously, but the same principle applies.

And the thing I said about pruning your prose here and

there – really just a tiny thing – you're generally very tight; it was only in places I noticed the odd super-fluous word. Now I think of it, it reminds me of Zadie Smith's recent article about writers and readers. There was this bit where she talked about how we shouldn't take the easy way out when we write. As in, there's this kind of vocabulary lethargy which sometimes rears its head – e.g., when authors find themselves using clichéd phrases like 'rummaging through a purse'. Perhaps because they're feeling 'too . . . thoughtless and unawake to separate "purse" from its old, persistent friend "rummage".' But as Zadie puts it, 'to rummage through a purse is to sleepwalk through a sentence – a small enough betrayal of self, but a betrayal all the same.' Sleepwalking through a sentence. That's lovely, no?

Sorry to go off on one, I just thought that was such a great way of putting things. Didn't mean to sound harsh before – about the LP stuff. If I was then, sorry. Speak soon.

Dx

Date: Tuesday 4 July 2006 13.59
Sender: justwilliam26@hotmail.co.uk
To: Daisy.Allen@paddingtonpress.com
Subject: Re: Re: Next chapter, DUENDE DAWN

That's spooky . . . I think I read that same piece, in the papers last weekend? I remember she said this other thing, which just made the hair stand up on the back of my neck (shit – there I go, sleepwalking again – sorry). Anyway – what was it? Hold on, I'll just look it up . . . Here we go (gotta love Google):

'To speak personally, the very reason I write is so that I might not sleepwalk through my entire life.'

I just love that. Don't you? And then later, there's this other thing she says, about how writing is all about, 'trying to express my way of being with the world', and how a novel is 'one person's truth, rendered through language'. I don't think I could ever put it better than that . . .

W

Date: Tuesday 4 July 2006 14.07
Sender: Daisy.Allen@paddingtonpress.com
To: justwilliam26@hotmail.co.uk
Subject: Re: Next chapter, DUENDE DAWN

Oh God . . . I devoured that article! I was going to mention those other quotes too, but was afraid you'd think me horrendously romantic and airy-fairy. I'm thrilled that you liked it too. Is that how you feel about writing? Is that why you write?

D

Date: Tuesday 4 July 2006 14.20
Sender: justwilliam26@hotmail.co.uk
To: Daisy.Allen@paddingtonpress.com

Subject: Re: Re: Next chapter, DUENDE DAWN

Well – yes, definitely. But also, for me, I think it's about trying to find a way to see life as clearly as possible. Like, if there was some great big technology store in the sky, where we could hire out all the most expensive equipment, then watch life in full colour, widescreen high-definition format. Second thoughts, is that a really mad, rubbish analogy? Maybe. It works for me . . . to an extent. But at the same time, you're not just watching life. By writing, I think you're really starring in it too. It's a way of saying, look, I exist. I really do. Even if no one else reads what I've written (least of all publishes it), it's still proof that I lived, breathed, had an imagination . . . all those things. Because at the end of the day, that's when I feel most alive, most awake, which I guess brings us back to the sleepwalking thing again . . .

You know, now you mention it, I've never thought about why I write. I've not been doing it long, but before I started this novel, I'd sometimes just wake up and think, what have I really accomplished in my life, you know? I'd sometimes just wake up with a burning need to write (he says, reaching for yet another slumberous cliché). It feels like it's just something I have no choice in. I never expected for a moment that anyone else would *like* what I've written – that's not what got me started. I feel as though I'm always striving to express something in me. but I can never quite reach it. The thing is, I've always had this other vivid analogy in my mind. When I write, it feels as though I'm on some sort of spring, and I keep bouncing back and forth, trying to touch this thing with my fingertips that's very nearly in my reach, but each time I move towards it, I stretch my arms out and the tips of my fingers are almost touching it – whatever this thing is – but I can never make contact. That's what writing is to me. Kind of a pessimistic view of things, but there you go.

Wx

p.s. I don't think you airy-fairy. Be as flowery and whimsical as you like, I'll never object.

Date: Tuesday 4 July 2006 14.25
Sender: Daisy.Allen@paddingtonpress.com
To: justwilliam26@hotmail.co.uk
Subject: Re: Next chapter, DUENDE DAWN

I don't think it sounds pessimistic. Maybe the more you write, the closer you'll get touching it, whatever the thing is?

OK, let me get this straight. Is this your first novel? The only thing you've ever tried to write? If it is, you're doing pretty well – am intrigued to know how old you are?! Either way, I'm very impressed.

I don't write myself, but if I did, I think I'd be with Goethe. Do you know this one? Maybe you'll think it cheesy or purple. I hope not: '*Whatever you dream you can do, begin it. Boldness has genius, power and magic in it*.' My dad told me that once. About the only good thing he ever told me – I've never been able to forget it.

Dx

Date: Tuesday 4 July 2006 14.29
Sender: justwilliam26@hotmail.co.uk
To: Daisy.Allen@paddingtonpress.com
Subject: Re: Re: Next chapter, DUENDE DAWN

I love that. It's beautiful. I'm writing it down.
I didn't realise the time . . . really got to go . . . but let's speak soon, OK?

Wxx

Just as she reached 'OK', Daisy sensed Belinda's perfume wafting into the vicinity, almost like a signal, warning her of her impending arrival three seconds later. Daisy's heart sank. It was the most awful wrench, being pulled away from all the stimulating ideas, the meandering conversations which had very nearly brought her to glimpses of more about this enigmatic Will. She wanted to carry on talking to him. She had so many questions.

'Daisy. We have a problem. That was Lottie on the phone – can you believe this, she's STILL in Minnesota. She was meant to be landing this morning! The trouble is, her mother's not any better, and she says she's got to stay there now until they switch off the machine.'

'Oh, really? That's awful,' Daisy said sympathetically.

'I know. It's bloody nightmare timing, with Edinburgh coming up.'

'Well – I meant it's a shame for poor Lottie.'

Belinda looked uncomfortable; as though her face was trying to feign compassion, but the lines on her face weren't used to this kind of choreography. After a few seconds spent screwing up her cheeks into an awkward arrangement, she gave up trying and wailed, 'It's a shame for us! There's a backlog of work piling up which Lottie was going to see to last week – when she was due back – but this is getting silly now.' She paced around the room and stopped by Daisy's wall calendar. She leaned closer to examine the days on it. 'Only 90 days till conference. No, the only thing I can think of is, we'll have to ask HR if they've got budget for a temp of some sort. Can you give Gareth or Katie a ring and sort that out?'

'Absolutely,' said Daisy. 'I'll go and see them now.'

Minutes later, Daisy was on her way back from the HR department. They had granted her permission to have a temp, and were now in the process of seeking one out. By the time she got back to her desk, she'd had a brainwave.

'Gaz,' she said down the phone a minute later, 'I've just realised – I know just the person. He'll save us a ton on agency fees. Let me just check he's available.'

She hung up the phone and quickly punched in a new phone number.

'Hello, is that Elliot?'

'Um, yeah. Hi, who's that?' he sounded nervous, and a little out of breath.

'It's Daisy! At Paddington?'

'Oh, hello! How are you?' he said, slightly on edge.

'Are you OK? You sound a little hectic, or something. Is it a bad time? Sorry.'

'No no! Now is good. Now is – fine. What did you want to talk to me about? Is it . . . What can I help you with?'

Daisy's forehead crinkled and she wondered why Elliot could be sounding so uptight. Was he a secret crack addict? Was that the real reason behind all his odd-jobbing?

'Well, it's just that Lottie – you remember, our editor? She's got stuck in America – she had a family emergency to attend to – and won't be coming back to work for a week or so. So we need someone to come and help out. Would you be able to do it?' She paused, then realised the major detail, 'Oh! And the best thing is, we can pay you! Imagine it, you'll be promoted from workie to temp! Please say you'll do it!'

There was a long pause.

'Elliot? What do you think? Will you be able to get away from the dead bodies and the charity begging for a week?'

There was a laugh. 'Well, when you put it like that how can I say no? Although I'm not sure the corpses will let me go . . . I think they've grown quite attached to me. I've managed to name them all now!'

'Haha . . . well, it's your call,' Daisy said, slightly surprised at Elliot's reluctance to come back. 'Um, couldn't you at least ask your bosses if they'll let you change your hours around for a week? Belinda says we'll even pay you £11 an hour – pretty good going, for publishing. Actually, hold on, that's more than I get as a salary! But never mind, what do you think?'

'Um,' Elliot paused for a while to consider, then finally added, 'OK, sure, I'll do it.'

'Great! That's fabulous! Thanks – I mean, Belinda will be so pleased.'

'Sure.'

'Great! Oh gosh, I've just thought, sorry for not asking sooner – how was your interview at Horsham Wyatt?'

'Not bad – OK, I think. Ish. They said they'd let me know by today or tomorrow though – so I'm not holding my breath. Anyway, I don't think it was really what I wanted. I really want to be doing fiction.'

'Oh well, keep at it; you'll get something soon, I'm sure. But this temping will be perfect in the meantime! So, I'll see you 9.30 on Monday, then?'

'Um, great, thanks a lot . . . yes, see you then. Have a great weekend.'

'And you, bye,' and they both rang off.

Date: Tuesday 4 July 2006 14.44
Sender: Daisy.Allen@paddingtonpress.com
To: justwilliam26@hotmail.co.uk
Subject: Re: Next chapter, DUENDE DAWN

Will

Yes, definitely . . . Sorry . . . got caught up on an urgent call. Hope you're still online and get this in time. Let me know if you ever want to meet for coffee and chat more about plotting etc.?

Good luck with the writing. Not that you need it.

Dx

Daisy clicked 'send' and stared at her inbox impatiently. Would he accept her request to meet up? Or would he blank her again, and fail to acknowledge the question as before? She sat. She waited. Five minutes. Ten minutes. Nothing. Her clock struck 2 p.m. She clicked out of Outlook, picked up her pen and notebook, and went to her production meeting.

In Between Hiccups

When Sunday came around, Daisy found herself in that common stance she knew only too well. If it was a yoga position, they'd call it the Waiting For Belle. One leg stretched out, the other bent leaning against the wall. Right arm down, left arm ninety degrees, and head bent forty-five degrees to the left, to see what time her watch said. Daisy sighed. The film was due to start in three minutes. She was just looking at her watch again and reminding herself of her favourite joke, that even Belle's gravestone would have 'Sorry I'm late,' written on it, when Belle came bounding up, rosy-cheeked and harassed-looking.

'Hello, my love. I'm sorry I'm so late.' Belle wiped her perspiring forehead and smiled apologetically, before flying off into a detailed monologue, 'You see, I left the house, walked all the way to the tube, and got there and I knew there was something wrong with the world – and then I realised – I couldn't see properly – that was it! I'd left my glasses. So then I walked back, got them, and headed back to the tube. And then I realised – this time I'd left my Oyster card at home! So I had an inner debate about whether to go back home and get it, or just pay again for a ticket – but then

I thought, in what possible universe can I afford to pay for my journey twice? Answer, NONE! So I went home and got my Oyster card, and had to go through every single jacket and handbag until I found it! Then I walked back to the tube, was about to go down the escalator, and guess what I'd forgotten? My efffing cinema ticket, which you gave me only yesterday! How annoying is that? So I stood there by the tube for ages, deliberating over what to do. I very nearly just gave up and went home, you know? But then I realised how sodding late I already was, and thought I'd have missed the film completely if I'd gone back again. So there you go, here I am, I decided just to come. Ticketless.'

'Well, that was silly, wasn't it?' said Daisy flatly.

Belle shrugged. 'I'm going to take my chances. You know. Find a sympathetic male to explain my story to. They should let me off – I mean, it's your card you bought them on, and you've got your one, so that should be fine, right?'

Daisy laughed cynically. 'Well, no – of course they won't let you in!'

But Belle was off. She'd spotted her victim. A pretty, blond-haired, blue-eyed usher who didn't look a day older than sixteen. Belle set about telling her woeful story to him. She explained in lucid detail her predicament – the spectacles, the Oyster card, the ticket... Sure enough, after four minutes twenty three seconds of this, he'd looked either side of him to check for any supervisors, smiled at Belle, and let her in. Daisy shook her head in amazement as she followed her sister into Screen Four.

Twelve hours later, Daisy was putting the finishing touches to Belinda's book-clearing bonanza, having got into work at 8 a.m. to try and get it cleared before everyone arrived.

Sealing the rim on the final batch of cardboard boxes marked Oxfam, she saw Elliot arriving. He strolled in, two coffees in his hands, and sporting a crisp, freshly ironed Fenchurch T-shirt and a broad, unshaven grin.

'Hey, stranger!' Daisy said, dropping one of her boxes. 'Ouch!' she squawked as it landed on the floor, just catching the corner of her left big toe.

'Oh, you poor mite. Here, let me help,' he said, lifting the box with manly ease and placing it on top of the tower of crates and boxes.

'What's all this? You guys finally moving into your bigger, trendier, air-con office in Soho?' he teased, putting one coffee down on his desk and handing the other to Daisy.

'Very funny. As if that will ever happen. No, they can't function without all this dust, creaky floorboards and mustiness. You know, it wouldn't be Mercury if it wasn't backward in some way. But thanks,' she said, lifting the cup of coffee to her lips, 'this is just what I needed.'

'How did I know you'd be here already, before anyone else?'

'Lots to catch up on,' Daisy said, perching herself next to Elliot on the edge of his desk.

'But that's meant to be where I come in, isn't it? I hope you've left me some work to do?'

'Oh, don't worry about that. There's tons to do. We can go through that in a minute. Meantime, how are you? What's new?' Daisy said with a chirpy smile, thinking quietly to herself how well Elliot was looking, even if his tan had faded slightly since the last time she'd seen him.

'Yeah, all good, thanks. I've moved down south . . . that's been the biggest event of the last month, I guess. I'm now in Streatham with a mate from uni. Bit of a shit-hole, but it's a start, and the rent's daylight robbery. Sixty quid a week, and no bills!'

'That's crazy cheap! Wow.'

'Yeah, so long as I don't get mugged, I stand to save a lot. And I've got a new job in a pub in Balham, which is going to help fend off the call centres for a while.'

'Oh, that's great news – that should be fun, shouldn't it? A chance to make new friends?' she teased, affecting a mock-maternal tone.

'Well – yeah, they're a nice bunch. Could really do with a proper permanent job, though . . . so anyway, how about you?' Elliot asked, slurping at the foam in the end of his coffee cup.

'Oh – I'm fine. Nothing much is new, really. Still living with my dappy sister Belle.'

'Oh, yeah, how's she?'

Daisy laughed. 'She's great, thanks. Actually, now you mention it, I remember thinking that you two would really get on . . .' She nudged Elliot pointedly.

Elliot looked surprised. 'Oh, really? Quite the little Emma, aren't you?'

Daisy smiled, surprised and secretly very impressed at his Austen knowledge. '*Moi*? Of course not.'

Elliot laughed. Then reluctantly – as though it was only polite to ask – he added, 'What does Belle do, then?'

'Well, there's a question. She's trying to break into singing, but the trouble is, they offered her the manager's job at the local caff, and that's made her want to quit. You see, it's sort of like death to your artistic career when you take an offer like that. She really is the most wonderful singer, but it's just so hard getting a break.'

'Surely not harder than publishing?' Elliot said, smiling.

Daisy laughed. 'Oh, you poor thing – have you still not had any luck yet? Even with all those letters you've been writing?'

'Nope. Didn't get the Horsham Wyatt job, either – which I didn't even want! What an insult. Oh well, I'll get something eventually . . . not to worry.' He shrugged. 'So anyway, what else is new with you?'

Daisy stopped to think, racking her brain for what was going on in her life. 'Well, there's still my kind of sort of maybe, can't commit won't commit stupid boyfriend – Mr Metcalfe.'

Oops. Suddenly she felt afraid that she'd said too much. She'd broken Miles's first rule of their relationship – that it was a secret. Ah well, never mind – one more person wouldn't hurt, would it? And besides, it wasn't as though Elliot would know him by his surname, was it?

But Elliot's face had already clouded over. 'Not as in the literary agent Miles Metcalfe?'

'Well, yes!' Daisy exclaimed, alarmed at his foresight. 'How on earth did you know that? He's only just been made one!'

'Oh, I don't know. I guess I just heard it somewhere.' Elliot looked away.

'Anyway,' Daisy began, not wanting to talk about Miles any more, 'there is this other amazing thing which has been on my mind pretty much most of the time the last few weeks. It all started – when was it – last Tuesday . . .'

Daisy was about to go into more detail when the editorial doors swung open, releasing a torrent of thick, dusty air, and with it a grumpy Belinda Bancroft, generously sprayed with eau de Monday-morning.

'Oh! Hello, Elliot, how are you?' she said as she walked

in, dispensing a smile to Elliot, and a 'Latte please, darling,' to Daisy.

'Hello – coming right up,' Daisy chirped, jumping into action and throwing her coffee to the bin.

Elliot stood up and lightly brushed Daisy on the shoulder. 'I'll get the coffee, Dais. You go get on with whatever it is you need to do. Remember, I'm everyone's slave for hire from now on . . .'

'Oh, thank you, Elliot.' Belinda said, looking disapprovingly at Daisy as she walked away to her office.

Daisy looked at Elliot guiltily and gratefully. 'Sorry, Ellie. I'll talk to you properly later.' She went to move away, then hesitated. 'Actually, you know what? Why don't we go for lunch today? Make up for how I couldn't the other week?' she asked breezily.

'Oh,' he said, a smile hovering on his lips, 'that'd be lovely – thanks.'

When Elliot appeared by her desk some hours later, Daisy was in a galaxy far, far away, completely absorbed in the words on the page and the thin red lines she was drawing all over them. Not daring to interrupt, Elliot stood quietly, studying her long hair, and the grim formation of the red marks.

'Good book, is it?' he tried.

'It is, yes,' she said, without looking up.

Elliot cleared his throat, and Daisy jumped. 'Hello?' she looked up, her eyes reflecting mild irritation at being distracted from the world of her manuscript.

'Sorry – are we off to lunch? It's a quarter past one.'

Daisy's green eyes were muddled. 'Oh! Right. Yes. Sorry.' Sliding her big black and red notebook over her manuscript, she stood up. 'Shall we go to Pizza Express?

You always know what you're getting there, don't you?'

'Certainly do. Plus, they do a great line in dough-balls.'

In just over half an hour, they were deeply involved in conversation, doughballs, and a sneaky bottle of red. Fortunately, Belinda was out at an editorial strategy afternoon with a group of other editors, and wasn't expected back for hours.

Elliot was busy stirring his *melanzane* with his fork, apparently unable to decide whether or not to take the next mouthful. 'So, what was it you were starting to tell me earlier?' he began, when a tall blonde waitress came over to their table and asked them, for the third time, if everything was all right, and did they need anything else to drink?

'No thank you, we're fine,' said Daisy, and watched the woman walk away. She smiled at Elliot.

'Right, well, the thing is –' Daisy looked around her, then turned back to face Elliot closely. Then she said quietly, as though confessing a dirty secret, 'For the very first time since I started my job, I've been reading some slush that I'm actually *enjoying*. This has never happened to me before, but this piece . . . don't tell anyone but . . . it's actually *not that terrible*.'

Elliot looked up from his food, which he'd still not started. 'Really?'

'Really. It's just your luck – you'd have very nearly read it yourself if you hadn't left! The story's actually half decent, and I think this person can really write . . .'

Elliot picked up his fork and took a mouthful of piping hot cheesy aubergine towards his mouth. 'So what's this "actually not that terrible" piece all about, then?'

'Well. It's very early days, and only part of it's written yet. I've just read the first few chapters, but so far it's about this guy who's kind of infatuated with this girl, who every so often he sees around in the art gallery where he works. She's an assistant to an artist, and for months it's been the same old story of almost bumping into each other, she doesn't know he exists, he fantasises about her and so on ... the usual thing. That is, until he goes to Seville on a research trip for the Summer. And, he didn't know this, but she's actually a quarter Spanish. It turns out she's there visiting her relatives, so one day they both serenpitdous – sorry, I just can *never* say that word, but you know what I mean—'

'Serendipitously,' Elliot said effortlessly.

'Thank you. Yes, seren— that word. Anyway, they suddenly find themselves in the same bar, in the same street, in Seville. Then for the next few days they have this wonderful, intense time just wandering around the city, getting lost in the romance of it, doing sightseeing stuff like the horse and carts, and getting to know each other ...'

Elliot put his fork back down on his plate, the food untouched. 'Sounds interesting, I guess. So, has this very romantic, not that terrible book, got a name?'

Daisy tucked into her La Reine pizza and cut off a perfectly oblong mouthful. 'Well, no – I mean, yes. The thing is, I'm going to suggest changing the existing one, so I should probably just tell you when it's confirmed.'

Elliot was puzzled. 'What's wrong with the one she's got at the moment?'

'She? Oh no, it's actually a "he". I know – so far, it sounds a bit romantic for a bloke to have written it. But I think that's going to be one of the selling points, if we can get it right. It's a completely different style of course, but I'm wondering if it'll be able to tap into the male romantics out there ...'

Elliot nearly spat out his red wine. 'Male romantics? I never knew there *was* such a phenomenon.'

'Oh Absolutely. In fact, I read about them only yesterday in one of those free London papers. If you thought romance was a purely female domain, think again. Apparently, there's a whole load of men out there who, as we speak, are sitting on sofas singing Eric Carmen at the tops of their voices. And according to this article, they're just as desperate as us women to find "the one"! Put it this way, they might not have as much of a penchant for Colin Firth in white shirts as we do, but that doesn't mean they don't secretly think *Pride and Prejudice* is their favourite novel!' Daisy said through giggles.

Elliot looked doubtful. 'I'm not sure I agree with all of that, but there's definitely a truth in there somewhere. We're not all kebab-swigging commitment-phobes, you know.'

'Shucks – you're not?' Daisy's eyes opened wider.

'Course not. In fact, lots of us think that once you meet the right girl, of course it'll be time to settle down, get down on one knee and do all that stuff. Personally, I've never really been into all that one-night-stand malarkey. I've had my heart broken one too many times. No, I think I err on the side of oversensitive wimp, if anything.'

Daisy laughed and took a sip of wine, studying Elliot closely as he talked. To spot him in a crowd, you would never have thought him the sensitive type. But the more Daisy got to know him, the more there was about him to surprise her.

'But never mind all that,' he said, 'why do you think this guy should change the name of his book?'

Daisy seemed deep in thought. 'Mmmm? Oh, nothing

major. I just don't think it's commercial enough as it is. But that's not important.'

Elliot was concentrating carefully on the patterns in his melanzane as Daisy went on enthusiastically. 'So, I should probably get you reading the book too – I'd love to know what you make of it, from a man's perspective! And then maybe we can brainstorm it, and see how marketable it really is. I mean, I could be very wrong about it . . .'

Elliot nodded enthusiastically, 'Yes, that'd be great. I'd like that.'

'Great!' said Daisy happily. 'Actually, the funny thing is, I can't seem to get the last bit out of my head . . . it's just really got to me for some reason.'

'Really?' asked Elliot, pouring out the last drops of red wine into both their glasses. Daisy took a long sip, realising that this would be her second glass at lunchtime. Which by her usual standards would mean that she was probably drunk by now. If not yet, it was definitely in the post.

'Yessss,' Daisy began. 'See, there's this bit where they go and watch flamenco together' – she broke off to release an impromptu hiccup – 'Oh! Scuse me. I sometimes get hiccups when I have a lot of – doughballs,' she said, relieved to see that Elliot seemed to buy this justification. 'Anyway, so there's this woman dancing . . . she's wearing this amazing, vibrant dress, and Will – that's the author – he really captures the image of it. The way it poofs out, with all the colourful ruffles and, well, it just made me remember this thing . . . OK, this is going to sound really silly now, so you have to promise not to laugh!'

Elliot managed a serious expression. 'I promise. What is it?'

Daisy giggled. 'It's this thing – this stupid, tiny thing, from when I was really little, and when my parents were still around.'

Elliot listened intently as Daisy told him all about her childhood growing up in and out of Harry the mustard-green caravan. Through hiccups, she told him about the time they'd stopped over in Madrid while crossing Spain one summer. They, all four of them – mum, dad and two daughters – had wandered into the town; hungry, irritable and in desperate need of a restaurant that wasn't closed for siesta. They were walking round the streets, past all the usual souvenir tat stalls, when the six-year-old Daisy had stopped just outside a small touristy shop selling everything from postcards to castanets.

Twenty-six-year-old Daisy took a sip of wine and went on reminiscing, hoping Elliot was still listening and not just feigning interest. 'Anyway, for some reason, I was just spell-bound by this set of silly postcards of flamenco dancers. They were so sweet! You see, they weren't just those ordinary dull flat ones that only had *pictures* of flamenco dancers. No, these babies were 3-DIMENSIONAL! You know – they had *actual stick-outy* ruffly skirts made of netting, which was attached to the card. Do you know the ones I mean?'

Elliot was nodding in amusement. 'I went to Spain years ago – yes, I know the ones.'

'So, anyway, I was all, "Dad, these are magical, look!" ' Daisy broke off into hiccups again. Elliot handed her some water, which she gulped down gratefully. 'So ... I remember tugging at my dad's sleeve, and chewing at the split-ends of my hideous hair, which used to be down to my bottom, as my mother would never let me cut it! And I was all, "Please, Daddy, will you buy me one?" and, you know, smiling sweetly at him, until he finally gave in and begrudgingly got me one – all the while complaining what a frivolous material thing it was to spend money on—'

Elliot laughed and looked sympathetic. 'Ah, poor little Daisy.'

'Hey! You promised' – hiccup – 'that you wouldn't take the mickey! Anyway, it's all very silly. Looking back, I don't know why I was so taken with it.' She began to laugh. 'I mean, they're really rather tacky . . . and faintly comical!' She burst into giggles as though this was the funniest thing she'd ever thought of.

Elliot was nodding, and laughing along with Daisy. 'No – I can totally see why you loved them . . .'

'Really, you can?' she asked before downing the rest of her water in a last-ditch attempt to stem the unrelenting tide of hiccups.

'Yeah, sure,' agreed Elliot. 'I mean, the world looks different when you're a child. Different things stand out back then, don't they? I have lots of similar memories of weird, tacky toys that seemed magical at the time and I don't know why. But I guess it's the little things you remember, isn't it?' He looked pensive. 'I think those little memories are really worth holding on to, don't you?'

Daisy looked at Elliot with interest. 'Yeah, you're right. I guess it was just funny the way the book made me think of that moment. I've still got it, actually, pinned up on my wall. It's the only one thing I've got that reminds me of Dad – of them both. I mean, when it comes to my parents, I hardly remember anything. It's like my brain's blocked most of the other memories out. So when one like that suddenly haunts me, it's really vivid. Strange how the brain connects things . . .' She trailed off, realising something. 'Hey! No more hiccups!'

'Oh, that's a shame,' Elliot's face broke into a smile, 'I was enjoying them. But . . . tell me to sod off for being a nosy git, but why have you blocked your parents out like that?'

Daisy never usually opened up about this sort of thing, especially not to people she didn't know very well. But after talking to Elliot all this time, and with two glasses of red wine inside her, she felt oddly comfortable talking about her feelings, and it suddenly didn't seem like such a serious, locked-up subject any more. Even more bizarrely, she'd barely thought about Miles all day. What the hell, Daisy thought, and took another sip of wine.

'Well, the short version is, they both left Belle and me when we were sixteen and eighteen. My aunt looked after us a lot of the time after that. It wasn't easy. I think I took it worse than Belle. She's the tough one out of us two – she always let's stuff bounce off her. Me, I can't help it, but I take everything to heart. So it was months, years even, before I stopped asking her when they were coming home. Then one day I just stopped saying it . . .' Daisy trailed off, felt herself pull back from the place in her head she didn't like to go. She brushed her hair out of her eye and sat upright. 'So yeah, there are lots of other things, but that's the main reason I don't tend to think about my parents. Until nosy gits bring them up, that is . . .'

'Sorry . . .' Elliot looked solemnly at Daisy, 'and sorry again . . . that must have been rough.'

She shrugged, 'Hey, it's fine. Could've been worse – at least they'd had the decency to bring us up until then, not everyone gets that!'

Daisy suddenly felt self-conscious. 'God! Sorry – I don't know why I just told you so much! I barely know you, and I've just rambled on and on at you about my childhood! You must think I'm so terribly odd.'

Elliot was laughing. 'Don't be silly. You're all the more charming for it.'

'Well, whatever I am, I'm all embarrassed now, so let's talk about something a little less deep for a bit, OK?' Daisy drank some more water, relishing in the freedom of life after hiccups. 'Um, let's see . . . what's your favourite film?'

'Uh . . .' Elliot looked at Daisy with wonder, as though he was struggling to keep up with her zig-zagging logic. 'OK – well that's easy. That would have to be *Withnail and I.*'

Daisy looked embarrassed. 'Oh – do you know – that's one of those films that I know I need to see, but I've never got round to . . .' Her voice shrank in volume as she saw Elliot's expression and became aware of the sacrilegious enormity of what she was saying.

'You've. Never. Seen. *Withnail and I*? Seriously?' Elliot looked deeply disturbed. 'Oh dear – I'm not so sure I can be your friend any more. It's a shame, too. I was starting to enjoy our little chats. Oh well.' He raised his glass to her and smiled.

Daisy laughed, 'Oh no! Please don't give up on me! I know it's a huge gap in my cultural education, but I promise to watch it, as soon as I've got time.' Daisy looked genuinely distressed.

'Christ, you're easy to wind up, aren't you? I was only joking you know! But in all seriousness, it *is* one of those films you have to see. It's got some of the funniest, most quotable lines . . .' Then, checking himself, he added, 'Oh dear, you'll have to stop me before I go off on one.' Elliot smiled. 'Still. It must've been fun – living in one of those vans. I took one round Europe – well, not just me, there were a few of us.'

'Really? Who were you with?'

'Well, to begin with there was a whole gang of us – but after about six months of it, it was just me and Alice – this girl I knew. And that's when I realised – those vans have a weird way of changing size according to who you're with. At first I thought there'd be loads of space and that we'd be rattling around in it. But no chance – suddenly it was tiny, and well, we were at each other's throats before long.'

'Were you . . . seeing each other as well?' Daisy probed, possibly a little too nosily.

'Well . . . yeah . . . kind of, to begin with. That was half the problem – anyway, it didn't work out, so we found someone to take my place and I came home. I think Alice is still out there now, heading into Egypt . . . although I haven't heard from her since I left her out in Hungary, sitting sunbathing out by Lake Balaton . . .' he trailed off, that same whimsical look in his eyes he always had when he talked about his travelling days.

'Shit! What time is it?' Daisy said, panic-stricken and realising she had no watch on, which was an aberration in itself. 'I feel like we've been here ages!'

'We have. But it's only a quarter to three.' Elliot raised his hand, caught the eye of a passing waiter, and mimed the 'please may I have the bill' action.

'Don't panic,' he said calmly, 'we'll have you back at work in ten minutes max. I'll tell Belinda it was my fault – you can blame it all on me . . .'

When they eventually snuck back into work a little later,

luckily no one was back yet, and the floor was deadly quiet. Daisy crept back to her desk, then realised even Hermione seemed to be out at an incredibly long lunch. Phew, she thought, and sat down at her desk, noticing that her work phone was displaying two missed calls. Both were from Miles's work number, so she quickly she called him back. There was no answer. But, clicking on to her emails, she was pleased to see there was a new one from Miles, informing her that he'd acquired some theatre tickets to see a new play at the National, and she must keep tomorrow night free. Hurrah, she thought, feeling relaxed, and resting her head on her desk for a ten-minute power nap.

'OK, that's me gone. I am *finally* going to go to the gym!' Daisy informed Elliot as she was leaving work late that evening; after they had both felt the need to stay late and ease Daisy's guilt after the extra long lunch. 'Right, I'm off to burn off all that wine and pizza! Please don't stay working on that filing of B's for too long. She was lying; it really can wait until the morning, you know.'

'I know, I'll go really soon, don't worry.'

'Oh, and here's what I've got so far of that book I was blabbering about at lunch,' Daisy said, handing Elliot her dog-eared printout of Will's book. 'I'd love to know what you make of it, if you can spare the time. None of the girls have read it yet, so you've got quite privileged access here . . .'

Elliot smiled gratefully. 'Well, thank you very much! I've a few others to plough through first, but I'll get to it as soon as I can. You have fun with the Lycra junkies, won't you . . .' he said, adding the pages to the pile on his desk.

'Oh, don't tease me – I hate it so. Anyway, cheers for

your help today, Ellie. And for a lovely lunch. Sorry about the hiccup explosion – it'll never happen again.' Daisy smiled breezily and went strolling through the double doors, Elliot staring after her.

He continued to gaze at the mahogany double doors long after Daisy had walked through them, and long after they'd finished swinging back and forth. He waited a good five minutes in the same position. A half-empty cup of Starbucks in his hand; his glasses perched on his nose, and a pencil tucked behind his ear. He checked to see that no one else was around. After enough time had passed, Elliot reached into his grey satchel and pulled out a set of key rings, attached to which was a small black memory chip. Looking around him, Elliot lifted off the cap and angled the shiny metal end towards the USB slot on the side of the PC. Checking it was lined up correctly, he pushed it into the slot.

He opened up Internet Explorer, bypassed the gossip columns and celebrity articles and went straight into Hotmail.com. Hastily he typed in the name that was now so familiar to him. He opened the inbox, ignored the subject-headings that were screaming out at him about Viagra and penis enlargements, and clicked on 'compose new mail'. He attached the Word file, typed a brief message. Scanning it for typos or any possibly identifiable traces of Elliot Thornton, he clicked 'send'. Then he closed the program and shut down the computer. He threw the coffee cup into the waste bin and picked up his coat and bag. He turned out the lights and strolled through the double doors. He ran down the three flights of stairs, through the main entrance, and out into the darkened street.

The All-New Adventures of Mr Bean

'I t's getting even better, you know,' Daisy told the girls at lunch the next day, having just torn herself away from a brand new instalment from Will. 'I know you don't know what it's about, but it's really hotting up now. They've both spent nearly a week together . . . and I think they're starting to fall in love. He's just unveiled all his paintings for her, back at his apartment, and . . .' Daisy trailed off, noticing the girls making eyes at each other. 'You know – I just can't wait to meet him now, and find out who on earth he is! Although he has such a sensitive voice that I keep wondering whether perhaps it's actually written by a woman. You know, pretending to be a man?'

'Don't be a cretin – why would anyone do that?' said Heidi. 'It's not like we live in the olden days, when women had to use a pseudonym. He's probably just a sensitive New Age guy. Oh!' Heidi almost choked on her sandwich with a major realisation, 'Holy crap! Maybe he's *hot* too! Did you ever consider that?'

Daisy's cheeks flushed involuntarily. 'I seriously doubt it! He's does seem very nice, personality-wise, though . . .

I mean, we've been having some really interesting conversations. But I'm still so intrigued about what he does all day. You see, since they started, the emails have always come at lunchtime, around 1 p.m. on the dot. And they've always stopped, mid conversation, just before 2 p.m. But then, last night, I got one for the first time at about 7 p.m. And then another today, in the afternoon. Which makes me think, maybe he's got a new job somewhere, or something? As in, he used to only be able to get online in his lunch hour. But now he has a job which gives him Internet access, perhaps?'

Heidi and Amelie looked at Daisy with concern.

'You really need to get out more, for the love of Mary!' exclaimed Heidi, 'So he's got himself a new day job, in an office or something. So what?!'

Amelie looked at Heidi sternly before trying a more sensitive approach. 'Aren't you even going to tell us what it's about yet?'

Daisy was itching to tell them all about it, but she hated the thought of them not taking it seriously, or making jokes about it and somehow undermining its brilliance. Maybe she was being a little precious about it – but until she felt more confident in her editing ability and her judgement, she felt reluctant to share. She also couldn't let go of the niggling feeling that maybe it wasn't very professional to be acting like this – to be getting this emotionally involved with a piece of work, and its owner? No, she decided again. Best to hold back a little longer.

'All in good time,' she said, trying to affect a mysterious, enigmatic look in her eye but suspecting that maybe Heidi and Amelie were trying not to laugh. 'But anyway, changing the subject, is anyone ready for the conference?

I mean, it's so exciting that we all get to go this year! Have you decided what you'll be wearing on party night?'

Out of nowhere, the Mercury Publishing Group Ltd. Sales Conference 2006 was now only seven weeks away. This year's three-day jaunt, to the girls' delight, was to be held in the centre of Venice. They, along with the more fortunate two-thirds of the company, would be whisked away to a luxury hotel for three days of presentations, ritzy dinners, excessive drinking and regrettable dancing. Sometimes, for the even more fortunate, there was a window of ten minutes to spare in which to leave the sanctuary of the hotel and take a fleeting look around the city itself. Simultaneously, every year, the unlucky, dejected third that got left behind would enjoy a three-day sojourn of short days and extra-long lunches, followed perhaps by some hours spent hunting for new employment. Fortunately, Daisy wouldn't be joining them this year; now that Lottie was held up in America, Belinda had asked that Daisy go in her place.

'I'll probably just wear what I wore to the Christmas ball. You know, my most prized possession – the only thing in my wardrobe that's not dirt-cheap from Primark.'

'Your lovely All Saints dress?' intercepted Heidi, all too aware of Daisy's austere clothing budget. 'A marvellous choice. Me, I'm *clearly* going to have to go shopping. Ams, shall we try and go next weekend?'

Not a fan of shopping (or anything else that involved making decisions), Amelie nodded reluctantly. 'I guess so.'

Heidi sat up suddenly. 'Hey, so it's great to see Elliot back in the building, isn't it? *How* did you swing it?' she said mischievously, looking pointedly at Daisy.

Daisy's eyes narrowed. 'Um, it's just because Lottie's

still stuck in America, so I got him in as a temp. He's very good. It's very – useful – having him around.'

'Well, good work, I say,' Heidi said with mock-parental pride. 'He's a hard nut to crack, that one. He never replied to my text ages ago, but I hinted that I'd like to go for a drink today when I saw him, and he didn't run a mile, so, touch wood . . .'

'So why don't you just ask him out then, get it over with!' said Amelie. Then, turning to Daisy, 'Did he not want to join us for lunch?'

'I don't know,' Daisy answered defensively. 'I did ask him, but he said he had lots of emails to send. He's really busy . . . trying to apply for permanent jobs and stuff . . .'

'Oh, before I forget,' said Heidi, suddenly bored with that conversation and commencing another one with the ease of flicking a switch. 'Do you remember Claire that I used to work with in my old company?

'Wasn't *everyone* called Claire in your old company?' asked Amelie.

'Well, yes. But anyway, tomorrow she's hosting a big, huge launch party for their latest Monica Ali type, and she said I could come. It's going to be around Old Street somewhere, and apparently loads of famous people are going. But they also want to make sure we make up the numbers, just in case all the interesting important people pull a no-show. So . . . if you both want to come, I can probably smuggle you in.'

'Mmmm, sounds good, count me in,' said Amelie. Then both she and Heidi turned to face Daisy, who paused from her lentil salad to look up apologetically.

'I'd love to. But Miles is taking me to the theatre. We got tickets ages ago – so I'll have to say no, I'm afraid.

Sorry.' Daisy was secretly pleased – both to be able to say that she had a date with Miles, and also to have avoided a launch. Privately, she wasn't huge fan of launch parties. She always found herself a little lost for words when it came to glittering small talk.

'Oh really?' said Heidi. Both she and Amelie looked pleasantly surprised. 'Sounds like things are starting to go well now?' said Amelie.

'Well, yes, I suppose it's going OK. At least, he's taken to sending me presents – which is something. Although the latest one was a box of chocolate oranges. I could swear he knows I'm allergic. But hey, it's the thought that counts, isn't it?' Daisy said stoically, reaching into her bag to pull out the latest chapters from Will.

'Well, yes indeed,' Amelie agreed, while Daisy was rummaging through the pages, looking for her place. 'I mean, I'd be lucky to get a Malteser out of Josh . . . no, pressies are a good sign, definitely. So long as they're from him, and not his assistant, that is . . .'

But Daisy wasn't listening. She'd opened up the manuscript and was quickly becoming absorbed in thoughts of burning hot sun, exotic palm trees, and a place called the Alcázar Palace.

'We've lost her,' Heidi observed, as she and Amelie stood up. They began walking back to work, leaving Daisy sitting alone on the bench – just Daisy and the words on the page.

According to Lauren, the Alcázar was one of Seville's greatest treasures. She lead the way through the grounds to a place called Mercury's Pool. As they wandered through the enchanted garden and went to sit by an indigo pool, just talking and enjoying the view, Daisy felt herself sinking into the world Will was portraying. The more she read of his book, the more she could feel herself being affected by his writing. After most sittings now, something about his world would always stay with her and continue to resonate afterwards. So much so that Daisy was now beginning to think of the manuscript as an old friend. Reading it felt reliable, sturdy; like curling up with an old favourite such as *Dombey and Son* or *Wuthering Heights*. It was becoming addictive too; even 'unputdownable', as they said in Mercury all too often. Daisy read on to find that in this particular scene, Lauren was telling off Ed again for taking too many photographs. Everywhere they went, there he was, watching everything through a lens, a stage removed, rather than experiencing it through his own eyes. Moments later, Daisy heard a loud, bellowing laugh. When she noticed that the people in the park were looking at her strangely, she realised it had been her. A moment in the book had tickled her – when Lauren had realised she didn't know Ed's surname, and he had been forced to reluctantly admit that it was in fact, 'Bean, Edward Bean.' At this, Lauren had burst into hysterics, and Daisy couldn't help joining her. 'So you're – like – Mr BEAN?' Lauren had taunted, perhaps a little more cruelly than was necessary.

But then out of all the light-hearted banter, a more bittersweet tone set in. It was Lauren's last night before she went away to New York, and so began the inevitable discussion about what would happen when they both got back to London. After lamely darting around the issue for a while, in the end they both agreed to postpone the conversation until they met again on September 15th – Edward with the painting of the flamenco lady in his arms, and Lauren, fresh from working out in New York, and with enough funds to pay for dinner for two (assuming the painting met with her approval).

Daisy picked up her pen. After reading this new section, she had a number of questions she wanted to go over with Will. She began making notes and marking up a few issues on to the text. But with each stroke of her pen, she felt a stab of guilt for tinkering with it. Part of her really was terrified to tamper with something so accomplished. What if she said the wrong thing? Worse, might she offend him by interfering? His prose was so well composed, and the writing so assured, she had to stop herself from adding a little 'sorry' in parentheses after each editorial note.

Just as she was writing a tiny note in the margin about consistency, she was interrupted by a beep from her phone. She went into her bag and retrieved it.

'Meet me tomorrow at our place on the South Bank at 6. Mx'

Hurrah. Daisy made a quick, gleeful note in her diary before going back to Will. She read through to the end of the chapter, through to the final parting moment. She felt her eyes almost welling up, and began feeling impressed at how well Will could 'do' poignant. Then, looking at her watch, she saw with horror that she was almost late for a meeting. She put the manuscript away and went back to work.

I'm a Cerebral Cortex, Get Me Out of Here

> Sweetness. Sorry again 4 cancelling on u. Don't b cross. I'll make it up 2u. If any consolation, I didn't get home from work until 2am. CU soon X M'

This was getting old, Daisy thought as she turned off her phone and walked the rest of the way up Bishops Bridge Road towards work. Once again, Miles had let her down by cancelling their theatre trip at the last minute. For once, though, she was determined not to be bothered by it. Yes, that was correct. Today she was going to try a new approach. The 'let it bounce off me and get on with life as normal' approach, otherwise known as denial. Brilliant. Soon she was back at her desk, shrouded in manuscripts and piles of book proofs. Rather than waste time rereading his text message and composing a reply, she defiantly threw herself into her work. Hurrah, she thought, until when Heidi's lunch email came around at one minute past twelve, she didn't feel in the slightest bit hungry. She could see that no appetite was likely to emerge, but decided to go and join the girls regardless. Elliot was fully submerged in a hunt for book jacket visuals from the Design department – which at the best of times was a bit like following an assault course or treasure hunt, and would no doubt have him engaged for most of the day. So once again Daisy found herself venturing out to join the girls alone. Walking through the gate to the park, she could see them talking earnestly; heads bent close together, hands gesticulating rapidly about some highly important topic. But as she got closer to them, this highly important conversation quickly came to a diminuendo. Daisy sat down to a hushed silence. Surely she was being paranoid, but she couldn't help feeling that both the girls were looking at her oddly.

'What? Why are you looking at me like that? What's up?'

'Like what?' Amelie blurted, just as Heidi delivered a breezy, 'Nothing. Nothing at all. How's things?'

'Fine. Yes, boring as ever,' said Daisy, expressionless. She wanted to tell them about Miles letting her down again, but part of her didn't want to admit it. She could sense the 'I told you so's' lined up in waiting, so she kept schtum about it instead.

'Rubbish weather, isn't it?' Daisy whined. 'I told you, that week of proper sun in June was all we were going to get . . .' she looked up at the cloud-covered sky, and frowned. 'I mean, *never mind* that it's the middle of July now! Still, at least it's not raining – that's something. So come on, tell me, then, how was the party?'

Amelie and Heidi looked at each other with pained expressions, and seemed unsure who should speak first. Eventually, Heidi rose to the challenge. 'Yeah, yeah, it was great! I mean, it was OK. *Gorgeous* canapes,' she said, pronouncing it without the accent at the end as she always liked to, for her own amusement, not because she didn't know the correct pronunciation. Daisy had never pointed this out before, but really, it wasn't funny. She wanted to tell her then that, actually, it was quite annoying. She kept quiet and began rifling through her bag, tidying through her things, tearing up redundant bits of paper and old receipts. Hoarding: the eighth deadly sin, she thought, as she threw any offending bits of clutter out on to the grass ready for disposal.

Heidi looked at Daisy with concern, and went on, upbeat as ever, 'Lots of those lovely mini mushroom tarts that you like,' she gushed, 'and a few *vaguely* starry people. But I think you'd have been pretty bored, really. Wasn't much crack going down.'

'Crack?' wondered Daisy with alarm, pausing from her rapid sorting frenzy for a moment. Since when did publishing soirées involve people taking crack?

Luckily Heidi could read Daisy's facial expressions like a book. 'Not the drug, Dais. It's an expression.'

Daisy was hugely relieved. 'I know that!' she insisted defensively. 'Durrr . . . But anyway, moving on – what were you both talking about before I got here? I got the impression there was something fascinating you were going to tell me! No gossip, then?'

'No,' both Heidi and Amelie said at once.

'Yep, none at all,' Heidi added, 'like I said. No crack.'

Daisy sighed. 'Oh. OK.'

'Anyway,' put in Amelie, 'H, how was your drink with Elliot the other day? You sly witch, you never told us how it went!' she said, looking pointedly at Heidi.

Daisy was surprised. 'I didn't know you two went for a drink? You never said, did you?'

Heidi looked muddled. 'Oh, yes! I can't remember if I told you. Yes, I think it slipped my mind – probably because it was so uneventful. But yes, yes, we went for a drink, and we had a really nice time. But that was just it. Nice. You know, the more I talked to him the more I realised – he's sooooo not my type! He's just way too nice!'

'Oh no!' exclaimed Amelie. 'After all that!'

Heidi nodded. 'I know! But . . . I think I was just blinded by the excitement of having a fanciable male at work, of any kind. We had all kinds of small talk, and then suddenly, about halfway through, this weird thing happened. Almost simultaneously, we both kind of decided that it wasn't going to happen for us. I was like, 'Well, no offence, but there's not really much of a spark here, is there?' and he was all, 'd'you know, I don't think we've got *anything* in common!" '

Heidi broke off, laughing, and Daisy and Amelie sat and stared in silence. 'It was like, both of us were trying to break it to each other. And then, it was really funny – we both just started talking about our relationship histories, and being agony aunts for each other! Nope, sorry, Daisy, I think he's way too serious and intellectual for me. Plus, I think I'm way too blonde and stupid for him! He honestly said to me that he tries to read at least three newspapers a weekend – you know, just to get a really objective look at the world. I mean, I barely even find time to read the *Metro*!'

Daisy felt oddly relieved. She'd never really have put those two together. 'Oh well, it sounds like it's worked out for the best,' she said simply. 'I'd better get back, I've got loads of conference stuff to sort out.'

'But it's weeks away still!' said Amelie.

'I know, but there's just so, so much to organise. I just wanted to hear how it went, and I'm glad you had fun. I'll catch up with you later.' And Daisy headed back inside, feeling overly introspective; her mind putting in extra shifts with wondering what the girls had been talking about when she'd first sat down. She decided to go back in and see if there was anything new from Will to escape into. Opening her inbox minutes later, she saw with disappointment that there was nothing from Will. Only Miles:

Date: Thursday 13 July 2006 13.10
Sender: Mmetcalfe@Agassociates.com
To: Daisy.Allen@paddingtonpress.com
Subject: grovelling apology

Daisy, are you ever going to speak to me again? It's really not my fault I had to work late. I know all these last-minute cancellations are awful, but just bear with me while I prove myself in the new role. I'm gutted – I know you were looking forward to seeing the play, too.

I humbly await your forgiveness, and am looking forward to you taking you out again soon.

M xx

Daisy sighed. Was she being too harsh? She began typing a reply. Then she stopped and deleted it all. Then started a new one. Halfway down the page she remembered her promise not to be bothered by him today, and closed the email down. She decided on sending out some rejection letters: a much more fruitful task than emailing Miles.

But then, after ten minutes of this, she found herself quite beyond all control, picking up her phone and dialling his work number; almost as though someone else was manning her faculties. As his assistant answered the phone, she numbly asked to speak to him.

'Oh no, he's out with one of his authors at the moment. Can I take a message?'

'Um, yes, it's Daisy,' she mumbled. Then, feeling worried that she'd broken their sacred pact, added, 'Sorry, Daisy Allen, from Mercury. I'm calling with reference to Gerard Bogaert.'

'Oh, right. I'll have him ring you.' The kindness in the girl's voice put Daisy at her ease. 'By the way . . . did you like your lilies the other day?'

'Oh – yes!' how sweet of her to ask, Daisy thought. 'They were lovely, thanks for asking!' She felt much more relaxed as she hung up the phone.

Three hours later, Heidi showed up on Daisy's call indicator.

'Hi, love, what's up?' said Daisy on answering the phone.

'Oh nothing. Just bored. Want to meet downstairs for a coffee?'

'Excellent. I'll just wait till B's gone down to her jacket meeting – see you down there in ten?'

Before long they were slurping on their lattes and talking loudly, when Heidi suddenly came over somewhat maternal. 'Are you OK today, sweets? You seem a bit down in the dumps about something. You didn't eat anything at lunch, either.'

'I did eat. I had some soup at my desk,' Daisy said defensively. It was important to be correct about things. But then, she couldn't hold it in any longer. 'Well no, actually, I'm feeling pretty crap, to be honest. I'm just really cross with Miles. I mean, he's let me down again . . . he's says he's really sorry . . . but I'm just not so sure I can trust him any more.'

'Oh . . .' Heidi's expression began to change from initial concern to a more serious look of worry.

Seeing this, Daisy began to feel worried herself. 'What is it? H?'

Heidi said nothing.

'What is it, what have I said? Tell me!'

Heidi was almost welling up. 'Darling, why didn't you say something?' she spurted. 'We had no idea you knew! How can you have possibly been keeping this to yourself all day long?! How did you find out? You mean, the rat actually *told* you? Well, at least he's honest, I'll give him that—'

'What in the name of bejeezus are you talking about?' screeched Daisy, 'Miles *told* me he had to cancel the theatre trip – of course he was going to tell me that – rather than just stand me up, I mean . . .'

Heidi's face grew pale. 'Right. Well, of course he did.' She nodded in understanding. 'How . . . how noble of him. So, are you going to forgive him? I don't think you should. I think this has to be the last straw with him. Why not just break it off with him?'

Now Daisy was terribly confused. 'H, it's not that big a deal! I'll probably forgive him, eventually. I'm just letting him stew a bit . . .'

Now Heidi looked as uncomfortable as Daisy was

confused. 'Heidi, is there something else? You're acting rather strangely – in fact, you and Amelie have both been acting strangely today. What's going on?'

Heidi shook her head, smiling saccharinely. 'No, sweets, you're imagining it. Nothing's happened!' She nodded firmly.

'Oh yeah, I know. No crack,' Daisy said sarcastically, watching Heidi closely. She stared at her friend as she continued to deny that there was anything else the matter, but the telltale sign was there. The left nostril of Heidi's nose crinkled up, in its dead giveaway manner, and that was enough for Daisy to know.

'Tell me. I *know* you're fibbing, H. Your nostrils always let you down. Just tell me.'

Heidi was insistently shaking her head now. 'No, Daisy, honestly. Nothing's happened.'

Daisy was getting impatient now. 'Heidi, just bloody tell me what's up! Is it to do with Miles?'

Heidi said nothing. Her nostril flickered again.

Quietly, Daisy said, 'Tell me. Before I beat it out of you.'

'Jeez, Daisy! Have you been taking rage pills?' Now Heidi was very afraid. After another long, edgy silence, she began to talk.

'OK. Don't freak out on me.' She paused, looking for the words. 'Um . . . we wanted to tell you earlier. Amelie was going to tell you, but I stopped her. We were going to see if he was man enough to tell you himself first. Clearly he's not, so . . .'

Daisy felt her stomach tense up. 'Please, can we just get this over with?'

'Sure,' said Heidi, looking apprehensive. 'OK, then. Right . . . well . . . Miles. You know he said he had to work last night? Well – he was working all right. At the party. As Gina Munir's agent's assistant. You know – the girl whose debut novel is being published by my old company?'

'The gorgeous, childhood prodigy one that's like eight years old,' Daisy said solemnly. 'Yes, I remember Miles mentioning her before.'

'She's actually seventeen, but I digress . . .'

Daisy nodded and she began to imagine the rest. She felt slightly giddy, and didn't really need to listen as Heidi went on, but she had a morbid compulsion to hear every last detail.

'So, he didn't see us there. Even if he had, I don't think he'd really have recognised us, least of all twigged that we knew you. But anyway, we kept seeing him around. To start with, he was just being his usual charming, effervescent self, floating round the room, working the crowd. But then as it got later, we both couldn't help noticing that he seemed to be getting quite chummy with Gina. And that, everytime we happened to look his way, they were leaning against each other, laughing and joking. And – sorry this is the tackiest bit – much later on, when lots of people had left, they started feeding each other bits of canapes! And I kept saying to Amelie – oh, it's nothing, harmless enough. You know he's just doing his job, looking after the client – so we forgot all about it . . . that is, until . . .'

'What? Just stop beating around the bush and tell me!' Daisy's face was growing pale, and she felt nauseous as Heidi told her the rest. All about how Amelie, right at the end of the night, had wandered off to find her coat.

'Of course, Amelie being Amelie, she couldn't remember which room she'd left it in, so she was just testing doors at random. And then there turned out to be this one door which she'd innocently assumed was a cupboard full of cloaks . . . and instead, it was a room full of Miles and Gina – his tongue down her throat, her Prada top slipping halfway down, and Miles's sordid little hands helping it along . . . and then, of course, Amelie promptly made it worse by squealing, "Oops, I'm so sorry!" Then she rushed off and grabbed me. We left the party as soon as we could after that . . .'

Daisy said nothing, but was concentrating hard on keeping her eyes from welling up. There was a long silence.

'How embarrassing for Amelie!' was all she could manage before she burst into tears.

'Oh, honey. Never mind Amelie! Oh Dais, I'm so, so, sorry.' Heidi put her arm around Daisy, and stroked her hair comfortingly. 'But you do believe me though, don't you? I'd hate for you to think we'd made this up. In fact, I so wish I *was* making it up. But sadly it's very true. Miles is a first-class shit.'

The more it sank in, the more the colour drained from Daisy's face. She could barely feel her legs, and her stomach was tying itself up in bits. 'Well . . . thank you for telling me,' she said calmly. Then, less so, 'I can't believe it. I know he's always had *issues* with commitment, but I didn't know he was actually seeing other girls! I mean, he kind of promised he wasn't, when we last had lunch!'

'Kind of? Well, exactly,' said Heidi, a little bit of 'I told you so' creeping into her tone. 'Well, at least now you finally know where you stand. What are you going to do?'

'I don't know,' Daisy said, a tear rolling down her face. Heidi leaned towards her and gave her another sympathetic hug. In truth Daisy wanted to throw dignity to the wind and crumble on to the centre of the floor right there in Chapter Ten, the staff canteen, and have a full-on crying fit. But instead she decided to settle for some good, old-fashioned denial.

'Actually, I do know. I'm going to go upstairs, and get on with my mountains of submissions. Sod him. I'll worry about him later.'

Daisy took her last sip of coffee, slamming the cup back down on the table in a gesture of defiance and strength, even though inside she felt shattered and broken into tiny pieces. With that she headed back upstairs in meditative silence, Heidi in tow.

Arriving back on her floor, she headed to her desk, catching sight of the vase of lilies on her desk. They weren't looking so well, despite how dutifully she'd been watering them, and how hard she'd tried to position them towards what little natural light there was in the office. It was two weeks since Miles had sent them to her, and they'd seen better days. Trying to muffle the voice in her head that was screaming at her all about symbolism, Daisy picked up the rotting lilies and ceremoniously dumped them in the bin. But in doing so, she caught sight of the card lying beside the bin, and had a flicker of a realisation. Suddenly it was all clear. How naive was she? Miles hadn't sent her these. Like Inspector Poirot when he'd just solved a crime, an imagined vision of what must have actually happened played out in Daisy's mind. Miles had probably just ordered his assistant to send some roses. That's why at lunch that day, he'd asked her if she'd liked the roses, not lilies. Perhaps, she conjectured, the shop had had none left, so the poor assistant had come up with the idea of lilies, having no idea that they happened to be Daisy's favourite. And the chocolates! No wonder they were orange-flavoured – the assistant had probably been in charge of those, too. Perhaps these were trifling details, but having an awareness of them seemed to open the door to new, unchartered levels of humiliation. Not only had he cheated on Daisy, but getting his assistant to send her faceless gifts? What was she – some sort of mistress, in a crap film?

Half an hour later, Daisy was hiding at her desk, after having committed the ultimate in professional suicide: walking round with puffy eyes at work. Each time someone had asked, 'Are you OK? You look like you've been crying,' she'd hated herself that little bit more. She sat thinking about this now, and that made her want to cry even more . . . which in turn made her hate herself even more. What a hateful roundabout of a predicament to be in. She felt all kinds of emotions – hurt, anger and, most of all, humiliation. But the absolute worst feeling of all? Despite everything, she still wanted to see him again. She couldn't stand the thought of not seeing him any more. She knew it was dreadful, but she was going round in circles. It should be so simple. Get rid of the two-timing arrogant fuckwit. Easy, surely.

'Hi, Daisy,' came Elliot's calming voice as he walked up to her desk with a nervous smile on his face. He placed a pile of marked-up manuscripts on her shelf, and took a sip from the mug of tea he'd just prepared for himself. 'Haven't seen you around much today. Is everything OK?'

At the warmth of his voice, Daisy felt the tears pressing at the corners of her eyes again, threatening to flood at any point. Don't you dare, she threatened, staring down at her page. She didn't dare look up at Elliot. 'Fine, yes. Just very busy. Thanks,' Daisy said, staring straight down at the page in front of her.

'You must be working hard,' he observed, 'I mean, you'd have to be, to be able to read that.'

Daisy looked up, confused. Elliot smiled sympathetically at her. 'Your manuscript's upside down?'

Daisy smiled wanly. 'Oh. How silly of me,' she said flatly, and turned it the right way round.

'You're not OK, are you?' he asked, real concern in his voice.

'No, you're right – I'm not really working. In fact, I haven't been working all day. I've got stuff on my mind. Stupid girlie stuff, that's all.'

'Want to talk about it?' Elliot asked gently, leaning on the edge of her desk. He held out his mug of tea for her. A smile leaked out from Daisy's maudlin face, and she took a sip gratefully. The tea was mildly comforting, and she felt momentarily revived.

'Hurrah! The first smile of the day. That's a proper breakthrough!'

Daisy laughed. Slightly.

'Result!' Elliot grinned, and took a sip of tea himself. 'Well. Look, I don't know what's happened to upset you, but if you want to talk, you know where I am . . .'

People being nice to Daisy when she felt depressed always had the odd effect of making her feel even sadder somehow. She needed to cry again, and felt tears nagging at the corners of her eyes again. Afraid that Elliot could tell, she began to feel embarrassed.

'Oh, it's nothing. I'll be fine. I'm just having a pathetic moment. It's my loser of a boyfriend – he's done something awful, and I think I might need to not see him any more. Only, he doesn't know I know yet, so it's up to me to tell him, otherwise we'll just be carrying on as normal. And I'm too scared to confront him on it, because as mental as this sounds, I don't want to lose him yet. I don't want to not see him – even though he's done his über-shitty thing. I mean, what kind of a pathetic loser *am* I?! Have I undone years of feminist progress just by saying that?!'

'No, of course not. You're only human. You can't control what you feel. Besides, whatever it is he's done, only you can decide on his punishment, and whether you want to forgive him or not. But hey, it's understandable . . . Miles is quite a dashing young chap . . .'

Daisy was surprised. 'How do you know what he looks like?'

'Oh, I saw his picture in *The Bookseller* a few weeks ago – you know, there was that feature on literary agencies, and all the young talents in the big ones?'

'Oh yes – of which he was one, of course. Slimey bastard.'

Elliot smiled with relief. 'That's the stuff. Let's see some rage. It's all healthy.'

Daisy laughed. 'You're right. Actually, I know what I'll do. I'll send him an email telling him what I think of him. You know, rather than talk to him in person, with his chiselled face getting in the way and putting me off. Yes! This way I'll be able to say exactly what I think, in a careful, composed manner. Excellent.'

'Indeed. Well, let me know if you want any help phrasing it. I'm very good at these sorts of things,' he joked, leaning his hand on her shoulder casually. 'You feeling a bit better now?'

'Actually, yes, I am a bit. It kind of helped just to talk about it a bit . . . Thanks.'

'Any time,' he said, and began walking away. Then he hovered, and thought for a moment before turning back. 'Um. It's just a thought, and it maybe the last thing you feel like doing, but, if you fancy taking your mind off things after work, I'm working at 'Under My Skin' tonight. I could probably smuggle you and Belle, or anyone else in for free. It's a ludicrous night out, but it's a real giggle, too, in many ways. So let me know if you fancy it . . .'

Daisy looked at Elliot, marvelling at his apparently limitless reserves of kindness. 'Thank you. At the moment I feel like curling up on the sofa and eating ten swimming pools full of chocolate, but if I change my mind, I'll let you know.' Daisy smiled and turned back to the manuscript she was line-editing, only this time the correct way up.

An hour later, she was just clicking 'send' on a curt email to Miles, having written ten different drafts, some more detailed than others. In the end, she'd gone with the short, cagey one, which curtly implied she knew more about him than she was letting on.

Date: Thursday 13 July 2006 17.10
Sender: Daisy.Allen@paddingtonpress.com
To: Mmetcalfe@Agassociates.com
Subject: Re: grovelling apology

Dear Miles

Thanks for your note. Hope you're well.

I think in light of recent events, it'll be good if we don't see each other for a while.

Best,

D

p.s. Thanks again for the chocolates. Belinda's loving them (I'm allergic to orange, but your assistant wasn't to know that).

Switching off her computer, Daisy grabbed her bags and got ready to leave. Out of the corner of her eye she caught sight of the Post-it note Elliot had written to her before leaving. Reading it now, she could see that it had the instructions for how to get to the 'Under My Skin' exhibition. She'd said no at the time, but now – in her present state of mind – she began to wonder whether this might not be the perfect distraction for her. Something that she would never normally do, looking at real, dead, preserved body parts – lungs, kidneys and hearts – there was always a chance that by seeing all these vital organs in their crudest, most glaringly red form, it would put into perspective the grim feelings in her own heart. Was there anything in that? Probably not, she thought as she put on her jacket, slung her bag over her shoulder, and left. But it was always worth a try.

Half an hour later she walked out of Earls Court tube station and stepped out on to a stormy Exhibition Road. She looked up at the sky and winced. Were those two weeks back in June the only bit of summer they were going to get, she wondered? She pushed out her olive-green umbrella over her head and squinted through the rain down at her A-Z. Looking up again, she clocked the huge sign in front of her that said in bold white letters, 'Under My Skin – season extended' on the side of the large exhibition centre. Well, that was painless, she thought. Grabbing her brown paper bag filled with chocolates – a Twix, a Mars and a Caramel, she marched up the road, dodging the puddles in her path.

Approaching the main entrance, Daisy retrieved the crumpled note in her back pocket.

'Look for a big, cuddly security guard with dark hair called Fred, and if he smiles at you, give him the chocolate.'

It didn't take her long. There was already a man of that description staring at her inquisitively. Daisy crept towards him, checking around her to see no one else staff-like was watching.

'Um, hello,' she said quietly to the Fred-like man, while brandishing the brown paper bag, half opening the top to reveal to him what was inside the bag.

'Ummm,' he said, smirking, a cheeky expression on his face. Clearly he wasn't going to make this easy for her. He was tall, extremely muscly from what she could tell, sporting a bulging white shirt and black baggy trousers.

'Are you – by any chance – Fred?' Daisy asked timidly, wishing she'd just played it safe and gone to the box office, which was only metres away, to buy a ticket. It was only £11, and well worth it for not feeling like a criminal. She was just about to give up and go and try the legal approach when Fred broke his vow of silence.

'Hi. Daisy, is it? Do you want to come with me?'

Relief washed over Daisy. She smiled, said nothing, and followed Fred as he strode through the foyer and through one of the black doors marked 'No Entry'. If Daisy felt incredibly nervous and afraid, she didn't show it.

As the door swung shut behind them and they set off down a bare white corridor towards a door marked 'Staff Entrance', Daisy said, 'Sorry – you *are* Elliot's mate, aren't you? Just so I know you're not abducting me?'

He laughed. 'Yes, of course. Follow me . . . Have you got a little something for me?' he asked as they set off walking.

Daisy felt relieved again. 'Oh yes – thank you.' Only then did it occur to her that she should've bought some for herself, the mood she was in. Too late. Stoically she offered Fred the bag of chocolates and he took them gratefully.

'Thanks very much! You totally didn't have to. I was *really* only winding Elliot up. Such an easy target, that one.' He looked in the bag, 'But good choices!' He nodded in approval.

'Here we are then.' He paused by the door and opened it for her. He pointed out the interior as she walked through. 'Now you're in the exhibition. Just go through here, round that corner, and you'll be straight into the Nervous System. To get to the start, you just need to backtrack through Urine and you'll be in Skeletal. Which do you want? Is it your first time?'

Daisy paused, thinking how little she cared which room she saw first. What was she doing here? Why wasn't she curled up on her sofa watching soothing American trash? 'Um, yes, it is. I'm not too bothered, really. Which one's the best?'

'Well, it's a matter of opinion. I think Reproduction's pretty fascinating. Gross, but interesting. Like most of this place. Anyway, must get back.' He smiled. 'Cheers for the choccies . . . and cheer up, you know it might never happen.'

With that, Fred was reversing down the corridor, leaving Daisy to wander into the Nervous system in search of some clue as to why she had come to this freaky place, and wishing that her eyes didn't still look so swollen from crying like a baby. Think positive, she told herself, just as she arrived face to face with the naked, overexposed spinal chord of a skinless man playing darts.

'Women blink nearly twice as much as men,' so read the panel in front of her on the wall two minutes later. Fair enough, Daisy thought, as she set off towards all the other skinless figures dotted around the room. Then a thought occurred to her. Why is that? Maybe it's so that women are genetically programmed to be less aware, when their guy's being unfaithful? A blink and you've missed it, sort of thing? There might be something in that, she thought. See, learning things already.

She walked into the Circulatory System, which was much darker and filled with pillars displaying bunches of red blood vessels and arteries. All the intricate lines and tiny branches were illuminated and looked like the delicate leaves of tiny trees, Daisy thought as she wandered around. Before long she came across the heart itself. Staring at this funny little organ in its odd display cabinet, she suddenly had a vivid picture in her mind of Miles with that other girl, both of them laughing together. She felt her eyes welling up and moved on further down the room, towards a darkened corner, and took quiet refuge next to a big red man holding a huge snooker cue.

'Hello, Cedric, how are you today?'

Daisy jumped, seeing Elliot standing next to her in the dark, addressing not her but the snooker-playing corpse.

'Oh – and hello, Daisy! Glad you could make it!' he said, pretending to have just noticed her.

Daisy went to give him a hello hug, but Elliot frowned and held up his hands in front of him. 'No fraternising with clients. Horse-face over there is watching, and she can't wait for an excuse to fire me.'

He indicated a blonde, crabby-looking supervisor at the other side of the room, who was staring daggers at them both.

Daisy backed away from Elliot quickly. 'Oh – right – sorry.'

'You enjoying yourself?' He grinned, a twinkle in his eye.

'Enjoying's an odd word. I guess I'm – learning stuff?' she tried. 'And I'm pleased to have the distraction – so thanks for getting me in, anyway . . .'

Elliot smiled. 'Have you met Nige here?' He lead her through to a dark, quiet corner where there was a tiny man posing in a yoga position. 'He's the absolute best yoga teacher I've ever seen. He's broken all known records for holding the Downward Dog.'

Daisy laughed loudly, inviting the woman opposite them to 'shhh' her across the room. Daisy mouthed 'sorry', then whispered, 'Have you actually named them all?' as they left the dark corner, Elliot leading the way into the next area.

'Absolutely . . . and we've worked out what they all did in their former lives, too.' Elliot paused, lightly rested his hand on one of the bodies' arms. 'For instance, Robin here was a teacher – you can tell by the way he's pointing, like he's trying to instil discipline into one of the naughty pupils. You see?'

He strode across to the other side of the room, and like a game-show host, went on to introduce the different bodies. 'Laeticia here, on the other hand, was a bit of a naughty gal. My mate George has her down as a definite hooker. You can tell by the way she's holding herself. Worldly-wise.'

Daisy looked closely at the scrawny figure in front of her, which seemed, stripped to its core, exactly the same as all the others. Suddenly, it was too much. She saw how ridiculous the whole thing was, and burst into compulsive giggles. Elliot joined in but then his expression dropped. 'Horse-face' seemed to be gesturing to him.

'Arse – it's Touch Pod time,' Elliot said, 'I've gotta fly. But give me ten minutes, and then you can come and spectate. Pretend like you don't know me, and then you can take part in our new fun quiz.'

Daisy laughed, 'What new fun quiz?! And what in God's name is the Touch Pod? Is it something to do with porn?'

'Ah, you'll see. We have to make up games. It's the only way to preserve our souls. Otherwise, well, we'd just slowly *become* dead bodies ourselves, and no one would even notice.' He smiled with mock self-pity. 'By the way, have you noticed how cold it is down here? They have to keep it that way so all the little buggers don't melt!'

'Gross!' Daisy said, feeling another rush of sympathy that Elliot had to work here.

After passing a further ten minutes in the Reproduction area looking at disturbing bits of preserved unborn children, Daisy headed into the main area to go in search of Elliot.

The 'Touch Pod' as it turned out, was a large semi-circular counter displaying multiple internal organs preserved in rubber. Behind the counter, two men stood in the guise of medical experts, poised in readiness for any questions. One of these supposed medical experts was Elliot. As Daisy approached, he was engrossed in a detailed explanation of how the spleen worked, demonstrating its various elements to a small red-haired girl with pigtails, who was smiling and nodding shyly. Walking slowly into earshot, Daisy could just make out what Elliot was saying. And, unless he was making all the details up, he sounded very convincing.

Satisfied, Pigtails nodded, dispensed a polite 'Thank you very much', and walked away. Elliot turned to face the front, assessing the number of people in the room. Without stopping to acknowledge Daisy, he turned, nodded to his sidekick, and then spoke up, loudly enough so that everyone in the hushed room turned to listen.

'Um – hello, everyone. Who would like to play a game?' He smiled nervously, as people turned away from their boxes full of red, bloody organs and listened to him. 'It's as educational as it is fun.'

Daisy felt herself laugh out loud, with a little too much zeal. She looked down, embarrassed, as people turned to look at her.

'So, we haven't come up with a name yet,' Elliot went on. 'Working titles are – "Who Wants to be a Megalosplenia?" '

Laughter filled the room.

'Or, "I'm a Cerebral Cortex, Get Me Out of Here." '

More laughter, and all eyes were now on Elliot. Daisy couldn't help feeling slightly nervous for him.

'So, you've got five of the body's vital organs here. Your mission, should you choose to accept it, is to tell me a) what it is; b) if appropriate, where it is; and c) if you're really a geek, one of its functions. OK? You've all got to work together as a team. And along the way we'll give you fun facts, and bonus points. Harry here's my glamorous assistant. He's actually a real medical student – not an impostor like me . . .'

Before long Elliot had charmed the room, and as he went on to play the game, the audience continued to laugh along with him, and seemed to be relishing this unexpected comic interlude in a rather sombre exhibition.

'OK, so what's this?' he said, pointing to one of the small, round blobs on the counter.

'Liver,' stuttered a shell-suited teenage girl in the audience.

'That's right.'

When no one knew where it went, Elliot held the blob up to beneath his ribcage, by way of explanation. 'See, it sits here. And here's where the portal vein goes, takes all the blood, then metabolises it. It also produces bile, which regulates the blood. Basically, your liver has to produce bile on demand. A little bit like top-up TV, if you get me.'

While everyone laughed, Daisy stared at Elliot in admiration. Watching how charismatically he dealt with the crowds, and how he'd managed to make what would usually be such a dull job interesting, she couldn't help feeling impressed.

A little later, Elliot was trying to move things along, but the audience seemed not to want the game to end. 'Well, that's about all you need to know about the venal artery.' Then he picked up a large grey, jelly-like object and held it up questioningly. 'Anyone?' he said, turning to Daisy for the first time.

All eyes turned to Daisy as she stammered, 'Uh . . . that would be the brain . . .?'

'Correct!' he screeched, and Daisy blushed.

'Function of the left side?' he fired at her.

Daisy suddenly felt very stupid. Which one was which? She was racking her brain. 'Oh – I've probably got this the wrong way round, but I'm going to guess. The creative stuff?'

'WRONG!' he said mock-scathingly, and everyone turned to her to laugh. Daisy forced a smile, sensing some people in the audience looking from her to Elliot with interest.

'It's actually the LOGICAL side,' Elliot said sternly, and Daisy looked down, embarrassed.

'Well, let's put the brain away shall we – that's the most boring one anyway.' He threw it to Harry, who caught it and popped it in a box under the counter.

'Actually, I think that about wraps things up,' he said, looking around. 'So, OK, thanks for playing "Who Wants to be a Megalosplenia"! You did the best yet out of any team, ever. What about that! Give yourselves a round of applause.'

An hour later, Daisy and Elliot were walking out of the exhibition centre, Daisy loaded up with all manner of ludicrous 'Under My Skin'-inspired souvenir toys – a spleen-shaped alarm clock, an egg timer made to look like a collapsed lung, among others. Daisy turned to Elliot and linked arms with him as they walked towards the nearest pub.

'That was really a lot of fun! I must say, you're a natural performer – I'm very impressed. Have you ever thought of being an actor?'

Elliot laughed. 'Christ no. Really, it's nothing. I'm just doing all I can to make the time go more quickly.'

'Either way – and I say this with genuine surprise – that was one of the funniest nights I've had in a while! Thank you very much . . . at least let me buy you a drink, to say thank you.'

Elliot pretended to stop and think for a moment. 'Mmm, let's see. Lovely green-eyed girl wants to buy me drink. I've got no money, and I'm in desperate medical need of some Stella.' He paused again, then nodded emphatically, 'Yeah. Sure. Works for me.' And they walked into the crowded pub.

'So,' Daisy said, as they took their seats, 'do you really know all that stuff, or were you just making it up to sound like a medical student, like the rest of them?!'

'Yeah, of course! Everything you heard was true. I've learned it all here, so I guess to some extent my time at the exhibition's been worthwhile. Ish.'

'Do you always tell them the correct facts about all the body parts, then?'

'Hell, no. I often tell people an anus is actually a venal artery. I mean, the other day, this fully grown woman asked me . . .' he broke off, laughing, 'she went to me, deadpan, "OK – so if this liver goes here, what about the other one?"'

Daisy laughed as Elliot went on, 'Anyway, I was like, well, if people really don't know their arses from their elbow and are really that daft, then maybe I'm not going to tell them the truth! It's totally mean of me, I know. But, the other day, I was the most bored I've EVER been in my whole life, so just to make the time pass I spent the whole day telling people that the gall bladder was a testicle, and vice versa. You've got to vary the monotony occasionally.'

Daisy shook her head disapprovingly. 'Oh, Ellie, that's mean. Those poor, misguided people . . .'

'I'm not proud of it, Daisy. I know it was wrong.' Elliot pretended to hang his head in shame, putting down his pint dramatically. 'Will you ever forgive me, if I promise not to do it again?' He turned to face her, his blue eyes blinking innocence at Daisy, and she fell about laughing.

'Well, since you asked so nicely . . .'

An hour and two glasses of wine later, Daisy was feeling the world become slightly out of focus.

'I've just realised, I haven't had any dinner. I'd better make this my last one, or you'll have to carry me home.'

Elliot was staring at Daisy as she said this, then he quickly looked down into his pint. 'Sure, yeah, we'd better get going. I've got to do two hours in the call centre first thing tomorrow.'

'*Before* Mercury? You're mad!' she yelled, slightly too loudly.

'Not mad. Just poor,' he stated factually, and got up to go. 'I've barely even made a dent into my credit card – I've still got horrific amounts of debt to pay off.'

As they both headed out the door and towards the tube, Daisy's mobile began to buzz in her pocket. 'Oh – scuse me,' she slurred as she reached into her pocket, and pressed answer without looking to see who it was. 'Ahullo.'

'Daisy, it's me. I'm on my way to your house now. Are you in?'

Ooops. Shouldn't have answered that, she thought. Too late now. 'Hi. I don't really want to see you,' she said, not assertively enough.

Elliot looked at Daisy and mouthed, 'Are you OK?'

Daisy shook her head. They were at the tube station, and it was raining now, even more heavily than before. Elliot leaned his arm on Daisy's, and she leaned back on to him, both of them supporting each other while she held the phone to her ear.

'Well tough,' Miles was saying, 'I'm on your road now. I just want to talk to you – I think there might be something I need to quickly clear up with you. Some sort of mis-understanding? I just want five minutes of your time. I won't stay the night, I promise. Just let me see you quickly?'

Daisy looked up to see Elliot, who was miming 'Noooooo' to her, and waving his arms about, obviously having guessed what was being said down the phone. She looked away, feeling embarrassed. But the trouble was, Miles was somehow so persuasive, without having to really try. Even at the best of times, Daisy was hopeless at saying no. But now she was drifting into drunk, she could feel all sense of logic and rationality disappearing behind her. So much so that, despite everything he'd done, she found herself really wanting to see him. it. She looked towards Elliot, who seemed to have twigged and was shaking his head. Daisy paused. She wanted desperately to say no – to tell him once and for all to go and take a leap out of a ten-storey building over a crocodile-infested gorge. But then, she reasoned, if she was going to break up with him, didn't social niceties dictate that she at least do it to his face? Wasn't that the decent thing to do?

Signing on the Dotted Line

Stony-faced, Miles and Daisy were sitting on separate chairs in her living room. Somehow, Daisy was calmly listening to what he was saying, rather than beating him around the head with a stick and then feeding him to a pit of hungry wolves as she'd been doing for so much of the day in her mind. She listened as he told her meekly that the compromising position he'd been found in at the party was in fact a one-off – and that all along, he'd just been doing his job. He'd begun by just being charming and friendly to the client, but it just got taken the wrong way.

'Look, it all just got a bit out of hand and silly. Everyone there was up to their eyeballs in booze, coke, what have you. I don't know how it happened. Look, you can tell me to go jump. But I just wanted to explain to you, Daisy, that despite what you might think, I don't make a habit of that sort of thing. I . . . haven't – you know – slept with her, or anyone else, either. If that helps.'

Daisy laughed. As she did so, she felt an aching in her jaw, which reminded her that she'd been laughing like a maniac for the entire evening. Which made her think – when was the last time Miles really made her laugh?

Which made her think – but never mind that – how could she ever trust Miles again? She sighed.

'The thing with this, Miles, is . . . technically, I don't have the right to be upset, do I? I mean, it's not like we're really exclusive, officially. The way you put it at lunch the other day, I guess we *are* allowed to see other people. So I don't see what I can do. I can't tell you not to. But at the same time, it makes me feel . . . just horrible . . . when I think of you with her. And that makes me think that, if there's any chance I'll end up feeling like that again, then I don't want to take the risk. I like you a lot, Miles – too much, probably . . .'

Miles looked at Daisy expectantly, new levels of humility and worry etched on to his face. 'And I like you a lot too, Daisy . . .'

Daisy smiled meekly. 'But the thing is, I have to protect myself.'

'I don't know what you mean. I don't understand where all this is coming from,' he said, visibly confused.

'Miles. Let's be honest,' Daisy went on, vowing to remain resilient, 'You see, we've come too far down this road now. It's like – we're there, we've hit that official crossroads point now. And one of us has to decide what to do – we either say we're together, openly, or we go our separate ways. And much as it pains me, I know I can't do this any more; this non-commital half-arsed relationship that you're afraid of calling a relationship. I hate to say it, but . . . I think we should break up. Even though, as you say, we're not officially going out. You see how nonsensical and cyclical this all is?! It's maddening!'

Daisy paused for breath, amazed at how long she had talked non-stop for; and also amazed at how long Miles had listened so attentively. Looking up at him, she was shocked to see that he looked upset, and even a bit shaken.

'Oh, baby. Please don't say that. That's . . . horrible. I don't want us to (and he held up his fingers as little speech marks) "break up". Look, what if I *swear* to you that it's over with her? That it will never happen again?' He looked fearful, and got up off his chair. He went to sit by Daisy on the arm of her chair.

Daisy shook her head, trying her hand at resolute. 'But that's like saying you promise to only be with me. And that's what you're so afraid of saying. You want us to be together, but at the same time, you're afraid of admitting it to anyone else. How shitty do you think that makes me feel? Face it, we're just going to be going round in circles here.'

'But you're just talking semantics . . .' He moved closer and put his hand on her knee.

'Don't.' She removed his hand, impressed at how well she was pulling off this being-strong business. 'I am not. I'm talking sense. You're the fuckwit here.'

Miles was dented. He was quiet for a very, very long minute. He gave a heavy sigh, drew a weary breath and then said, slowly, 'OK, all right.' Then, after another breath, he blurted loudly, 'OK. FINE! You can call me your sodding boyfriend, if that's what it takes! Fine! Where do I sign?'

'And they say Romance is dead,' was Amelie's caustic response over lunch the next day in Chapter Ten. It being one of those British summers that really couldn't make up its mind, the girls were confined to the canteen again, sheltering from the rain.

'Well, exactly. And whoever "they" are, they were definitely on to something,' agreed Heidi, after Daisy had finished relaying her account of the night before.

'Look – I know what it sounds like to you guys. Enough mugs to open a tea-shop. But the fact is, he's finally giving me what I want! An actual, verbal commitment! We're finally on a new path, going in the right direction, and all that . . . you know, we've made it past the crossroads at last!'

Heidi and Amelie were nodding slowly, reluctant and unimpressed respectively.

'Look. You know what it all comes down to here? I'm not ready to give him up. You see, there's a much, much bigger problem here. I've realised – I think I'm really, properly falling in love with him. Sure, there's a chance this will still turn to shit, but I'm just not ready to give the bugger up. If there's the teensiest chance that we'll work out in the long run, I have to see. Does that make sense?'

'Daisy, you sound delusional, you really do,' said Heidi, just as Elliot walked into the cafeteria. He glanced over from the other side of the room and smiled. Daisy watched as he bought a takeaway filled baguette and then quickly headed back out.

'Question. What is up with that boy?' Heidi asked, following him curiously with her eyes. 'I think maybe he's avoiding me – ever since we went for that drink he's been a bit funny with me.

'What do you mean?' asked Daisy almost defensively, 'He is a little quieter today, I suppose, now you mention it . . .'

'It's not just that. I mean, why does he never join us for lunch any more? It must be me.'

Daisy shrugged. 'I don't know. He's not been himself for ages.'

'Actually,' said Heidi, flicking conversational switches again, 'I've got major gossip.'

'What?' Heidi and Amelie said in unison.

'Man gossip. Beautiful man at the gym has just become Beautiful Jim at the Gym.'

'Oh, stop talking in riddles,' Daisy said sternly. 'What are you on about?'

'I mean, the beautiful man I've been admiring from afar, ever since I joined the gym, has finally started returning my looks – it must be my new gym gear! So anyway, now we've been chatting every time we go, and I'm going every day at the moment. Plus, we're going on a date this weekend. Well, after our workouts, that is.'

'That's disgusting!' opined Daisy. 'How can you possibly be attracted to someone who's all covered in sweat and smelly?'

'Easy. He's gorgeous, he works in the City, and has his own flat in Docklands. Sweat is soooooooo not a factor.'

Later that day, Daisy was getting ready to meet Miles for dinner. She walked up to Elliot's desk, having hardly seen him all day. She was enjoying having him around again – as were the rest of the department. He'd been back for almost a week, and already the department was functioning far better. He'd been writing reports for Daisy, taking minutes, ordering stationery. He'd even been speaking out in meetings – something even the most tenacious of assistants wouldn't dare attempt, so scary were Belinda's put-downs. But before long, he'd fashioned a fully fledged role for himself within the department, and even Belinda was beginning to thaw slightly, just through having his sunny disposition around.

'Hey you,' Daisy said, standing by Elliot's desk. 'Have you got enough to do? Oh, of course you have . . . sorry . . .' she said, noticing the obvious stacks of books, manuscripts and to-do lists all around him. 'Um, look . . . I'm sorry that last night ended rather stupidly. I have to admit, I was having a really fun night until then.'

Elliot put down his pen and looked up at Daisy. 'Oh, yes, plenty. And hey – no problem. So did you take great pleasure in telling Miles to go jump?'

'Well, yes. Initially.' Then Daisy looked down at her feet and said quietly, as though she wasn't very proud of herself, 'Except, well, then he kind of wouldn't let me.'

Elliot looked up, surprised, as Daisy went on with her confession, 'He ended up talking me round, and, well . . . I'm kind of giving him another chance. I'm seeing him tonight so he can try and make it up to me. You see, he's finally said he's ready to be "official", as it were. But I'm not holding my breath, to be honest. I'll see how it goes.'

Elliot nodded. 'Well, exactly. See if he makes it worth your while or not.' He paused, thinking.

'Anyway, thanks for coming yesterday – it livened things up a bit more than usual. Oh, and Fred thought you were lovely, by the way. I think you've got an admirer there.'

Daisy giggled. 'Must have been all that chocolate I gave him. Seriously, though, I had such a fun night – thank you so much for getting me out and showing me how to laugh again. I owe you one.' Daisy prepared to leave, before adding, 'Don't work too late today, OK?' She pushed through the double doors, and was gone.

'Don't worry, I won't.' Elliot said quietly to himself,

watching the doors swing back and forth until they became still, before pulling out his memory stick, plugging it in and opening up a Word file. Then, remembering something, he went out into the hallway. Checking to see that every last bit of Paddington editorial had left the building, he went into the small kitchen and studied the half-empty bottles of wine lined up, all going to waste after somebody's birthday drinks. He grabbed a wine glass from the cupboard and poured himself a modest glass. Back at his desk moments later, he stretched out his arms and fingers in front of him in traditional writerly style. Now, he was almost ready.

He was trying not to panic, but there was still so much material to get through. So many new ideas to get down, and so many new thoughts to write up from his Moleskine. He looked through the notes, thinking. He sat. He drank another sip. And he waited. He moved his hands to the keyboard, and stared at the screen.

Ten minutes later, nothing.

Half an hour later, he was still there, staring straight ahead of him. He opened up his iPod and put on some classical music to see if that would help – he'd once read somewhere that Bach was meant to make you more intelligent. Nope. Nada. Still nothing but an empty vessel.

Eventually, he started bashing at keys randomly here and there, just to try to get himself going. But little of any sense was coming out. His brain cells felt claustrophobic, blocked – his mind inarticulate. Every sentence was ineloquent, every phrase awkward and clunky. He drank another sip and concluded that this was useless. Everywhere he looked in his mind, in every corner, every annal of thought, she was there. There was no escaping it. No escaping her.

But then, neither was there any escaping the reality that he *had* to get something written. It was days since he'd got any new material down. With a resigned sigh, Elliot drank another sip, and began to type. Anything was better than nothing, he decided, and gradually, after writing pages of incoherent drivel, he felt his muscles loosening, his imagination stirring. Eventually he broke through to the other side. An hour later, he was still there, absorbed and finally in thrall to the flow of his inspiration. Downing his last sip of red wine, he bashed at the keys furiously and rapidly.

'Is anyone still there?' An hour later, Freddy Rhubarb poked his head round the door into the editorial department, and flicked the lights on and off.

'Yes . . . Sorry, I'm just about heading off – sorry.'

Of All the Bars in All the World

A week later, Belle's dream to perform in the Bedford Arms's open-mike night had almost made it to fruition. While Belle was fussing around backstage and choosing which colour beret to wear, Daisy was back at the flat immersed in ironing – a feeble attempt to distract herself from the fact that Miles was half an hour late already, and that maybe he'd forgotten. Just as she was beginning to think how real a possibility that was, and deciding that what the hell, she'd go on her own anyway, there was a buzz at the door.

'Hello, beautiful one.' Miles leaned in to kiss her cheek as she opened the door to let him in.

'Hello!' she said as he walked into the flat and went to sit down, 'I'm glad you could make it. Was *almost* giving up on you then!'

Miles quickly dispensed one of his wry, lopsided smiles which had always made Daisy melt in the past. Tonight, annoyingly, was no exception.

'OK, you're forgiven. But we'd better get going. There's no time for a drink here any more.' With that Daisy grabbed her blue handbag and frogmarched

Miles back out through the door.

'Quite the Little Miss Bossyboots when you want to be, aren't you?' Miles commented as he led the way to his car.

Arriving at the pub twenty minutes later, it was almost at capacity already. After some tough negotiations with the bouncers to be allowed in, they pushed their way through all the people and headed upstairs to the even more crowded balcony room. Looking around her, Daisy could see an array of Belle's friends, exes and fellow musicians. In amongst the growing din of instruments being tuned in and voice warm-up exercises, she could just about make out a sound she recognised.

'Ya-Ya-YA-ya-ya-ya . . .'

Daisy didn't have to look far. Her sister was doing her warm-up wails and chants in the corner. Clad in skinny-fit black jeans, an oversized red jumper, a black beret and thick red lips, she looked every bit rock chick and ready to go.

'Hello, hon!' Daisy went bounding up to her. 'Good luck times a million . . . not that you'll need it.'

'Did Arse-face stand you up?' Belle asked bluntly, hardly bothering to look around her as she spoke.

'Belle! Shhhh. I assume you mean Miles, and *no*, he didn't! Don't be so mean. He's actually gone to the bar to get me a drink! Which is lucky – he might've heard you otherwise!'

Belle looked doe-eyed and innocent. 'Sorry, but he's not with you now, is he, so how was I to know?'

Daisy shook her head dismissively, 'Never mind! Want me to see if he can get you one, if he's still at the bar?'

'Oh shit, yes please. Deffo need something to calm the nerves. JD, straight up – and a double, if he's paying, please!'

'Less of the cheek, missy moo,' Daisy said as she walked up to join Miles who was at the bar being served. As she crept up behind him, she was planning a surprise embrace from behind, but something she could hear held her back slightly.

'I SAID I wanted a pint of Bitburger. This, on the other hand, is a *half*-pint of Bitburger, planted into a vessel twice its size, and then filled to the top with an airy foamy head.'

'I'm really sorry. I'll make you another one,' came a tired, oppressed voice from behind the counter. 'We've just changed the barrel, that's why – the beer's playing up a bit.'

Daisy stood quietly and listened as Miles went on with his tirade. 'I'm not really that interested in the hows and whys – I'd just like my pint the way it should be, if that's not too much trouble. And I can tell you, I'm not going to be handing over my hard-earned money for that the way it is now, I'm afraid.'

'Miles?' Daisy said, moving closer to him, shocked to hear him brandishing this aggressive side that she'd never seen before.

He turned to Daisy, his face contorted with indignation. 'Bloody south Londoners – they don't know *what* they're doing!'

'Miles! What are you getting so worked up about? I've never seen you so belligerent!' Daisy couldn't help feeling sorry for whoever was at the receiving end of Miles's tirade, and turned to look apologetically at the barman. She did a double take. With complete alarm, she saw that the man standing behind the bar and trying hard to remain calm, was Elliot.

He cast a quick glance in her direction. As his face grew more and more inflamed, Elliot looked from Daisy back to

Miles, and seemed to be thinking rapidly. Elliot stood, his cheeks growing hotter, as he asked Miles for the money.

Daisy was mortified that Miles had been so rude to poor Elliot, but she didn't know what to say. Silently she fumbled around for the words, but in the end decided to try and go with friendly and breezy.

'Well, hello!' Daisy threw on one of her warmest smiles, and tried to send messages of apologetic encouragement to Elliot through her eyes, meanwhile feeling Miles's burning stare on her face. 'I remember you said you worked in Balham, but how funny that it's here! So, how's it all going?' she asked, then instantly wished she hadn't. Ouch. Of course, it was going like a train wreck. How ridiculous of her to ask.

Elliot remained mortified, but gave a noble attempt at a smile, 'Fine, fine. Yeah. Busy tonight, but we're getting on with it. How are you? I didn't know you drank in here? Of all the bars in all the world . . .' he said, an amused, enigmatic look in his eyes.

Daisy smiled. 'Indeed,' she said, and just as she did, she felt a nerve sparking off inside her. She stopped and thought for a moment. Where had she heard that phrase recently? She felt a niggle of déjà vu, but couldn't think why. Miles, meanwhile, was looking from Elliot to Daisy in astonishment.

'You two – you *know* each other?' he blurted, interrupting the synapses jolting about in Daisy's mind.

'Yes, Miles,' Daisy said sternly. Then, turning back to face Elliot, 'I don't normally. But it's Belle's first time here at the jam night, so we're all here to cheer her on . . .'

'Oh right. Which one is she?' Elliot asked, his face gradually regaining its normal shade of tanned.

'The one all stunning and dolled up in red and black – you see? Look, chain-smoking in the corner – looks like she's chatting up the host guy. Oh, hold on – no – she's seen us all staring at her, she's coming over! Oh, quick – she wanted a double JD, please . . .'

Miles, perhaps feeling somewhat left out, seemed unsure how to deal with his previous blunder. He cleared his throat. Daisy and Elliot ignored him and continued chatting, when Belle appeared.

'Hello! Thank you so much for coming!' She turned to Miles. 'Hi – I'm Belle. You're Miles, aren't you?' She looked at him with obvious scrutiny.

Miles held out his hand. 'Indeed. I am he. Hello.'

'I've heard *so* much about you,' Belle said, the phrase 'most of it bad' not very well suppressed in her voice. Miles seemed to want to reply with a jovial 'most of it good, I hope' in that way that people do, and yet in this particular scenario, something held him back.

Daisy rushed in to plaster over the silence quickly, 'And this is Elliot . . . he's working with me at the moment, but he's also working here to pay off some of his travelling debts. Elliot, this is my sister Belle.'

Belle and Elliot shook hands. Belle smiled warmly at him, looking him up and down with interest. 'Lovely to meet you. I've heard lots about you, too. Thanks for the drink, by the way.' Elliot smiled back and glanced at Daisy, who now seemed to be in charge of this awkward new social gathering.

Reluctantly, Daisy added, 'Oh, and Miles, this is Elliot.' Mutual grunts on both sides. Then, with their drinks poured, they all moved away, leaving Elliot to tend to the ten-deep queue at the bar. Daisy still felt terrible about

Miles's behaviour, but decided she'd make it up by apologising to Elliot the next day at work.

Belle downed her drink in one go before rushing off. 'Well, this is it – see you afterwards, and for God's sake wish me luck! Oh – and also, sorry in advance – we're all just improvising, so it could go either way, I'm afraid . . .' She smirked, then walked away.

Miles and Daisy looked around for a place in the audience. Finding an unoccupied large corner sofa, they were soon huddled together by a window. Seconds after they'd sat down, Miles leaned up close to Daisy, planted his hand on her thigh, and a casual kiss on her cheek. Daisy wanted to reprimand him for his earlier behaviour, and to demand that he apologise to Elliot. But she also wanted to enjoy the rest of the evening. Plus, he *was* looking particularly fine with his new haircut. Reserving her willpower for later, she cuddled up to Miles and kissed him back. She'd talk to him about it afterwards; maybe even try and get him to apologise to Elliot. Pleasantly surprised, Miles put down his pint and took Daisy in his arms. He put his hand on her cheek, turned her head so that now she was facing him, and kissed her some more.

Some moments later, the sensible half of Daisy attempted to make contact with the other Daisy, who was entirely lost in the moment and the kiss. Eventually, sensible Daisy won, and Miles flinched as she pulled away from him.

'Not here,' she cautioned, remembering they were in a packed pub, 'everyone can see us . . . we don't want to be told to go and sit in a corner or something!'

'We *are* in a corner. Don't be a prude,' he scolded, moving his hand further up her leg.

'OK then, smarty pants. We'll get asked to leave. Or worse, told to get a room. Besides, we don't want to miss Belle, do we?'

Daisy turned to face the stage just as Belle walked up to the podium and took the mike. The guitarists, pianist and drummer were all finishing setting up around her. Daisy looked across the stage and caught sight of Elliot's blue eyes behind the bar, looking over in her direction. She smiled over at him, and then looked away as Belle started singing.

Then, after two hours of improvised wailing, strumming and banging from the stage, Miles began to appear increasingly restless. In the 'Are we nearly there yet?' voice of a car-sick toddler, he asked how long before they could leave.

'I can't leave yet! Not until Belle's finished – she'll never forgive me. Here, let me go and get you another drink. Would that help?'

Miles shrugged, 'I guess so. Same again – but preferably a beer without the head this time, mind . . .'

Daisy rolled her eyes and headed off to the bar, hoping to catch Elliot. She scanned the busy counter and saw him engaged in counting out a customer's change. She moved closer, and waited until he caught her eye.

'Hello. I'm so, so sorry about before.'

Elliot shrugged and continued going about his highly important job of stacking the glass-washer. 'No bother.' He looked away, fully absorbed in what he was doing.

Perhaps he was just busy – the bar was very crowded – but Daisy couldn't help thinking he seemed much less attentive than usual.

'No, really,' she went on, 'I don't know what got into

him! He's been under a lot of pressure at work lately, but that's no excuse for taking it out on you, I know . . .'

'Hey, like I said, don't worry about it.' Elliot looked around at all the people waiting at the bar to be served. 'Look, what can I get you?' he fired.

'Oh,' said Daisy, surprised at his bluntness. 'Um, same again for Miles . . . and . . . I'll have a rum and Coke, please,' she said, smiling and hoping he might reciprocate. No such reward.

'Are you OK?' she gave it one last attempt.

Elliot was absorbed in pouring Miles the perfect pint, but looked up for a second. His eyes were washed out; he looked tired and emotional.

'I'm great. Just great. Everything's fine – really. Don't worry about me.' Slowly, he lifted the pint, with its perfectly formed, immaculate 1cm head. He slammed it down on the counter, narrowly avoiding a major spillage. 'Here you go. And yours is here,' he planted her rum and Coke next to it. 'Enjoy.'

Daisy handed over the money, feeling fraught with guilt; wondering whether anything else was upsetting Elliot, or whether it was just that his pride had taken a proper bashing back there, and he had yet to recover. She picked up the drinks, and got ready to go.

'Well, thanks for these. And if I don't see you later, have a good night and I'll see you tomorrow?' She smiled meekly.

He nodded and smiled back numbly. He moved away and went back to stacking his glasses.

The End of the Line

It was hard to say when the change happened. She couldn't pinpoint it. It had been very gradual; almost like the change in seasons. There's that day when you first feel it's time to don your musty winter coat again – after months of floating around in sleeveless tops and flip-flops. It's very subtle, the change, but it happens. That was how it was with Elliot. One day he was her friend – making her laugh every day, bringing her tea, sharing a silly anecdote from one of his jobs from hell. He'd be doing his best to lighten her load and defend her from the boss from Hades. But somehow, over the past month that he'd been working there, he'd morphed into someone altogether different. These days, he would come in every day, exactly on time. He'd nod a curt hello, go and sit at his desk, cool and work-like. Occasionally he'd make flaccid remarks about the weather, before burying his head in his work, barely muttering another word. When it first happened, Daisy had made an attempt to see if he was OK, and to try and cheer him up. But now, having had her fingers burned one too many times by him snapping at her and shooing her away, she'd started to keep her distance. She didn't know what was wrong with him. Everytime she asked, he'd shrug it off and say he was fine. She wondered whether it might be girl trouble – maybe that girl called Alice from his scabby backpacking days was back on his radar, causing him romantic issues? Whatever it was, and however sad she felt to have lost a friend, she didn't want to push it. For now, she decided there was nothing to do but keep her distance.

This plan was working fine until one fine Wednesday, when Daisy had just got back from another lunch in the park with the girls. Once again, Elliott had refused her invitation to join them. But to her delight, she could see him now coming over to her desk. Hurrah, she thought optimistically. Maybe he's got over his problem? Maybe he's finally going to be sociable and friendly, she thought, smiling up at him expectantly.

'I'm afraid I'm going to have to make this my last week.'

Daisy failed to contain both her surprise and her disappointment. 'But that's such a shame! You can't be serious?' She looked at Elliot with genuine disbelief. '*Can* you? Don't tell me! You've been offered a proper job at last . . . in publishing or something?'

Elliot looked down at his feet. 'Well, ish . . .'

'Oh my gosh! Congrats you! But where? We'll all be so sorry to see you go!' Daisy looked mortified as an important, horrible reality sunk in. 'But, oh my gosh! It's the sales conference in six weeks – we'll need you around to help with that – we really, really need you around if you can possibly stay?'

Daisy was surprising herself at how relentlessly she was begging – it wasn't like her to argue her case this much, she was normally so polite and demure.

'I'm really sorry. It's just the pub; they've gone and offered me a manager's position. And I can't take that on if I'm still working here ... you see, they've said they can either give me that job or they'll have to get someone new in, and I'll be out of a job altogether ...'

Daisy was openly shocked. 'But that's – blackmail, isn't it? And besides, Lottie's not coming back for ages – we really do need your help. Please, at least think about it ... at *least* stay until the middle of next week, until the first conference rehearsal? Drat! I really need your help with all the Powerpoint presentations, there're so many jackets we still need to get hold of ...' then Daisy remembered the full enormity of this situation – there was a whole other dimension she hadn't even acknowledged yet. Her face fell even lower. 'Oh my gosh! Belinda will do herself an injury! Crumbs! She'll probably have me fired!'

Elliot looked uncomfortable as, one after the other, *Malory Towers* expletives fell from Daisy's mouth unchecked and she became increasingly panicky at the prospect of him leaving. He shuffled his feet nervously, his eyes darting around to avoid hers.

'I know – I really hate to let you down. Jeez, I'm sorry – I didn't think you were going to take it this bad.' He looked around and added, guilt-ridden, awkwardly, 'OK – listen ... I *suppose* I can ask them if I can start next Thursday instead ...'

Daisy was studying him closely, feeling ever more confused. 'I don't want to sound like I'm telling you what to do here, Ellie. But you leaving – it makes no sense! You don't want a career in the hospitality industry, do you? I thought publishing was where you wanted to be? I'm sorry, but I really think you're making a mistake!'

Elliot looked at Daisy intensely, his eyes washed out. 'Maybe you're right. But I'm sorry, I've made up my mind.' He looked away, his face solemn. Then he walked over to his desk, turned a page on his batch of manuscripts, and began copy-editing in silence.

Daisy felt hurt and confused. Why was Elliot being so cold, so dismissive? Hmmmph. Part of her couldn't help thinking, if he really believed that a job in a pub was going to do him more good, then, fine, good luck to him. If this was how he showed his gratitude for all the help she'd given him, then good riddance to him. As a distraction, she emailed Miles, and made a list of suggestions for what they could do that weekend, in the way of culturally nourishing activities. She'd been hinting all week that wouldn't it be nice to go away for the weekend, what with the weather being so good at the moment. Now that it was Thursday, she had fingers crossed that he might've caught on and have something planned.

Friday morning, Daisy went to check her emails, hoping there might be news from Will or Miles. She didn't fancy admitting it to the girls, but lately she'd noticed a distinct break in her deliveries from Will. It had been three weeks since her last fix! She'd begun by checking her email religiously every day. But now, the disappointment being too much to bear, she didn't even like to check any more. She'd get to work everyday and feel the same sinking feeling as the inbox loaded up, watching all the little new envelope icons line up on her screen, scanning them hopefully every day for one from Just William26, with news from Lauren and Ed. No such luck. Just Miles, with news that he'd booked 'somewhere special' for dinner.

Sitting in a quiet, intimate restaurant in Mayfair that evening, Daisy was admiring the cosy, candlelit coves where each couple had their own little corner. She couldn't help thinking that it seemed like the kind of place you could imagine being proposed to in. Of course she didn't dare mention this to Miles. Instead she proffered a quiet, 'It's lovely.'

Sometime into the meal, as the waiters brought out the dessert menu, Miles began talking about his brother, and how he was 'buying in leafy Barnes'. Daisy listened patiently while he told her all about it, when after a moment, a thought occurred to her.

'D'you know, I was only thinking about property the other day – and how everyone I know seems to be brandishing that awful phrase about – you know, "getting on the property ladder" and all that.' Daisy sighed. 'The whole thing makes me feel quite queasy! You know? I mean, look at us – we'd never be able to afford to do that, would we? What, with us both being in publishing!'

A shadow passed across Miles's face. 'Well, no. Certainly not.' He shrugged, then opened his mouth as if to begin another conversation.

'You know – it does make you think, though . . .' she went on despite herself, throwing caution to the wind, 'You know, maybe it's not out the question. I mean, we could think about it, a year or so from now when we might be on better salaries . . . and it's always cheaper when you move out a bit – you know, maybe into zone three or four at least . . .'

Miles remained alarmed. 'Ummmmm . . . Easy, tiger . . . slow down a minute there. Living together? Who said anything about us *living* together? We've never mentioned this before! Have we?' He looked perplexed at Daisy.

'Well no – I know.' Daisy frowned. 'I was just speaking hypothetically, that's all. Since, you know, we've been seeing each other well, nearly a year now,' she began on a gabbling, nervous path. 'Well, I mean, on and off, that is, so to speak . . . not including all the "on a breaks" that we've had . . . But *obviously* I'm still nowhere near ready for that either. I'm just saying – a few years down the line' – she hovered, seeing his face losing a little more colour – 'if we're still together, I mean,' she added, in a transparent attempt at aloofness.

'Want some of this chocolate mousse? It's to die for.' Miles thrust a spoon in Daisy's face, signifying the end of the conversation.

When the bill came, Daisy got out her debit card to pay for her half, but Miles put up his hand, made a big show of pulling the bill saucer towards him, depriving her once again of the opportunity to pay.

'Please, let me give you something for it,' she insisted.

He shook his head. 'Next time,' he said, looking into her eyes expressively, his hand covering the bill.

'Suit yourself,' she said, 'But I'm going to have my way next time!'

They stood up and slipped on their jackets. Moments later, they were walking towards Green Park tube, discussing the highs and lows of their dinner.

'Well, that's you on your tube now,' Miles said as they got to the station, 'I'll call you soon. Thanks for a lovely evening.'

Daisy was affronted. 'You're not coming back to Stockwell with me?'

'Um, yeah, about that. I've got a big lunch on tomorrow,

and I need to be up and at 'em early, so I should probably stay at mine tonight. Also, since I'm already halfway home, it makes sense for me to get a cab from here, so . . .'

'Halfway home? What are you talking about? You live in Hoxton!'

'Yes, I do. Thank you for reminding me. No, it really is quicker for me to cab it than to get the tube.'

'No, it's not – you could easily just tube it to Islington from here and then your cab will be lots cheaper. Here, let me show you . . .' Daisy opened her handbag and pulled out her tube map.

Miles was shaking his head in irritation, 'I know, I know, get the Victoria line up – put your map away! God, why are you always so sodding organised? Do you think, for once, you could come out without your *A-Z*, or without your map?'

'Oh, I guess I could try . . . but there's usually someone that needs it,' replied Daisy defensively, knowing she was making it worse on herself by talking, but feeling crushed that he was lashing out at her like this. 'OK, then – go whatever route you like. But either way I can't come back to Hoxton with you, as I don't have my spare contacts with me. I won't be able to see to get home tomorrow . . .'

'Oh well, never mind,' he said, without even trying to talk her round like he'd normally do. 'You and your removable eyes,' he'd usually say, 'why don't you just carry a spare set in your handbag? Then you'd be able to be a bit spontaneous for once!'

None of that tonight. Instead, he seemed oddly keen to move things along. Daisy couldn't help feeling flummoxed – they'd been getting on so well until now. She was gutted that they wouldn't be spending the weekend together. It was news to her that he had all these plans of his own. Then she had a thought. Is this what all those *Men are From Mars* devotees mean when they go on about men 'needing to go in their cave sometimes', and be on their own? She had vague memories of Heidi going on about a cave analogy of some sort. Or was that Plato? Either way, Daisy decided, it was nothing to worry about. Miles just needed some precious cave time.

'OK, well. Thanks for dinner, then,' she said, and went to kiss him on the cheek. He took her in his arms and kissed her firmly on the lips, and she relaxed and began to assume that perhaps everything was, in fact, OK after all. Yes, you bugger off to your cave for a bit, she thought, but didn't say. After they'd exchanged goodbyes, she walked down the steps and headed into the tube station. Midway down she turned back to give Miles a final wave, but he'd gone.

Stepping on to the stuffy southbound Victoria Line train a few moments later, Daisy began replaying the evening over and over in her head. She took a seat on the half-empty carriage that was still hot from a typical August day of being crammed with overheated and cramped commuters. She mulled over the conversations and the looks they'd exchanged. To anyone watching them in the restaurant, they'd probably looked like the perfect happy couple, in the early throes of passion. But now, looking back, something just didn't feel right. Maybe it was the hot, clammy air in the carriage muddying her brain, making her feel trapped and thinking difficult. Or maybe it was something else?

She couldn't put her finger on it. Staring at the window on the other side of the carriage, she hardly recognised the girl reflected back at her. She seemed tired and lost.

Daisy's eyes shifted to the right a little, and landed on a couple. A girl's head lay resting on a man's shoulder, and they were both sound asleep. Daisy couldn't help admiring how peaceful they looked. Just then the man opened his eyes, looked through his blond fringe of hair to his own reflection in the mirror, admiring the woman resting her head on his shoulder. He smiled contentedly and then closed his eyes again, without even noticing Daisy staring. The girl stirred, shook out her arm, and cuddled up to him. Daisy sighed, suddenly feeling overwhelmingly sad. She tried to imagine her and Miles being that comfortable with each other. Tried to picture them sharing the same levels of affection and being so natural with each other. She tried, but she just couldn't see it.

Arriving home half an hour later, a tear-stained Daisy knocked on Belle's door. It was just gone 1 a.m., but by some stroke of wonder, Belle was home.

'What's up? I'm asleep,' Belle grunted, sitting up in bed and rubbing her eyes. Seeing Daisy's bloodshot eyes and red cheeks, she shifted along the bed, patting a Daisy-shaped area for her to sit on.

'Come here. Tell me what he's done now.' She took Daisy in her arms and gave her a big Belle-hug.

'It's nothing he's done, really. I think it's more me,' Daisy sighed, 'I've just had some sort of epiphany on the tube home . . . That he's never going to give me what I want. You should have seen his face when I accidentally mentioned the idea of us moving in together one day! It wasn't like I was suggesting it, either, it just fell out! Silly man. No – I've realised, he's never going to be my man on the tube . . . he never even catches the tube, dreadful snob that he is!'

Belle rubbed the sleep from her eyes, looked a little confused, but listened attentively as Daisy went on.

'It's just – ever since the horrible thing with that girl at the party, I don't think it's ever felt the same between us . . . and even though he says he's my boyfriend, I don't think he'll ever really truly be able to commit, no matter how many forms I get him to sign! I'm joking, Belle, I really didn't make him sign any forms!' Belle looked genuinely relieved.

'But Belle, I've realised – there's more to this than just him just being a caveman . . .' And now Belle looked genuinely confused, but Daisy went on regardless, 'So, anyway, as much as it pains me, I'm thinking that maybe I should just give up on him. Be done with it . . .' Daisy looked up and Belle was nodding sagely, emphatically. She went on, 'But the weird thing is, now that I've finally decided, I feel all right about it. I feel a kind of relief, really. Like, at last, I'm free of his games! Hurrah!' And she burst into tears.

Belle smiled gleefully and began manically jumping up and down on the bed. 'That's just marvellous! I never liked him anyway! Cocky bastard, he was! Oh, what was it about him? He just seemed like he was always trying to *be* a certain way – like he was always a bit *affected*, or not quite comfortable with himself. Like being charming didn't come naturally . . . you know?'

Daisy nodded. 'I know *exactly* what you mean.'

'Not like little Elliot. Who, by the way – I meant to say – is lovely! Can I have his phone number, please?'

'Oh . . .' Daisy hovered. Even though she'd always thought Belle a perfect match for Elliot, she now felt strangely reluctant to give out his number. 'Sure. If you like. I'll get it for you tomorrow.'

Belle was looking at Daisy closely. 'Cool – thanks. Never mind that now . . . I'm so glad you've come to this decision all by yourself. I think this calls for a celebration!' Belle dashed into the kitchen and began attacking a bottle of Cava. 'Don't you?'

A tear rolled down Daisy's cheek, and she nodded.

Spring Clearing

Are you sure you want to permanently delete the selected items? You cannot reverse this action.

Quite sure, thank you very much, thought Daisy the following Monday, as she moved her mouse over to the 'YES' on her PC. She hovered a moment, then clicked. She was mortified but thrilled as, piece by piece, line by line, all her emails from Miles – each of them lined up for virtual execution in her recycling bin – faded into nothingness. How therapeutic was this? Why hadn't she done this months ago? How marvellous to finally have clarity of thought, to finally have made up her mind where Miles was concerned! No more fretting, no more analysing his every word and action. No more feeling like things were never enough, but pretending they were. No – instead, she felt liberated. She couldn't help being reminded of the 'he's just not that in to you' eureka moment in *Sex and the City*. Hurrah! What she felt now with Miles was the same sense of freedom. Desperately sad, wretched and lonely to the point of suicidal – admittedly she was all these things – but at least it couldn't be said that she lacked self-respect. Now, newly cleansed of his non-commital-ness, she could think about beginning her life again.

As it happened, he hadn't taken it so very well. She'd gone round to his the next evening and told him straight away, without further delay. She was 88 per cent sure she'd imagined it, but as she'd said the words 'the end of the road,' she was sure she'd noticed a subtle change in the colour of his face – from hazel-tanned to a milky pale. He'd sighed heavily, and looked genuinely stricken. Leaving him, Daisy had felt faint, dizzy and a little sick in her stomach. But in her head she knew the right thing had been done.

Next up, following Belle's advice, was the text messages. A lump in her throat, she read through every last one of Miles's sweet messages to her then deleted them all. The sentimental part of her (i.e., most of her) desperately wanted to hoard them all – to keep a log of them some- where, as a little potted history of their romantic journey – a time capsule preserving the biggest, most significant relationship she'd ever had. But then the vaguely audible voice of pragmatism within her decreed that this would be anathema to what she was doing in the first place – trying to dispose of him. To latch on to memorabilia of any kind would therefore be unhealthy and dangerous. Far better to say goodbye to them all, perhaps mourn and grieve them all one by one for a moment, and then finally dismiss them and start with a clean slate, she decided.

'Uhm . . .' burst in Belinda, appearing almost as an apparition by Daisy's desk, 'Have you got me all the jackets I need for tomorrow's rehearsal yet?' Her shrill tones trampled all over Daisy's own private wake, and reminded her of the work that was piling up on her desk, especially now that Elliot was leaving. Which Daisy was still putting off explaining to Belinda.

As expected, when the time came to tell Belinda that 'the best workie they'd ever had' was leaving, she immediately hit amber alert levels of rage and fury. Naturally the whole thing was entirely Daisy's fault rather than Elliot's. And yet, in a rare show of generosity, Belinda offered to put some money behind the bar at the Black Bird, Mercury's local pub. This offer was gratefully taken up and on his last day, a small leaving party was thrown in his honour.

Heidi having been attached to Elliot for most of this particular evening, Hermione was struggling to put up a good fight. (Although Heidi had denied that there was any spark there, she still enjoyed the rivalry against Hermione.) Daisy, on the other hand, had barely been able to squeeze a few words into the banter. She just stood watching him, surrounded by his coterie of adoring females. She'd barely been able to speak to him all week, what with all the work to do before Venice. It was only a three-day trip, but somehow it still required months of preparation. Even in the small gaps where they might have been able to take a sneaky coffee break, Elliot had been glued to his screen, saying he had letters to write, work to catch up on, and flats to hunt for. From 9 a.m. until 5.30 p.m., he'd scarcely left his desk.

Daisy stood leaning against the dilapidated brown walls, clutching her gin and tonic. She stared at Elliot, who was in the middle of throwing back his head at the sheer hilarity of one of Hermione's apparently classic jokes. As Elliot leaned across to thwack Hermione around the head playfully, Daisy couldn't help thinking how much she was going to miss him.

After half an hour of people-watching, she decided to admit that she really wasn't in the party mood, and prepared up to leave. She approached Elliot's table and saw that he was now submerged in what looked like a deep, serious conversation with Heidi. Daisy daintily cleared her throat. Nothing.

'Well, I've got to be getting off.'

Elliot looked up, alarmed. 'You're going? Already?' He made to get up, and various excuse me's later he succeeded in channelling himself a clear path through the clusters of people.

'Oh, you didn't need to get up,' Daisy said, not wanting to disturb him.

'Don't be daft. I'll come and say a proper 'bye.' He ushered Daisy towards the door. Daisy dispensed her goodbyes to everyone else – to Amelie, who was on her mobile, deep in some kind of heated discussion with her boyfriend, and to Heidi and Hermione, whose eyes were still fixed on Elliot. He looked over at them, then turned to Daisy. 'Breath of fresh air?'

Daisy nodded, and followed him outside, feeling the eyes of the H and H double act boring into her back as she walked. Outside, Daisy leaned against the wall while Elliot opened up a pack of cigarettes, offering one to her. She shook her head. She hated cigarettes, and yet despite herself, she couldn't help finding them strangely alluring when attached to other people – particularly men. Cancer sticks. Evil, poisonous things – an addictive, and in no way attractive habit – she tried to tell herself, despite watching as Elliot lit up and thinking how well it looked on him.

He took a long drag and smiled. 'So . . . I just wanted to say a proper "thanks again" for everything. And that I hope we keep in touch.'

'Oh, definitely.' Daisy nodded emphatically, 'Absolutely. I've loved having you around – you know we're all sorry to see you go. So just – well, good luck at the Bedford, and don't forget what it is you *really* want to do with your life, OK?'

Elliot nodded. 'I won't. I promise. And – don't you forget to look after yourself, OK? Don't let that horrid Miles man mess your head around any more than he already has, OK?'

Daisy gave a bittersweet laugh. 'Well thank you. That's very good advice. It's just a shame there's no chance for me to take it any more . . .'

Elliot's eyes flickered with curiosity. 'What do you mean?'

'Oh, I mean, we've split up. For good this time, I think . . . *and* it was my doing too – which I'm really rather proud of !'

'Oh, I'm sorry. I had no idea,' Elliot stumbled quickly.

'Well, we've not really had the chance to speak much, have we? What with it being so busy this week – and you have to admit you've been keeping your head down a lot lately . . .'

Elliot looked down, 'Yeah – I'm sorry about that. I've just had – some stuff on my mind to sort out. Are you OK now?' He looked at Daisy, his eyes blinking concern.

Daisy nodded. 'I'm fine, thanks. Break-ups suck, we all know that. The trouble is, one way or another, he's kind of been the love of my life. You know, I thought he was "the one", and that we really were in it for life . . . now I can see that I was being a bit naive. So yes, it's been horrible getting over him. But, cliché of clichés, I think it's for the best – you know?'

Elliot's eyes looked heavy. 'Right, yes, of course.'

'But never mind me – you'd better get back to your leaving party. Your groupies will be wondering where you are!' she teased.

'Yeah, you're right . . .' Elliot looked through the window to the pub, then looked back at Daisy, hesitating, as though there was something he wanted to say.

Daisy waited for him to speak. An awkward silence ensued, which she couldn't bear to leave unfilled. 'So, I'm sorry for being lame and leaving so early . . . I'm just so knackered after work and everything.'

'No worries,' he said, a little over-casually. 'So, um – Daisy . . .'

'Yes?'

Elliot paused. 'I just – thanks for everything, OK? And, don't be a stranger . . . keep in touch.' His eyes were melancholy as he gave Daisy a big goodbye hug.

'Absolutely. I'm really glad we met. And I hope everything works out for you. So just make sure you drop me a line every now and again, OK?'

Daisy hugged him back, planting a friendly kiss on his cheek before breezily walking away. Halfway down the street, she turned back to wave goodbye. Elliot was leaning against the pub door, watching her walk. He raised his arm, gave a half-smile, and went back inside.

18

In Between Days

Date: Friday 25 August 2006, 13.15
Sender: DaisyAllen@paddingtonpress.com
To: elliottthornton@yahoo.co.uk
Subject: Hello

Dear Elliot,

I hope you're enjoying your new life in the hospitality industry. I'm sorry if that sounded sarky. I didn't mean it to. I just wanted you to know that we're all missing having our favourite elf around. Everyone says hi. Even narky Belinda.

Listen, I just wanted you to know – if you change your mind, you'll be welcomed back with open arms. Rumour has it that one of the workie muppets we've had here in the past will be coming to fill your shoes. But I can tell you now – her kitten heels won't be a patch on your weathered old Gazelles.

I trust no more pompous men in suits are giving you

grief over head sizes, and that the new job's going great.

Daisy x

It had only been a week since he'd left, but already Daisy was beginning to feel Elliot's absence; both in her workload and in her general state of mind. She'd felt in low spirits over the last week, and this coupled with the complete and total absence of Miles in her life (she was even missing having enigmatic emails to deconstruct) meant that for the first time in years she was feeling that she might be on the brink of a real, full-blown depression. No matter how many shopping trips and romantic comedies Belle and the girls had sat her through, and no matter how many tubs of Ben and Jerry's she'd consumed, nothing seemed to help. She just couldn't seem to snap out of it. Fortunately, there was the lure of Venice ahead, which was getting closer and closer, and with it the blissful promise of escaping everything for a few days. She was counting down the days on her calendar. Today was Friday 25 August. She drew a thick red line through it. So that meant a total of five weeks and two days until she'd be on a plane, flying far away from everything. She couldn't wait.

But with each day she crossed off and got that bit closer to her goal, she also felt a twinge of sadness, for it was also an indicator of the distance between now and when Elliot had been there. She'd had no word from him since he'd left, and she was beginning to worry. He'd left so abruptly, she hoped he was all right.

Daisy lived out most of September in this vein – worrying, waiting, and wondering; crossing out the days one by one. As the weather began to worsen, and long lunches sunbathing in the park became a distant memory of merrier days, Daisy found herself working through all her lunches, busying herself with the fourteen hundred presentations there were to prepare for Venice. She kept her head down, threw herself into her work, and tried to forget about Miles. Things carried on like this for weeks, until one day she received a fragment of new material from Will, and decided that this must surely be the perfect excuse to email Elliot again.

Date: Friday 8 September 2006 15.15
Sender: Daisy.Allen@paddingtonpress.com
To: elliotthornton@yahoo.co.uk
Subject: All quiet on the Elliot front

Dear Elliot,

Just a wee note to check your email's working – I sent you one a couple of weeks ago, but I've not heard back, so wanted to check all's OK and that I have the right address. I guess you're not finding much time to check your mail in your new line of work, so I may as well keep this brief.

I hope it's going well for you, and that you've not been mugged yet in Scary Streatham. One thing, if you ever want any advice about getting into the book world again – you know, once you've paid off some more of that mahoosive debt of yours, then just give me a shout any time. And remember – life's not just about money. Try to think of yourself, what you really want –

not the rent cheques and credit cards looming over your head. I'll be thinking of you.

D

p.s. I'm attaching another bit of Will's book which I've just had in – hurrah! I don't know if you've had a chance to finish the last part or not, but I hope you enjoy it. Let me know what you think, and whether it's beginning to give you the shivers or not. It is me. It's really sad at the moment, too. Now that Lauren's left, Ed's been playing the tortured artist all summer, painting prolifically in memory of her, but also in an attempt to get her out of his head. And the thing is, E, I get the feeling that the mood is all about to take a turn for the worse? The writing's got – I don't know – a sudden darker undertone, like it's not the romance I thought it was any more. I don't know if you'll agree, but I get the feeling it's crossing into more of a mystery now . . . I don't want to give too much away, though! Sorry. Anyway, here's a bit more.

Just as she'd clicked 'send', Daisy turned back to reading the new delivery from Will. True enough, the novel was taking on a much darker tone now. The location was back in London again, and Daisy could feel it changing tack, into more of a different, moodier genre. As she read on, she felt that it was becoming more than just a love story now. No, she thought, seeing the hyperbolic cover blurb in her mind; this was moving into 'high-octane literary thriller' territory now . . .

Daisy looked up from the manuscript and began to

think about what was next for Will. If she was serious about wanting to make him an offer for his book, she'd need to have more of a clue what she was talking about before she went any further. How much could they offer him as a reasonable advance, for instance? And what kind of contract would he need? She soon realised that there was no way she could actually do any of this deal on her own. The way she saw it, she had two options, both of them hugely unappealing. There was Belinda – terrifying, but a necessary evil at some stage. Or there was Miles, the person she knew best in publishing, who would be most likely to know the answers to all her questions. In her mind, she flirted with the idea of calling him, and felt herself meandering into various fantasies and daydream scenarios where he dispensed advice and wisdom over a bottle of wine, and one thing led to another ... But it wasn't long before she admitted that this was just a cheap ploy to get to see him again; the pathetic truth being that she was still missing him. No, it would have to be Belinda – but not just yet. She'd show her when there was more material, and when she was more confident with the editing she'd done.

In the meantime, she still needed more background information from Will. She made a note of this on her to-do list in shiny purple ink. Of course, none of this had anything to do with the fact that she was completely *dying* to know a bit more about him. *Was* he the strange man she'd met on the train? Either way, how old was he and where was he from? What was *his* story? And all the other questions in between ...

A few days later, Daisy ran out of patience entirely and

decided the only thing to do was to chase Will on both these things, and to try to extract some more information out of him.

Date: Tuesday 12 September 2006, 13.15
Sender: Daisy.Allen@paddingtonpress.com
To:justwilliam26@hotmail.co.uk
Subject: BIOG AND MEETING UP

Hiya Will,

Thanks very much for sending me more new material, which I'm all the way through now and must say I'm still completely loving. Clever, clever you. I've not got my editorial notes ready on these new sections yet, but will do soon.

I was so sorry to hear about your flat and everything – being evicted sounds awful – there's no need to apologise for your being held up, please don't worry about it. We'll get there when we get there – and when you're ready. Anyway, I hope that you've been able to get back to a bit of normality. Are you back from staying with your parents in Ireland yet? Have you managed to find a new place?

Meantime, I've just got a quick request for you – I'm going to be getting in touch with some agents for you, who I think might be interested in taking you on, but before I do, I'll just need a bit of a potted biog from you. Just a few bits and bobs about you, where you're from, your career until now, how old you are. Just so

224

they can have a picture of you as a person, and a package. If it's easier, a CV will do just fine.

Let me know when you think you'll be able to have that ready for me. And also, there're a couple of things I'd like to discuss with you about the book, but rather than do them over email, would you be able to meet up for a coffee some time in the near future?

Kind regards,

Daisy x

She was just putting the finishing touches to another daydream about the real Will, and what he must look like (unless he was the man on the train – whom, she had to admit, at the time had seemed moderately attractive, if a little old), when a new envelope popped up on her screen.

Date: Tuesday 12 September 2006 13.37
Sender: elliotthornton@yahoo.co.uk
To: Daisy.Allen@paddingtonpress.com
Subject: News from the Elliot front

Daisy,
I'm sorry I've not been in touch. Don't be cross. I just needed to take a bit of time out – I'll tell you about it some time. Just need to work some stuff out. Thank you again, for everything.

E

Hurrah that she'd heard from him! But a slightly odd response, Daisy couldn't help thinking. Now she felt even more concerned. But she didn't want to harass the boy any more than she had done already. She knew she should probably leave it before she replied, so as not to seem stalkerish. She also knew from other sources (Belle) that he was still alive and living in Streatham. As it happened, Belle had texted Elliot a few times, and they had been enjoying some nice long chats on the phone. But strangely, it had all fizzled out before even getting to the first date stage. Daisy couldn't deny that she was slightly relieved. She really hadn't wanted to see a friend of hers subjected to the two-week 'use-by' treatment from Belle. She'd seen so many men before him suffer from it, and it wasn't pleasant. No – that he'd not called her back again was probably for the best.

Over the next few days, Daisy immersed herself in her work once again, and after a few more days of anguished, impatient thumb-twiddling whilst waiting to hear from Will again, she was mildly disappointed when his reply finally came:

Date: Friday 15 September 2006 13.08
Sender: justwilliam26@hotmail.co.uk
To: Daisy.Allen@paddingtonpress.com
Subject: BIOG AND MEETING UP

Hi Daisy

Thanks for your email, and I'm sorry I've taken so long to reply. Thanks times a million for being so understanding about it all. The trouble is, I'm stuck in

Ireland still, and I don't see how I'm going to be able to move any time soon. I've got time to write though, so I'll still be able to send you stuff, but I don't have any of my CV stuff with me, so the biog is a bit tricky. Also, it means I won't be able to meet you yet but I hope that can wait also, until I'm back?

Sorry to be such a pain about it all. In brief, this is me: twenty-nine years old, studied a degree in English, in Scotland. More to follow . . .

Wxx

Daisy was not satisfied with this, and emailed back immediately to let him know, with a hint of sternness in her voice, asking for more information about him. It was most unusual for an author to be so aloof and unforthcoming, she said, trying to instil a polite, cordial sense of urgency in between the lines. Trying to sound calm, she bashed out ad hoc questions to William. Where in Scotland did you study? Are you Irish, or does your mum just live over there? And so on. She had so many questions, and all these answers were vital before she could even think about approaching an agent. So far, his biog was scant at best. She was trying not to sound harsh, but she hoped that finally, this time, she'd get something out of him.

But no reply came. Not for weeks.

Half a World Away

Date: Monday 2 October 2006 15.15
Sender: Daisy.Allen@paddingtonpress.com
To: elliotthornton@yahoo.co.uk
Subject: Re: news from the Elliot front

Hi Ellie

Thanks for your email. Thrilled you're alive! If I can be
of any other help at all, let me know. I'm sorry you
seem to be having a troubled old time – I hope you're
OK, and it's nothing too serious. Listen, one thing I
know: when it comes to most things, you have to
follow your gut. Or is it heart? It's one of the two.

But anyway, it'd be lovely to catch up over coffee
sometime. I'm off to Venice in the next hour or so, but
I'll be back in three days. If you ever want to chat, you
know where I am.

Dx

Daisy clicked 'send' and then stood up to give her shelves a good clean for the third and final time that day. She took a pen and put the finishing touches to her four-page 'How things work' encyclopedic list of things to do for Siobhanna; scribbling the last few bits:

> If in doubt, call me on my mobile . . . and here's the number of the hotel – oh, it's called the Hotel Regina and Europa. Don't worry, we'll be there the whole time, from noon until night. And here's Hermione's and Belinda's – but for God sake only ring Belinda's in an absolute emergency and if you can't get any of us on our numbers. Anyway, we'll see you on Thursday. Have fun and good luck, Dxx.

That should do it, she thought, and deposited the note on to Elliot's old desk, pausing for a moment to wish he was still there.

'Are you coming or what?' demanded Hermione, who was suddenly standing next to Daisy, looking petulant. 'The coach is outside, and they're about to start boarding.'

Daisy was alarmed. 'Really? But it's early! OK – let me just get all my stuff together. I'll meet you down there in two ticks.'

She crossed over to her desk, remembering that thing which Belle always used to whine when she was running late – that earliness of any sort was a complete and total discourteousness to others. She'd never understood it before but it now seemed strangely appropriate. She was just about to shut down her computer when she saw an envelope pop up on the screen. Her heart skipped a beat. There on the screen, twiddling its thumbs, was the email she'd been waiting for, for over two weeks. She clicked on the email with excitement, poised for her curiosity to finally be sated as to the true identity of Will Marwood. She waited for the message to open. And then it stopped. Maddeningly, her PC was doing that freezing-up thing which it liked to do when she was in a rush. She waited, tapping her fingers on the desk, for it to unfreeze. About forty-five seconds later it finally finished loading up. She opened the email, but then to her surprise and frustration, there was still nothing in his message about who Will Marwood really was, or anything vaguely biographical. Instead, just a short, jovial note indicating that, after a long burst of inspiration, he'd finished the whole book. And here it was, attached. Her heart in her throat, Daisy opened up the three-hundred-page document and pressed 'print'. She looked at her watch. The coach would have to wait. Never mind the gondolas, the Italian men, the seafood linguine. There was no way she was leaving the country for three days without this entire manuscript on her person, she thought, as her mobile phone began to bleep and she went in frantic search of A4 paper.

Hope ur having a great time hon. Flat feels empty without u. But stop press have met gorgeous new hunk of man! Going on date ce soir! (I finally got another text from little Elliot but don't think it's happening – have suspicion he's gay.) Ho hum, miss u, bring me back some nice Venetian choc or suchlike x x

Feeling oddly relieved, Daisy snapped shut her mobile phone and sat back down on the luxurious, bigger-thanking-size bed in her five-star hotel room. She surveyed her room, and the entire contents of her suitcase, which were spread all around her in piles. She was trying – failing – to decide what to wear for the first formal dinner. It was hopeless. She picked up her hotel phone, dialled one of the four-digit extensions she had scrawled on to a Post-it, and waited for the foreign pips to beep.

'Hello!' answered Amelie, 'are you having traumas too?'

'Complete and total. Can I come and join you?'

'Sure. I'll call Heidi. Just bring your best options, and we'll see what we can work out between us.'

Daisy hung up the phone and surveyed the gargantuan suite, which she had all to herself for the next two and a half days. Her eyes panned around the room, surveying the array of chocolates, tea and coffee, deluxe minibar and fridge, fully stocked with all manner of midnight snacks. She stood up and walked into the adjoining marble bathroom, which was piled high with free cosmetics, and thought for the fifth time since arriving, how ludicrous it was that all this belonged to Daisy, and only Daisy, for three whole days. What a waste, when she could easily have shared it with two other people! How funny it was that a huge company like Mercury, which could only afford peanuts for salaries, could afford to be so lavish in ways such as these. But, it could be worse, she thought as she rolled over in the luxurious, warm and fluffy bed, peeled off the lovely cosy white duvet and jumped down to the floor. She could be at home in her ex-council den in Stockwell.

Daisy quickly made the bed, grabbed a handful of clothes, and put them neatly into her Mercury-branded canvas bag which she'd been given on arrival at the hotel, along with all manner of Mercury-branded goody-bag contents – stickers, tattoos, a baseball cap, a fridge magnet and some chocolate body paint. All of which were stamped with shout-lines, celebrity endorsements and hyperbolic tidings of next year's bestsellers, and all of which would almost certainly never see the light of day outside the hotel. Emptying some of these items into the bin, she packed in a few more options to wear. Then she went towards the door, catching sight of Will's manuscript poking out of her suitcase en route. Feeling a twinge of guilt that she'd not managed to read any of it since leaving England, she picked up some of the pages, shoved them in her bag, and went to join the girls.

After that, the manuscript followed her everywhere, in small bite-size chunks. Down to breakfast, smuggled underneath her morning paper. And in all the presentations, she would sneak glimpses of it in between Powerpoint segments, or even during the talk from Philip Hunt, Mercury's chief executive. In Daisy's defence, Philip's presentation was invariably a mixture pie charts, squiggles and management-speak mantras which went straight over Daisy's head at the best of times. She knew if she was caught reading at this time she'd probably be reprimanded at best, fired at worst, but she just could not bear to leave the manuscript alone. The further into the book Daisy got, the less she had to carry, shedding the layers of each chapter and leaving them behind in her room, piece by piece. Until finally, by halfway through the second day, only twenty pages remained unread – the rest of it scattered and dog-eared, all over her once pristine room.

When, on the second day, there was a break of one hour, they were permitted some 'free time'. While Amelie and

Heidi were now gagging to go shopping, Daisy instead decided to steal herself away for a wander round the little backstreets, taking Will's writing with her. Venice was quite the most romantic, enchanting place she'd ever seen and she couldn't wait to explore. Clutching the remaining pages of manuscript, she slipped them into her black satchel and headed out, armed with her *Time Out* guide, determined not to get lost. She set off through the meandering streets, scrolling through her list of must-see spots. Reaching the water, she saw a sign which – if she wasn't mistaken – pointed to San Marco both to the left, and to the right. That wasn't very helpful, was it? Squinting at her map, she decided to head for the next thing on her list instead. Eventually, after much walking she stumbled upon the Rialto. She walked over the bridge, stopping for a moment to look out longingly at the gondolas, wishing she could afford a ride in one. She marvelled at the way the sun's glow was casting tiny white flecks of light over the water, and thought once again how like a fairy tale this place really was. Wandering back on to the little side streets, Daisy window-shopped her way round the little market stalls, before weaving her way through to the Piazza San Marco. She strolled to the other side of the square where a bandstand of musicians were just reaching 'Summer' in Vivaldi's *Four Seasons*. Daisy took a seat under a yellow canopy and ordered a cappuccino in broken Italian. Even though Vivaldi was doing a great job of making her think it was summer, she could feel from the strong breeze in the air that in the real world it was definitely early autumn now. Still, Daisy being Daisy, she slapped some precautionary sunscreen on to her nose just in case. She always burned on her nose – the fact it was mid-October would be no exception – it was just one of those lovely things about being a redhead.

When her coffee arrived, she took a sip and sat back in her chair. She opened up her manuscript, to find Ed back in his flat in Finsbury Park, giving the painting of the flamenco dancer the final once-over. He'd done the best he could in the time given, he was thinking. And even if he hadn't, it was too late now, he realised as he headed out to go and meet Lauren.

Just as she was feeling herself drift away back to London, Daisy's mobile began to exert a hideous bleeping sound. She looked around, hoping no one in the brasserie had been disturbed by this embarrassing Nokia ringtone, which she still had no idea how to reset. She looked at her phone and turned off the alarm. Bugger – she was just getting into it! How could it be time to go back to the conference already? Reluctantly, Daisy finished her page, shoved the manuscript in her bag, and wandered through the winding streets back to the hotel. Still two more hours of talks to go – involving high-tech Power-point presentations, and fancy dress skits of some painful description. So that meant she could probably squeeze in a teeny bit more reading time before the formal dinner and last-night booze-a-thon would kick off later that night, in all its glory.

Spruced up in her most treasured item of clothing, the green All Saints dress, Daisy was playing with her sesame seed bread roll at the dinner table. She didn't want to ruin her appetite by eating it, so instead she was squishing it with her fork and watching the seeds fall off while she talked to the other people on her table. She'd been seated with a mixed assortment of Mercury employees, most of whom, she gradually came to realise, she'd never met before Venice, and might never see after Venice. Garold from the Web Team, Shauna from Accounts, and Hannah Wilbert, the Head of Distribution from Mercury's warehouse. Not only that, but Daisy also slowly realised that most of the people on her table were based out in Chingford. So even though it was always nice to make new friends in the company, Daisy did wonder what long-term difference it would make to their daily lives. She smiled and nodded as Hannah told her all about a day in the life at the warehouse. She laughed and 'oh-really-ed' her way through Garold's rant about the ins and outs of DDA compliancy (some kind of Internet thingamyjig that was of the utmost importance to every digital decision which Mercury made). Fortunately, Amelie was also on this table, listening to Howard from Production talk about new trends in spine widths and a new, cheaper type of paper that Paddington were considering using. Although they were at opposite ends, Daisy and Amelie both occasionally got to exchange looks of pain, with which to pass the time. But by the time dessert came around, Shauna from Accounts raised her trump card, that she'd recently given birth. Complaining of fatigue and depression, she excused herself and slipped away to bed.

'Cunning, very cunning,' said Amelie, slipping into Shauna's spare seat while no one was watching, 'I mean, if only we had newborn babies as an excuse!'

Daisy laughed. 'I know – and that's if she's telling the truth! I mean – we'll never know, will we? She could be playing with the fact that neither of us works out in Chingford with her!'

Amelie sighed and took another bread stick to her mouth. 'God . . . To think, we were all so looking forward to the conference. And it's just not all that great, really, is it?' Daisy nodded, and they both sat watching their various colleagues growing increasingly inebriated and animated by turns.

An hour later, the girls were still in the same position, polishing off remnants of cheese and downing final drops of wine. Daisy looked at her watch. 'Do you think anyone will notice if I go upstairs for a bit and then come back? Only, I really want to get back and finish the end of the book.'

Amelie groaned and rolled her eyes. 'And miss all this?'

Daisy looked at Amelie doubtfully. 'Seriously – I'm so into it now. There're about fifteen pages left, and I just need to know what happens! Honestly, Am, it's so sad right now, because Ed's gone to meet her on the 15th of September, like they arranged, after two months of waiting to see her again, having worked all summer on this special painting for her, and . . .'

Amelie put her chin in her hands, pretending to look thoroughly bored.

'Just let me tell you, quickly!' Daisy persisted. 'Anyway, he's waiting for her at the gallery, and he's totally looking forward to seeing her again and stuff – but then, it's so sad, she just isn't there! It's so weird, because we know that something's not right – like they were both really in love, and there's no reason why she'd stand him up . . . plus she won't answer any of his calls, and he's been leaving these sad and hopeless messages. And the last bit I just read, he's just called her and her phone line's gone totally dead, like it's not even working any more. So now he's running around Islington trying to find her . . . it's like maybe she never existed, was just a spirit all along, a bit like the girl in Ali Smith's last book?'

Amelie nodded, 'The Accidental, right . . .'

'Back at the gallery, everyone's being all mysterious about her – none of them has seen her since before the summer. You know, her contract was finished in June, and so they'd pretty much assumed they wouldn't be seeing her again. So then he's like – OK, I'm not going mad, she did exist once, but he's thinking, she just doesn't want to know him any more. He's heartbroken, and after mooching about for ages, he pulls himself together, remembers he's got an exhibition to prepare for. And then he decides that, since she's not bothered to come and collect it, he'll just put the flamenco girl painting straight into the exhibition. But he gives it pride of place, and in the blurb panel beside the painting, he writes 'For Lauren Harper, I owe you dinner.'

Amelie, who had been fiddling with her nails, engrossed in the task of removing a bit of trapped cheese, looked up to say, 'Ah, that's sweet, isn't it?'

Daisy went on enthusiastically, 'So, just let me quickly tell you the rest. The exhibition's been running for a week, when one day this really strange, creepy guy comes to look round the paintings. He walks round the whole exhibition, and then at the end, he pulls Ed to one side. He tells him that he's from the local police station, and that the parents of a girl named Lauren Harper have recently reported their daughter as missing. But that's not all, Am. This guy – he's all suspicious of Ed, like he suspects that Ed might have got something to do with her apparent disappearance. So before he knows it, Ed's being arrested and dragged down to the police station for questioning. But as he's sitting there in the interview room, fielding loads of rude questions from the narky cops, he's got this big huge grin on his face – he's relieved, because all this means she didn't stand him up, that she's not still in New York, that she might even be alive somewhere still . . .' Daisy stopped, realised how long she'd been talking. 'Sorry – I'll leave it there, for now! Better not spoil any more for you. I think you should definitely start reading it . . .'

Amelie, having sparked up while listening to this recent development, now seemed interested. 'Well, I'd love to, actually . . . I was only joking about it being dull. Really, I thought you'd never ask.'

'Hooray!' Daisy was delighted to finally have some backing from someone else in her find-Will-a-book-deal project. 'Hurrah. I'll go grab it from my room later.'

Amelie smiled. 'Great! Jolly hockey-sticks!' she joked, in a gratuitous mockery of Daisy's Enid Blyton-Tourette's syndrome.

'Stop it!' Daisy poked Amelie in the ribs.

'Sorry,' Amelie smiled guiltily, looking around the room. 'So . . . shall we – I don't know, have a dance, or something? I mean, I know everyone looks kind of ridiculous – but that's really the only thing which will pass the time, isn't it?'

Amelie pointed to a small dance floor, cordoned off by chairs. If the layout, lighting and music were anything to go by, it was all alarmingly reminiscent of a school disco. On the small dance floor, the movers and shakers of Mercury Publishing were moving and shaking. They had all linked arms, and before long all of Amelie and Daisy's worst fears came into fruition. Daisy watched, wide-eyed as representatives from Marketing, Editorial and Production all joined together in a disjointed rendition of the conga, marching around in an almost circle, arms flailing, skirts slipping, bra straps sliding, cleavage gaping.

'You *really* want to get involved in all that?' Daisy asked unsurely.

Amelie shook her head. 'No, you're right. We're nowhere near as drunk as we should be. Come on,' she said, standing up. 'Let's get to the bar.'

Daisy looked over towards the small bar in the corner of the room, 'You're right. It's the only way. And by the looks of things, Heidi needs rescuing while we're at it . . .'

Amelie followed her gaze to where Heidi was standing by the wall. A tall, balding man with alarmingly visible sweat patches, was wobbling and leaning into Heidi, in an attempt to steady himself. Heidi had the face of someone who didn't quite know how to extricate herself without being rude, so, like a martyr, was remaining still for the sake of being kind.

'Looks like Mario the "Assistant Webmaster" has had one too many again,' Amelie commented, and they marched, solidarity in their every footstep, towards the bar to rescue their friend from a fate worse than death.

When ten o'clock came around, Daisy was heading back to the party from the ladies, feeling two things: a) she was a good deal more drunk than before, and b) that she'd almost certainly danced to enough Grease mega-mixes and Whigfield covers to last a lifetime. When 'The Birdie Song' came on, and Belinda squawked 'Yessssss!' at the top of her voice and jumped up on to a podium, Daisy knew this was her moment to slip away quietly. If she was quick, she could just sneak off to her room, finish off the last twenty pages, and then re-emerge, born again and no longer being eaten up by the curiosity and the all-consuming not-knowing-ness. She knew she was showing mild signs of obsessive behaviour, but she just had to know whether Lauren was dead or not. Watching Amelie and Heidi strut their stuff along with Garold, Hannah and Hermione, Daisy decided that now was probably safe. But in mid-scurry, she was spotted.

'Just where do you think you're going, missy moo?' demanded Amelie.

Daisy blushed. 'I'm just going to the loo! I won't be long, I promise!' and she hurried away, fully intending to re-emerge ten minutes later.

Before long she forgot all about the carnage going on five floors beneath her in the dance hall and returned to the manuscript, where she found Ed sitting in the foyer of the police station, having finally managed to convince the police that a) he wasn't a serial killer with a penchant for chainsaws, and b) he should be allowed to go free. When the detective came out of his office, Ed stood up, gathering his things together ready to leave. 'Actually, if you wouldn't mind sticking around, we've just had a call you might be interested in.'

Daisy took another large sip of the red wine she'd brought with her, and felt the thickness of the pages in her hand – only a few left to go. She read on as the police explained that they'd just had a call from Charing Cross Hospital. Two weeks ago they'd had a Jane Doe admitted, with severe bruising to the head, among other injuries. She had only just regained consciousness, but in doing so had no memory of who she was, where she came from or what she was doing there. Because of this, and her complete absence of personal possessions that might help trace her identity, it had taken the hospital a while to connect her as the missing person. Daisy read on, intrigued, as the doctors revealed that this Jane Doe was now suffering from severe amnesia, having experienced a traumatic attack of some kind.

Daisy looked at her watch, hoping Amelie wouldn't be too annoyed at her for leaving the party. As she read on, the police were keen to get down to the hospital to continue their investigation. Ed's first impulse, however, was to rush back to the gallery in Islington, to reclaim the painting of the flamenco dancer. But, as Ed discovered when he got there, someone had already put in an offer for the painting. After two hours spent arguing with the curator as to why he now needed the painting withdrawn from the exhibition, he eventually hailed a taxi back to the hospital.

Daisy read through the next few pages and turned into the final chapter. She listened as the doctors gave the rest of their diagnosis. The severity of her amnesia was such that, although Lauren might eventually recall her sense of self, she might never remember the last few years of her life. As Daisy read on, Ed walked into the room where Lauren was half dozing, waiting to be taken for scans. She smiled a polite stranger's smile. Ed held up the painting in front of her, and stared at Lauren, earnestly hoping for a flicker of recognition in her eyes – any flicker at all. Daisy held her breath. Surely this, the one painting that had been fashioned out of both of their memories, would help bring her back? If not, the whole connection they'd shared in Seville would be severed for ever.

Daisy jumped as her mobile phone vibrated and beeped. She looked down at the handset and saw that it was Miles.

What was he doing calling her again? They'd not spoken in weeks! Besides, why was he calling her now – it was probably about 4 a.m. in London – was this his debut drunken 4 a.m. phone call? That was never normally his style.

'Hello?' she answered tentatively.

The line was crackling noisily, but she could just about make out a distant, slurring, 'Daaaiiissy . . .'

'Er, hello?' she said nervously.

'Daisy! *Ciao!*'

The crackling in the line had stopped, and, on hearing the voice, Daisy felt a jolt in her stomach. 'Miles? What are you doing calling me? You know I'm in Venice, don't you?'

'Daisy, darling . . . I miss you. So, so much . . .' through drunken slurs, he added, 'Please . . . can we see each other again?'

Daisy slumped down on the bed. It was so nice to hear his voice, and yet so sad. Already she could feel all those neatly buried feelings being horribly resurrected. 'Um, Miles . . . please . . . no . . . we've been through this. It's for the best, OK?'

'Please, Daisy, please just give me one last chance. I won't let you down, I promise!'

Daisy was affronted. She'd never heard him like this. He sounded desperate, weary, and, for the first time ever in his life, a little needy.

'Miles . . . I'm kind of in the middle of something. Couldn't we do this another time?'

Ray-of-hope-wise, this was all Miles needed. He grabbed to it with both hands. 'You mean you'll see me? Great. I'm on my way. I'll be there in fifty minutes . . .'

Daisy felt her stomach lurch. 'What do you *mean*, fifty minutes?'

'I mean, baby darling, that I'm in a cab. I'm just approaching the Tangenziale ring road. You're in the Hotel Regina and Europa, right? See you very soon.' And he rung off.

Daisy wanted to scream. What the hell did he think he was playing at? She couldn't believe what she was hearing – he sounded like a completely different person, Humble, grovelling, egoless. And what did he mean by turning up at her hotel? In Venice, which was officially the most romantic city – Paris lacked gondolas – in the world? Of all the inflated romantic gestures in the history of romance, this surely had to be up there with the best?

But what was she going to *do* with him when he got there? She began to feel giddy, and her stomach was tensing up. She couldn't imagine what she'd say to him. Against all the odds, she'd actually been getting on just fine without Miles the last few weeks. How completely like him it was to wait until then, and then decide to come and undo all the good . . .

Time out, she thought. All these anxieties could wait a few more minutes. She'd tend to them in a minute – in the meantime, she had a book to finish. And so, for the first time in her life, Daisy filed away all feelings and concerns relating to Metcalfe, Miles neatly in the shelf in her mind marked MISC, and quickly found solace in the words of Will's final pages. She found Ed, a few days on, rummaging through his flat, looking for the one thing that he'd suddenly realised might be able to nudge Lauren's memory into bringing her back. He was rifling through his room, throwing his belongings about, looking for something. Finally he found it, and ran to his car with it. Daisy's curiosity was mounting over what it could be. She looked at her watch, prayed that Miles's cab was wedged in some traffic somewhere, and read on. Ed was sitting in his car outside the hospital, turning the postcard over in his hands, thinking what he would say. He looked at the postcard in his hands, at the picture of the girl flamenco dancing, wearing a vibrant, ruffly skirt. Daisy stopped reading for a second. Something in all of this was eerily familiar. Something about it was giving her a murky feeling of déjà vu. Daisy read on, butterflies niggling at her stomach, as Ed walked into the hospital room and opened his mouth to speak.

'And there's this . . .' he said, nervously handing her the postcard. 'Complete with ruffly skirt,' he added sheepishly. Daisy read on, feeling like the awkward third person in the room, invisibly watching as Lauren took the card and stared at it, transfixed. After about a minute of her staring at the card, Ed gently tapped Lauren's foot.

'Lauren?' No reply. She just kept on staring. 'Lauren . . .' he tried again.

After another moment, Lauren looked up from the card at Ed. Then she looked at Ed, then at the painting resting against the wall, and finally back to Ed. She narrowed her eyes. 'I've no idea who you are . . . but I think I owe you dinner?'

As the last page fell drifting to the floor, a tear slipped out of Daisy's left eye and rolled down her cheek. She'd never experienced it before, but right then she knew exactly what people meant when they said someone had just walked over their grave. She looked up from the page, and wiped her eyes. That detail about the postcards – how could Will have possibly invented something out of thin air that was already so personal to her? Not only that, but to have made it into such a pivotal part of the novel? She ransacked her brain. Had she ever emailed Will to tell him about her weird penchant for postcards with ruffly skirts? Granted, it wasn't the best opener – 'How was your weekend, get much writing done? By the way, I have a fetish for weird tacky Spanish postcards.' But then, that wasn't the only similarity she'd noticed. There was the line in the book 'of all the bars in all the world' – where had she heard that recently? Now she thought about it, there were other moments in the book, which were oddly reminiscent of recent things in her own life. But why hadn't she noticed this until now?

She flicked back through the rest of the manuscript. Impatiently, she thumbed back and forth through the pages, searching for any other echoes of herself, or from her life. Just as she was mentally chastising herself for such narcissistic behaviour, her eyes fell upon the scene at the Alcázar Palace in the centre of Seville, where she noticed that the pages had been drastically amended, and new material inserted. Where Ed and Lauren were sharing a moment beside Mercury's Pool, there now appeared to be a new conversation, where Lauren was confiding to Ed all about how the woman in the flamenco dress reminded her of her childhood. 'It's strange,' Lauren said, 'it made me think of the funny old days when my dad was still alive . . . made me think about those 3-D postcards he used to send me . . .'

Daisy felt like she'd been dealt a blow to the stomach. There was no way this author could have just imagined something like that and chosen to write about it, was there? To be sure, there was no way Will could possibly have known all these things, just from her emails to him. She knew she had a habit of overzealously reading in between the lines, but surely this was too much of a coincidence to ignore? No – there had to be a sensible explanation for all of this.

Pacing around the room, Daisy ran through all the options in her mind. One thing seemed clear. If this detail about the postcards was based on her childhood story, then logically, she must know the author. She didn't know anyone called Will. Therefore, there were only two possibilities: either 1) Will was a friend of someone she knew, or 2) Will was not his real name – it was actually someone she knew. Option two ruled out it being the mysterious man on the train. No, now that she saw that Will Marwood might well be nothing but a pseudonym, she began to realise that really, this author could be anyone she knew.

But then, who could have known about this postcard story of hers? The only person she remembered ever telling it to was Elliot. It wasn't the most interesting story in the world, so chances were no one else (except Belle of course, and her father) would have any reason to know it. So maybe the connection was her father? No. That was too crazy. For all she knew, her father wasn't even alive any more. No, it was far more likely that Elliot was the link. Maybe Will was a friend of Elliot's, or connected to him in some way? Or . . . perhaps Elliot was trying to help a friend get published, by sneaking his friend's manuscript on to the slush pile. Hurrah, that was it! Daisy heard about that kind of thing happening in publishing houses all the time – she was often asked to do similar things herself. But then her heart sank as she realised the implications of this. It meant that Elliot would have to have gone blabbering about her personal childhood details to his friend, which really, really didn't seem like his style. He was more discreet than that, wasn't he?

Hovering by the window and looking out over the Grand Canal, another more radical idea popped into her head. What if Will *was* Elliot? That was impossible! He'd surely have told her – they were too good friends for that, weren't they? But then, thinking back over all the contact she'd had with them both the last few months, she began to feel very stupid. It did make a mad kind of sense. Suddenly all she wanted was to get home. To get back to London, to Belle, and to her computer – she had a desperate urge to go through and analyse both Will's and Elliot's emails for any clues that could be buried in between the lines. But she knew the earliest she could get online would be the day after tomorrow, back at work. She began to feel panicky. Suddenly she was all too aware of the levels of alcohol inside her and felt increasingly queasy. She ran to the bathroom, feeling an ever-increasing need to heave with every step she took.

Sitting on the bathroom floor, hugging the pristine luxurious five-star toilet basin, she had a complete and total thunderbolt of a revelation. Daisy took a deep breath (regretting it quickly as she remembered she was hanging over a toilet basin). If it *was* Elliot (and that was a big if), why on earth would he do this? Why wouldn't he have told her? The only reason that she could think – crazy conjecture thought it was – was that he was doing it because he *liked* her in some way? Maybe that would explain how cool he'd been with her when she was in the pub that time with Miles? No – this was surely too far-fetched? But then what if all this deception, and using intimate details about her childhood as a pivotal plot device, was his rather long-winded way of expressing the depth of his feelings for her? Was there any likelihood at all in this: that Will Marwood's book was a hugely elaborate, *love letter* to her? If so, how did she feel about him in return? Somehow, deep in the recesses of her mind, she was beginning to wish this idea into existence.

Her mind was spinning with all the different possibilities. Suddenly it was all too much. She was driving herself mad! Why was she like this – why did she have to *obsess* so much about every little detail with things? Why did everything always have to *mean* something? It didn't, was the answer. She decided to do nothing. She would just ignore this supposed similarity, and go and rejoin the party. She thought about standing up.

But then – it was all so strange – she felt like she knew this author intimately, and yet she still didn't really know *who* he or she was. One thing was clear, though; she was now more involved with this book than ever. She'd been so involved with the text since its conception, through all the editing she'd done with Will, that now – unless she was imagining it all – the novel seemed to be inextricably linked to her. She was just smiling to herself over the relentless irony of it all when there was a knock at the door. She jumped in surprise, bashing her head on the bidet in the process.

Allowing the stars spinning around her head to settle, Daisy stood up and splashed some water on her face. Wondering what Amelie would be doing chasing her already, Daisy went to open the door. She hadn't been gone that long from the party, had she?

Her heart skipped yet another beat when she saw who was standing there.

'Hello, beautiful girl!' Miles swept Daisy into his arms, carried her into the bedroom and playfully threw her on to the bed. Although he looked thoroughly EasyJetted, Miles seemed very excited to see her. And with Daisy being so distracted, the small detail that Miles was looking especially handsome barely even hit her radar.

'OK, I know this is a shock, but – shit, it's good to see you . . .' he moved towards Daisy, to kiss her on the cheek, but she backed away.

'Please – just give me one hour of your time,' he demanded. 'Then I'll go all the way back to London, if that's what you want. But just please, come with me for now, and hear what I need to say . . .'

Daisy shook her head. 'No way – no-no-no-no-no!' and farcically, she ran to the other side of the room, as though he had some rare kind of lurgy that he'd come all this way just to share with her. 'No really, I don't want to hear it; whatever it is. I'm having kind of a trauma right now and I don't have time for you to make things even more complicated! No-no-no-no!'

And yet, after only fifteen minutes of manly persuasion and charm from Miles, Daisy's stock reserves of willpower had been all but chipped away. Soon she was sitting waiting on the terrace outside their hotel, wearing her pashmina around her head almost like a burka (both for warmth and disguise purposes – she was afraid of being seen 'breaking out' of the hotel enclosure before the end of the conference – especially with a man). Quickly and with his usual suaveness, Miles pinned down a gondola, and held out his hand to help Daisy climb into it. She wobbled slightly, gave a discreet hiccup, and sat down. Next, Miles revealed a bottle of champagne.

'Wow,' Daisy gushed with attempted sarcasm, but it just ended up sounding genuine, 'You've thought of everything.'

Miles nodded. 'Cover your ears,' he commanded, knowing the pop always gave her a fright.

Daisy ducked down and put her hands over her ears, giggling and cowering while a loud 'pop!' entered the night air. She smiled and pulled her hands down again. 'Sorry – I'm such the biggest loser. But thank you,' she gushed, taking a beaker of champagne from him. She took a sip, and leaned back in the copiously cushioned gondola. No one had ever mentioned how gloriously comfortable gondolas were, she thought to herself, admiring the enchanting views of the Santa Maria della Salute Basilica from close up. As they set off down the canals sipping champagne, Daisy had to admit that – fuckwit or no fuckwit – this night was becoming a tiny bit special. As much as she tried, after a while she admitted defeat and gave up on holding back the smiles.

'Amazing, isn't it?' Miles remarked.

Daisy nodded. 'I have to admit, yes it is. To think, none of us have even been out here at night yet! It's nuts! I mean, take this week – if we weren't trapped in the conference room watching talk after talk, we were in the hotel bar every other minute, being plied with booze . . . meanwhile, all this amazing gorgeousness is just sitting out here, waiting to be seen!' She gave Miles a spontaneous bash on the arm. 'You're such a bugger, but thank you . . . I'm really glad you got me out to see all this, especially at night. It's just like something out of a fairy tale, this place . . .' she trailed off, and leaned her head back to look at the night sky.

'You're welcome,' said Miles, in his best rendition of humble. 'Now, don't laugh at what I'm about to say, OK, but—'

Daisy felt herself gradually tensing up. 'What?'

'It's just that . . . Daisy, you just look so beautiful, I mean, you should see the way the moonlight's reflecting off you, and the way your eyes are shining . . . Here, I've got to get a picture of you . . .'

Whatever, went the voice of her inner chaperone as Miles took a picture of her on his mobile and then snapped it shut. Just breathe in and out, Daisy thought, keep smiling from ear to ear until we get back to the hotel. Do not under any circumstances buy into any of this formulaic attempt at romance – this is nothing but textbook, transparent sleazy talk. Daisy said nothing – she simply smiled and nodded as they glided along. She stayed at the Safe Distance of at least five inches away, drank in all the romantic lines, and tried her best to remain cynical and unwooed.

'It really is lovely to see you, Daisy. I've missed you so much.' He leaned over, pulled down her pashmina-cum-burka, and moved to run his hand through her hair. 'I've missed this hair – your lovely red hair – I missed your cute smile, your silly hiccuppy laugh . . .'

Against her better judgement, Daisy could feel the ice melting around her a little. She wanted desperately to discourage him, and to keep up her wall of resistance, but something about the sensation of gliding along in a gondola had rendered her quite incapable. So incapable that, eventually, she gave in and let him kiss her. No, worse than that, she kissed him back.

When Daisy opened her eyes again, the gondola had turned off the Grand Canal and begun weaving its way through the labyrinth of smaller canals and back alleys.

Wait, Daisy suddenly thought, sitting up and reinstating her burka. Was there more to all this? She let go a smile, while thinking to herself, what was this man – this all too gorgeous man whom she'd never been able to trust before – really up to? She thought for a moment, grappled for some adequate words.

'Um . . . that's very nice of you, and everything. And it's very lovely of you to do all this. But seriously, Miles, what are you actually doing here? What's it all about?'

The gondola was heading towards a low bridge. Miles put his hands in his pockets, and turned to Daisy. The gondola slid under the low bridge, and they had to quickly huddle down together so as not to lose their heads in the bridge. As they came out the other side, Miles was bending down, crouching on his knees as though he'd lost something.

'What's wrong? What are you looking for?' Daisy asked, 'Here, let me help you.' She slid off her cushion and squatted down next to him, so that now they were both crouching together on the base of the gondola, earning them a strange look from the gondolier. Oops, there goes the safe distance, Daisy thought, wishing she could temporarily gag her inner chaperone. How close was too close? she wondered, catching the scent of his aftershave and feeling a sad twinge of nostalgia at the recognition of it as her old favourite. 'Miles, what've you lost?' she asked innocently.

He shook his head. 'Nothing. I've found what I'm looking for.'

Daisy was muddled. 'Miles, just stop talking in rid . . .'

she trailed off, seeing Miles's hand extended before her, containing a small, glowing object, twinkling almost as much as the stars.

'Daisy dearest. Dozy, dazey Daisy Allen. I'm trying to ask you to marry me.'

Sorry? she wanted to shout, but didn't. She couldn't speak. Was any of this actually real? She took the ring in her hands and studied it. She kept thinking; despite all this – the romantic setting, the glinting diamond – Miles was still Miles. He was still a commitment phobic, he still had a slight penchant for infidelity, and he was still a man with many different personae. Turning the exquisite ring over in her hands, Daisy had a strange prosaic feeling that if she was going to stick with this man, she'd have to be prepared to see all of these quirks of his again and again, many more times over. Then suddenly, she remembered what Belle had said to her all those months ago. That she wasn't in love with Miles, but rather a projection of her own ideals. Similarly, Miles seemed to have constructed a designer image of himself according to how he wanted to be seen by others. Standing watching him now, suddenly all she could see was constructs. Like a city built on water, their relationship now seemed lacking in a solid foundation, or anything real, and solid. So much so that, the more text-book romantic gestures Miles sent her way, the less she felt able to believe in them any more.

Miles held his hands up to fend off any rebuttals. 'Look, I know what you're thinking. But just hear me out.' He took a deep breath. Unless it was all a very brilliant affectation, Miles did look very nervous. He seemed to show a vulnerability Daisy had never seen in him before. As he spoke, the gondolier was turning the gondola around, and they were heading back the way they had come. Miles looked intensely at Daisy, and went on, 'Listen, while you've been out of my life, I've had a bit of an epiphany. Being without you all this time, and trying to see other girls, it's just made me realise that one hundred and ten per cent, now and for ever, I want to be with you, Daisy, and no one else.' He looked up at Daisy as though to check she was listening, and went on, 'Move in with me – we'll get married, we'll have lots of little mini Mileses and mini-Daisys . . . and we'll move back to Southwold or some other little place in Suffolk. Our kids could even get the same school buses together as we did!' His face became serious. 'Daisy, I want the lot. With you. Can't you see it? Think how great we'd be together! Really – we'd have the best life! Imagine it!' He held his arms out high in the air, smiling ardently at Daisy. He brought his arms down again, seeing her befuddled expression, and stopped.

'Dais – I'm so, so sorry that I messed you around so much in the past. But I promise you that I'll more than make up for it. We're so good together. Look, at least think about it. I mean, we don't have to get married right away – I was thinking it could be one of those really long engagement things. Besides, who else can offer you this much financial security? I mean, Daisy, can you believe what I'm saying? I'm finally ready!' Miles leaned back down on his seat, oddly triumphant. By the time he'd finished his speech, they were back at the hotel. The gondolier was hanging over the edge of the gondola impatiently. 'Romance is over – time is money,' his eyes seemed to be saying as he waited for Daisy and Miles to climb out. Daisy was still silent, struggling to find the words – any words at all would help.

Here was a man offering her everything she'd ever wanted, on a great big shiny Italian platter. Being proposed to in a gondola, under a moonlit sky. What else was there? Possibly this was more romantic than any novel she'd ever read or edited. So how could she turn him, or *it* down? That would be to commit a disservice to Romance itself, wouldn't it? Or at the very least, it would betray everything she'd ever believed in, wouldn't it?

20

Popcorn And Proof

Venice was stirring. It was only 7 a.m., according to the brass alarm clock on the bedside table, but already the noise and clatter of the canals, the gondoliers, the tourists, was beginning to seep through the thin glass of the window. Daisy rolled over and turned to study the tanned, gorgeous figure sleeping next to her in the bed. He looked strangely calm and humble in his sleep, she thought, watching the brown strands of his hair falling over his face and rising up and down in line with his breathing. She couldn't believe he was here. She replayed once again the events of last night in her mind, and her stomach began to tense up. She thought about waking him, but decided some moments to herself right now, in the circumstances, would be a good thing. There was a lot to think about.

She slipped out of bed quietly and wrapped her huge, fluffy white dressing gown around her. Stepping into her unthinkably soft hotel slippers, she went to gently open the shutters. She tiptoed out on to the balcony, and then sat with her glass of water, watching the birds and the sun rising over the sparkling Grand Canal. She watched the seagulls congregating across the water, on the piazza in front of the Santa Maria Della Salute Basilica, which they'd been so close to only a couple of hours ago. Along with the seagulls, there were crowds of people in elegant dress, perhaps gathering before a wedding. What a glorious place to get married, she couldn't help thinking.

'Hey, lovely,' Miles said, stepping out on to the balcony.

'You're awake!' she said, mildly irritated at having her quiet reverie interrupted. 'Great! Right then, you can get going now, can't you?'

He tried for a kiss, but Daisy backed away. 'No-no-nooouuuuu! Christ, Hermione's only two doors down! What if she sees you out here on the balcony? Get back inside right now! I'll get in such trouble for having a man here!'

'Shit – good point,' he said, looking either side of him to ensure that no one from Mercury was out slurping their morning coffee on any of the adjacent balconies. He hurried back into the room, Daisy following after him, agitation personified.

'Quick – you've got to go! before anyone *sees* you!

'*Right* now?' he asked, shocked, grinning cheekily in response to her schoolmarm-meets-Monica-from-*Friends*-ish manner.

'YES now!' she shrieked. 'I only let you stay here on the condition you'd go on the early flight back this morning. You know that.'

Miles gave the smile of a schoolboy trying to wangle his way out of a another detention. 'But now I'm here, why don't I just stay on for a bit? Yes – we could both stay on for another few days, spend some quality time together . . . you know, I'll get us another room here, or another hotel – maybe even out on the Lido. That'd be nice, bit of beach time, eh? I mean, it's kind of sunny for October – we could try and work on our tans. Come to think of it, this place is twinned with the Exelsior Hotel. I'll make some calls now,' he said, as though it was a fait accompli. He picked up his jacket and went rummaging through it for his mobile.

Daisy was aghast. 'Miles! There's no way I'm staying here – or the Lido – and having to explain to my boss why! I'm due back at work tomorrow! And the flight to Heathrow is leaving this morning!'

'Oh you really are a true unromantic, aren't you?' he whined sarcastically, trying to pull her back towards the bed. Being plenty stronger than her, it wasn't long before he'd manoeuvred her next to him on the edge of the bed. She was still anxiously trying to keep her distance, but was failing under his pressure. He pulled her in closer, towards the bed, her gown slipping off her shoulders. He stroked her cheek, his hands wandering down her back as he kissed her. Daisy let him go on kissing her, thinking how nice it felt as his hands drifted further a field, until finally her inner chaperone awoke with a sudden bolt, and Miles was forced away.

'Shit! You've got to go! I've got to get to breakfast, and to pack all my stuff up before checkout! Crumbs – please don't let anyone from here see you, whatever you do!' she jumped up, headed to the bathroom. 'I'm going to have a shower, and when I'm out, please can you not be here?'

Daisy slammed the bathroom door, feeling she might be on the threshold of a huge fit of self-loathing. She was intensely regretting letting him stay here last night. The trouble was, the more she pushed him away, the keener he became – a recurring theme with this boy, she thought, as she stepped into the shower and pulled the curtain across. Seconds later, he was back, poking his head round the corner of the bathroom door. 'Can't I join you first? Then I'll go?'

She drew the curtain back just enough so she could poke her head out. 'NO! Please just go back home! Oh, and watch out, Ronald and Hermione are both on this floor – so just keep your head down, OK?'

'OK, OK . . .' he gave in, looking despondent. 'I'll go now. And I promise to be invisible. Look, I'll even wear my hood up so they don't see me! But on one condition,' he smirked cheekily. 'You give me your answer before I go.'

Daisy rolled her eyes, beginning to shiver with cold and wishing he'd leave her to get on with her shower, 'My answer, Miles, is that I'll think about it. I can't do better than that right now. You've got to give me some time.'

'Fine. I'm leaving the box and the ring on your bed. Think about it. Look, I know this isn't easy, but just take all the time you need. I'll be in Rome for the next week anyway, so I'll be in touch when I'm back.'

Daisy nodded slowly. 'OK, I'll see you in London.' Sternly, she drew the curtain back, jumping as the powerful jet of water spurted all over her face.

'Seen it, seen it, seen it.'

Twelve hours later, Daisy was curled up on her sofa at home, and was idly flicking through channels in search of something light and funny which would whisk her away from the indecision encircling her mind, the guilt from spending the night with Miles, and the turmoil over his proposal and what to say. And, not to mention, the still unsolved mystery identity of her enigmatic favourite author. She had a serious gut feeling that she knew who it was, and yet she had no real proof.

She scanned the piles of loose manuscripts which were stacked up all around her, and the dozens of popular genre books she'd been given at the conference – from crime, to romance, to history . . . Out of all of them, not one of them seemed capable of sustaining her attention for more than three lines. Instead, after a few more minutes of dedicated channel surfing and mental aerobics, Daisy eventually stumbled upon something that seemed interesting on TV. It looked like the 1970s, somewhere in London – was it Camden or Kentish Town maybe? It was one of the two. In a dimly lit, filth-ridden flat, two impoverished, emaciated-looking men – or possibly students – every chance they hadn't showered in weeks, were arguing. One was diving into some rat-infested washing-up, in an alarmingly filthy kitchen. The two men seemed to be in the midst of a ferocious argument of some sort. And even though dirtiness of this calibre usually had Daisy averting her eyes, in this instance she found the dialogue strangely captivating, and quickly found herself settling down to watch the film.

An hour later, Belle turned up and started chattering loudly over the top of it. Suddenly she needed to hear all about Venice and share her gossip, right then, that second.

People talking over the TV was one of Daisy's pet irritations. 'Shhhhh . . . let's talk when this has finished. It's really good.'

'Of course it is,' said Belle, in a 'Duuurrr' kind of tone. 'But you must have seen it before, though?'

'No, I don't think so,' Daisy said without looking at Belle.

'Oh well, I'm going to put some popcorn on,' Belle got up and went into the kitchen. Putting the bag of kernels into the microwave and shoving it on high, she ran back in and sat on the sofa. '*How* have you not seen *Withnail and I?*' she asked, amazed.

'What is it with everyone and that film?' Daisy asked, irritated.

'You mean this film.'

'Eh?'

'Well, this *is Withnail and I*, silly.' Belle looked at her sister in confusion. 'What? You mean you've watched nearly the whole film, and you haven't even figured that out?' Belle shook her head in amusement. 'God, sometimes I really wonder why it is that everyone calls me the dappy one! It's not fair! You can be *ludicrously* scatty sometimes!'

'Well, how was I to know?' Daisy said in her defence. 'It's not as if we ever do organised things like own a TV guide, is it?'

'Whatever,' Belle said, quietening down to watch as Richard E. Grant was walking through a park in the rain, a bottle of wine in hand.

'Oh, this is my favourite bit. It's just beautiful . . .'

As Withnail came to the end of his *Hamlet* soliloquy, the rain began to drench him through and the music was getting louder. The screen faded to black and the credits began to roll. 'Well, I must say, I really enjoyed that,' said Daisy, leaning back in her chair, 'I'm glad I've finally—'

She went silent. Her face was losing some of its colour.

'What? What's wrong with you?' Belle asked, looking at Daisy, then turning to see what she was looking at, following her line of vision. There, moving slowly up the screen, was one simple word.

'Oh my gosh . . .' Daisy said quietly, her face breaking out into a bemused smile. 'How stupid am I . . . Marwood. Well, that settles it, then.'

'Settles what, then?' asked Belle.

'It's the final piece in the puzzle!'

Belle stared at her sister with growing concern, and launched into a rambling lecture all about how the 'I' character is really called Marwood, but it's never mentioned in the film. Meanwhile, Daisy's mind was quietly working overtime. Of course Elliot was Will – he was William Marwood! All along there had been traces in the writing, the characters tinged with a haunting familiarity. But now here was actual proof, that he'd lovingly ripped his pseudonym out of his most favourite film. Daisy was itching to call Elliot then and there to confront him. But she knew she had to be cleverer than that. Too much was at stake.

'What are you thinking about, oh darling ditzy sister?' asked Belle, apparently relishing her newfound discovery that Daisy had scatty tendencies of her own.

Daisy suddenly turned to Belle. She screwed up her nose, and worry quickly washed over her face. 'Belle, is that the sweet smell of burning?'

'SHEEEETT! The popcorn!' Belle jumped up and ran into the smoke-filled kitchen.

Mountains Out of Moleskines

Date: Monday 9 October 2006 8.17 a.m.
Sender: Daisy.Allen@paddingtonpress.com
To: justwilliam26@hotmail.co.uk
Subject: Re: THE WHOLE LOT
Importance: High

Dear Will,

Hi – thank you so, so much for sending me the whole m/s, which I've now read twice, from beginning to end and throughly adore. I think it's completely brilliant and I've shown it to my boss and she loves it too.* We'd very much like to talk further with you about the possibility of publishing it. But we can't do that without meeting you, so would you be able to come in for a meeting? Let me know how you're fixed this week or

---

* This wasn't strictly true. Daisy was going to talk to Belinda later that morning about it, but for now she wanted Will to think he had no alternative but to come in and finally meet with her right away. In truth she was dreading what Belinda's reaction would be – but far better to make Will think that things were already moving.

early next. Can you please call me so we can arrange a time? I've also been speaking to a few agents, and still need a biog from you – or would you prefer it if I just give you their details?

Either way, I look forward to hearing from you. And congratulations – I think you've written something really great. Well done.

Daisy xx

Having come in early again the next day, Daisy had spent most of the morning ploughing through and analysing all of Will's and Elliot's emails. She was enjoying looking for subtle differences in their email style, and was almost certain now that Will was Elliot. But she had to credit him – he'd been very careful not to give his Will emails any conspicuous Elliotisms. Rereading all Elliot's emails, she had to keep explaining to people what was so amusing when she kept bursting out laughing. Looking back over them now, the emails formed a kind of catalogue of how their friendship had developed over the last few months. Only now, looking at the words on the page, did she fully realise how close they'd become. She clicked back on to her inbox and waited for a reply. Nothing yet.

There was one more very important thing she couldn't put off any longer. She allowed herself a few moments to compose herself and summon up some courage, before she gathered all her editorial notes together with the manuscript pages, and walked around to Belinda's office.

She crept round the corner, and gently knocked on the door.

'What?' Belinda barked through the door.

'It's just me,' she said through the door. Terrified, she pushed it ajar. 'I wondered if you have time for a quick chat at all?' She peered nervously into Belinda's huge and immaculate office. 'Don't worry if you're swamped,' she added, recoiling and hoping that Belinda would be busy, and would send her away again.

'No, fine, I've got a few minutes. Anything to distract me from this dull-as-shit book on bus shelters . . .' She watched as Daisy hovered uncertainly by the door. 'Well? Come on, then, I haven't got all day.'

Daisy began to think perhaps she should postpone this little chat until she was in a more receptive mood. She was full of dread – that Belinda would despise Will's book, throw it across the room and officially declare it a true member of the slush pile for ever. Nevertheless, she went in and sat down.

After Daisy had finished enthusiastically pitching the book, she watched Belinda's face closely, trying to assess which way her wrinkle formations were going to go – would they be voting in favour of a smile or a frown? She held her breath. Belinda pursed her lips tightly together, her eyes squinting in disapproval. Daisy's heart sank.

'It's not the story I have a problem with here . . .'

Daisy's heart lifted. There was hope.

'It's the lopsided, hare-brained way you've gone about doing all of this. What on earth possessed you to give him his editorial notes all the way through as you went, rather than waiting until it was all done? That's just not the Paddington way! For example, how am I, now, meant to make head or tail of what you've done?' She picked up various different sections of the novel which Daisy had laid out;

some of them with multiple versions and drafts, unedited and edited. Belinda fussed with them all, leafed through them as if trying to demonstrate just how anarchic it all was, and then dramatically threw them all back down on top of one another, leaving the table in disarray. Belinda's desk now looked as though someone had come in and sprayed the room with a manuscript gun, with A4 wads of paper as bullets. 'Can't you see? It's the most frightful mess!'

Daisy was mortified. Few things upset her more than mess. But mess that she'd caused? She grew red in the face with shame. 'I'm sorry, Belinda. I should have come to you sooner. I was just so excited by it, and I must have got a little bit carried away.'

She began tidying up the papers. 'But really, it's quite straightforward to see what I've done editing-wise. I'm sorry again. I hope this doesn't affect what you think of it. It really is the most fantastic book.'

Belinda appeared to soften. 'Well, be that as it may, I'm not going to read it in its present state. Clear all of this up and give it to me in a more ordered fashion, so that I can read through it, see what you've done to it, and decide if it is, in fact, as you say, publishable, or not.'

Daisy looked visibly relieved, and collected all the papers together in her arms. 'Of course. I'll have it back with you right away. Thank you, Belinda. Thank you so much. And I'm so very sorry for not coming to you sooner.'

Belinda was no longer listening. She was staring at Daisy as if to say, 'why are you still in my office?'

Daisy soon got the hint and scuttled away.

Returning to her desk, both mortified and disappointed, she was then delighted to see an email from Will perking up her inbox.

Date: Monday 9 October 2006 09.17
Sender: justwilliam26@hotmail.co.uk
To: Daisy.Allen@paddingtonpress.com
Subject: Re: THE WHOLE LOT
Importance: High

Hi Daisy

Thanks for your email. I'm really happy that you
enjoyed the ending. Sorry I can't call you just now as
my mobile is playing up and I don't have a landline. As
soon as it's fixed I'll call you, though.

As for my coming in for a meeting, that sounds great,
too – but I'd actually rather wait until I've secured an
agent before I come into Mercury and meet everyone,
as I think that might be jumping the gun?

Best wishes and thanks again for your nice comments,

Wx

p.s. If meeting really can't wait, though, I suppose I
could meet you in a café instead?

Date: Monday 9 October 2006 10.30
Sender: DaisyAllen@paddingtonpress.com
To:: justwilliam26@hotmail.co.uk
Subject: Re: THE WHOLE LOT
Importance: High

Great – how about we have lunch this Thursday? Do

you know Paddington? How about Pizza Express? If one's OK with you, I'll book a table? Smoking or non? Really looking forward to meeting you finally!

Dxx

When she filled the girls in on all the developments over lunch in the park, to begin with they were stunned. But once they'd pieced together the whole of the story, it wasn't long before they found the whole thing delightfully amusing.

'Well, who knew?' asked Amelie, smiling broadly. 'I think it's fabulous news. I can't quite get my head round it, but I think it's great. And I think you and Elliot would make the *loveliest* couple.'

Daisy felt her face grow hot. 'Don't be silly. He's not interested in me like that! We're just friends.'

Heidi shook her head. 'Oh, you'd be surprised. I got the impression he liked you when we went out . . . you know, I was telling him about my man at the gym, and he was telling me about a girl he fancied, in a pathetic, unrequited-love kind of a way . . . and I just guessed it could be you, even then. But I didn't want to rock the boat with you and Miles . . .'

Daisy shook her head. 'That's nonsense, that really is.'

Heidi shrugged. 'But anyway, back to the issue at hand – what's next in your plan, Daisy?'

Daisy laughed. 'Well, you see, I decided I may as well pretend like I still had no idea it was him. As if it's not totally obvious, I mean!' Daisy laughed slyly. 'Well, two can play at his game now . . .'

Amelie giggled, 'You mean, he still doesn't know that

you know? And you know that he might not know that you know?' She paused, her eyes indicating the whirring and screeching of cogs within her brain. 'Although, on the other hand, he might know that you know, but might also be pretending not to know that you know. Either way, you're both pretending that you don't know until you meet in person? Is that right?'

Daisy stirred her spag bol, and began winding some strands of spaghetti around her fork. 'Yes – that's right. There's just too much to say . . . I don't want to mess it up by doing it over an email or on the phone.'

Heidi's face contorted with confusion as she, too, tried to think all the details through. 'But hang on, both of you. You still don't know for certain that it's really Elliot, do you? Aren't you jumping the gun? What if it's someone totally different? A really ugly fat woman? What then? Or, worse, what if it's secretly Miles?'

Daisy threw her head back and laughed. But then a shadow moved over her face. 'Oh. My. God. Why, in the name of SHIT, hasn't that occurred to me before? H, I think you might've actually hit on something there.' Daisy's stomach tensed up again, and she was too distracted to even notice the girls' shocked reactions to her language which was much bluer than usual. She was too busy thinking. Miles – he had always wanted to be an author – and only she knew this! What if, all along, Miles had been Will? That would explain about the overlap with all her own intimate details! Maybe she'd not told him recently about the Spanish postcard thing, but there was always a chance she could have rambled about it when she'd had one too many one evening? Or maybe Belle could've told him the story once, in a playful attempt at embarrassing

her sister one night? Daisy's heart sank as she realised that
this was actually all quite possible. Why on earth had this
thought not occurred to her before? In fact, it was actually
more likely to be Miles, thinking about it, because she
knew that he was a closet aspiring author. He was always
secretly hinting at how much he wanted to write, flashing
his Moleskine around like a trophy, and forever whining
like a repressed artiste. Whereas she had no reason to
think of Elliot as a writer, had she?

She put her head in her hands. There was the time
when Elliot had looked away when he'd mentioned that
he'd heard of Miles. Maybe this was proof of a prior
awareness of literary agents and the 'how to get published'
scene? And there was the fact that Elliot had once been to
Spain, so he might be writing the scenes in Seville from his
own experiences. But that wasn't in any way conclusive.
Suddenly, with anguish, she realised that it could actually
be either of them, equally. But then, if it was Miles all
along, why did she feel disappointed? Why did her heart
sink at the idea of it not being Elliot? Were her feelings for
Elliot more complicated than she realised?

'Daisy?' Both Heidi and Amelie interrupted her reverie
and were staring at her.

'What, sorry, who?' Daisy blurted, landing back in the
park with a thud.

'I *said*, what are you going to say, Dais? When you
finally meet Will?' asked Heidi.

'Yes,' put in Amelie with a hint of sternness, 'and what
about Miles?'

'He's been in Rome for a week. That's bought me some
time . . .'

'But what are you going to say to him anyway?' put in

Heidi accusingly. 'About the ring, and all that? Never mind whether he wrote the book or not! You can't just leave him hanging! He's Miles Metcalfe! You've got a decision to make, girl!'

Daisy frowned and pushed her food away, untouched. 'I know. I . . . I don't know. I don't know! I guess I'll do whatever it is that girls do in novels, when stuff like this happens . . .'

'And what's that, then?' asked Amelie.

'Follow my heart . . . Isn't that what they always end up saying?'

In Between the Lines

When Thursday finally came around, after two days of excruciating waiting, Daisy arrived at work early. She was amazed to discover that Belinda was already in her office. Sitting down at her desk, Daisy caught sight of a note, scrawled by the hand of Belinda. 'See me,' it said, balancing atop Will's manuscript which appeared to have been read and returned to her desk. She felt an uncontrollable wave of nausea. No, not today of all days, please don't rain on my parade and tell me that I've been a complete dunce and we can't publish it after all?

Daisy walked as slowly as possible to Belinda's office. Walking in, she was faced with something she'd never, ever seen, in all her three years at Paddington. There, in front of Daisy, sitting at Belinda's desk, was a full-blown, un-edited, unadulterated smile. Not only that, it was backed up by friendly dialogue.

'Hi there,' she began, 'good news. I thought your little book was really quite charming. It needs a bunch of work doing, particularly the ending – I think that needs a bit of untangling! But I can definitely see the potential. I mean, off the top of my head, I'm thinking this is sort of a Laurie

Lee meets Michael Cox meets Carlos Ruiz Zafón and enters into a flirtation with Hemingway – kind of thing. You know?'

Daisy sighed with immense relief.

'But not only that. I also want to commend you on your editorial skills. Now that I can see what you've done with the original – and I'm not saying I agree with all of your comments – on the whole, I think you've done an excellent job. I think you'll make a fine editor. I think you're well on your way, Miss Allen.'

Daisy was grinning from ear to ear. 'Why, thank you! That's such great news!'

Belinda's smile then swiftly vanished, only to be usurped by a torrent of business speak. Which agents to approach, who internally would have to read it and approve it before they could offer. Then what sort of an offer they should make, would it be for foreign rights or just local, and where would they squeeze it on to the already congested publication schedule?

There was so much to think about. As Daisy left Belinda's office, she couldn't wait to tell Will, to tell the girls, to tell everyone. Her first book deal! She was so excited. But she had to remain calm – as Belinda had pointed out, Will hadn't technically even said yes. For all she knew, he might have zillions of other offers to choose from. It was by no means a done deal, but having the blessing of the Boss From Hell certainly meant Daisy was one step closer.

Lunchtime having almost arrived at last, Daisy was putting the finishing touches to her appearance in the third-floor ladies' room. As she applied another layer of lipgloss, she couldn't decide – was it her career she was dressing up for? For her first one-to-one lunch with an author? Or was it more because she wanted to look nice for whoever her author turned out to be? Be it Elliot, Miles, or even Freddy Rhubarb, for all she knew? Either way, as she finished getting ready, she felt enough somersaulting trapeze artists galloping round her stomach to fill a circus tent.

For the first time in her life, Daisy was watching the minutes tick by on her watch, and not doing everything in her power to be early. It pained her not to rush around, get ready and leave Within Plenty of Time, like she had done every day in her life. But today was different. She needed to be fashionably late. She needed to get there after him, that way she could steal a glance at her mystery author and prepare her reaction accordingly. This being late stuff was harder than it looked. She was struggling. She felt panic rising in her stomach, took a glass of water, and sat waiting. Eventually, about five years later, ten past one came around and she headed out.

Rounding the corner on to Bishops Bridge Road, Daisy headed down towards Pizza Express. Her throat began to feel even drier. Her hands grew clammy with nerves as she realised she was only nanoseconds away from seeing the culmination of everything the last few months had been all about; from finally knowing the true identity of the man with whom there was every chance she might be falling in love. She ran a hand through her hair, checked her face quickly in her hand mirror. Adequate. Then, just as she was about to turn into the courtyard, her mobile began to bleep. Miles. Without thinking, she cancelled the call and put the phone on to silent. She took another deep breath, and snuck up to the restaurant. She looked out, her eyes quickly scanning the sea of faces in the courtyard, perusing menus, tucking into pizzas, clinking glasses, celebrating the impending weekend. She took in the couples, business contacts, colleagues – luckily none from Mercury, by the looks of things – and then finally her eyes rested on one corner table where there was one man sitting alone, his eyes staring down at a newspaper and his fingers tapping a glass of wine in time to his iPod.

She stood and watched for a moment, preparing what to say. She hadn't banked on him looking quite this good. He was more smartly dressed than usual, and seemed more well-groomed and clean-shaven. Why had she never noticed how handsome he was? Suppressing the cacophony of nerves sparking off in her stomach, she walked into the courtyard.

'Well I never,' she said, in an attempt to feign surprise, but not really managing it.

Elliot looked up sheepishly, his face growing slightly red. Then, as though it had only just occurred to him, he stood up quickly, almost knocking his wine glass over but saving it at the last second. 'Sorry – Hi . . .'

Daisy leaned in and kissed him hello on the cheeks. This was going to be more awkward than she'd imagined.

They sat down in silence. Suddenly Daisy couldn't think what to say. She'd prepared so many things in her mind before, but now all she could think was that this felt kind of strange. Seeing both Will 'the wordsmith' and Elliot 'the lovely-and-really-quite-gorgeous friend' together and in front of her like this for the first time, was nothing short of surreal. Small talk seemed completely out of the question. So, instead, they both sat in silence for approximately four days, staring intermittently at one other and down at their empty plates.

'So, I'm really sorry,' he stammered, finally trampling over the silence like it was a bush of bristly brambles. 'I mean, for not being straight with you. But the thing was, I think I thought that the spell would break, if you knew. And that somehow you'd treat me differently . . . and well, there're other reasons, other stuff . . . it's complicated . . .' He looked uncomfortable, and picked up his menu to hide beneath.

Daisy pulled Elliot's menu away from his face, 'Shhhh . . . don't be silly . . . it's fine, you really don't need to apologise. It was a nice surprise. Although obviously, I'd pretty much figured it out before I got here.'

'You had?' He was alarmed. 'But why didn't you say anything?'

'Well, I wasn't a hundred per cent sure, so I had to be professional about it and wait, rather than confront you over the phone. Say I'd been wrong, that would've been awfully embarrassing . . .'

Elliot nodded.

'But hey, never mind all that cloak-and-dagger stuff – that's all water under the bridge now, isn't it? Honestly, all that stuff about living in Ireland! You're a very good liar, you know! But, the fact is, I completely and utterly adored your book. Where did you learn to write? And why didn't you tell me? And all those sorts of questions!'

Elliot began to blush uncontrollably now, and fortunately the waiter came over to relieve him from the spotlight. 'Can I get you anything to drink?' the waiter asked.

Daisy looked at Elliot questioningly. 'Yes, sure – same

again?' Daisy said, referring to the Cabernet Sauvignon they'd both enjoyed the last time they were there. She ordered it, and he nodded.

The waiter nodded, took the rest of their order and then went away.

'So, I'm really glad you liked it. Thanks so much for all your comments,' he said humbly, 'so what did B say about it?'

Daisy was surprised he should be bringing up Belinda already. 'It turns out that she's also a fan.'

He smiled with relief. 'Does she – you know?'

'Does she know that instead of being our dear, sweet, humble workie elf, you're actually a lying, scheming wannabe author? No, I didn't tell her about that yet. Like I said, I didn't know for sure – even though the Marwood thing was a bit of a dead giveaway!'

Elliot looked surprised. 'It was? I thought you'd never seen *Withnail and I*?!'

'It just so happened to be on the other day. I must confess I really, really liked it actually! You were right . . .'

'Well, of course.' He nodded sagely. 'So does she . . . does she think she can fit my book into her busy schedule?' he pressed.

'Well, yes, I think she'd like to slot it in somewhere. She's getting the bigwigs to read it first before we can make a formal offer. But in terms of timing, yes, she was thinking of slotting it into – assuming everything goes to plan – July next year. And that way we'd have a shot at getting you into summer reads and all that promotional gubbins . . .'

Elliot looked stunned.

'It sounds a long way off, I know – but as you know, the

timeline on books like this is normally quite long-drawn-out . . .'

'Oh, I know that – I'm not complaining! It's just so exciting to be talking about when it will be out there. In shops and stuff. It's mad!'

'I know. It's very exciting,' she said, pouring out the wine.

'Hey, anyway, here's to you – congratulations!'

They clinked their glasses and laughed, their spirits rising.

Elliot took a sip of wine and began to look pensive. 'So – Daisy . . .'

'Yes?' she asked, admiring how his hair was so much neater than before. Had he had it cut, she wondered? Newly styled?

'I remember last time we were here, you mentioned that you didn't like the book's title?'

'Oh, I don't *not* like it. It's more that I think Sales, and people like that will want to change it to something more accessible. I mean, I personally think it's lovely, but it does assume a certain amount of knowledge, as in, what "duende" means, which a title for this sort of book shouldn't really do – as immediately you've lost some people straight away. I think Belinda wants to have a think about it too. But if you feel *really* strongly, we don't have to change it . . .'

'Oh no, it's cool. Whatever you think's best.' He smiled. 'Boss.'

Daisy's heart swelled. He was so sweet, she kept thinking, and looked so well. It was weird seeing him in this way – as a client, as an author. Now they'd been talking a while, she couldn't help noticing he seemed different somehow. Much more self assured, and focussed – professional, even.

'Great. Oh, and before I forget, here are some more of my editorial notes. Belinda will come back with some too, but she's going to email you separately, I think. She's looking forward to meeting you too. Although – do you want me to let her into the secret now?'

'Yeah, that's fine. No worries.' He smiled, and then began to slowly, one by one, ask Daisy questions about the deal. How much of an advance would he be entitled to? How many books would the deal entail? And what royalties would he be getting? Daisy answered them all to the best of her knowledge, but as soon as she'd finished with one question, he'd come back with another one straight away, and continue quizzing her. Daisy kept thinking that he seemed at that moment to be so much older, more assertive than the quiet, self-effacing boy who had first come in on work experience.

They pressed pause on the business talk briefly, to comment on and share bites of their Neopolitana, and Pepperoni pizzas respectively. But quickly the negotiating began again.

'And like I said, you really ought to get an agent to advise you,' said Daisy. 'They'll be able to explain the figures much better than I can. I'm afraid my maths isn't up to explaining your royalty calculations just yet!'

'Oh don't worry . . . Will do.'

'Great. And, it goes without saying, I'd really love to have first dibs on it . . . unless you'd like to shop around first.'

'Oh no . . . no shopping around for me.' Elliot smiled shyly, 'I mean, I have to say that after the way we've been working together so far, and the editing you've been doing, I can't imagine going elsewhere with it.'

Elliot looked meaningfully at Daisy, and that was the precise moment when her heart sank, and her perception of the world changed. Suddenly something was candidly clear. From all Elliot had been saying so far, there was absolutely nothing there to interpret as flirty, overly friendly or romantic. She could see now: Elliot wasn't interested in her in *that* way – he was really only interested in her on a professional level, as an editor, and in securing himself the best deal. At best, he saw her as a friend, and as someone who could help him out. What had she been thinking, imagining that there could be more to it?

While Daisy disappeared in her own head for a while, Elliot excused himself and went to the toilet. The more Daisy mulled it over, the more stupid she began to feel for ever imagining he'd written about her in any way. All that time, she'd seemingly *found* things in his writing – noticed similarities – in the conversations, the people, and the ideas in his novel. But now, looking back, she felt so stupid and naïve. How self-absorbed of her to think that he might have used her as his inspiration, his muse! The sad truth of it was, Elliot was simply doing what all writers must do all the time – they take elements of their own experience, snippets of conversations with people, and they weave them into the wider world of their own imagination. So of course it didn't *mean* anything that there were parallels in Will's book. That's just what happens with writers. Silly Daisy, she told herself as she signed for the bill; always looking for hidden meanings in everything. She decided right then and there to stop being such a hopelessly romantic dreamer, and start living in the real world.

Just as she did, a huge unexpected dose of reality hit her, in the form of one name. Alice. Of course. Suddenly Daisy was overcome with reality. Alice was the girl Elliot had talked about, the ex-girlfriend he'd travelled around Europe with, which must have been around the time he was in Spain, and probably also when he'd started to write his novel. She'd thought nothing of it at the time, but he *had* had a funny look in his eyes when he'd talked about her. So there it was, then. Proof that if Elliot had ever had a muse, Alice was sure to be it. There was no mistaking it; suddenly everywhere she looked, all she could hear was nails shooting into coffins. Now she was worried – had Elliot ever picked up on a vibe from her that she might like him in a more-than-professional way? How wrong she'd been. How embarrassing. Could the ground swallow her up, please? Once again, that evil blurry dividing line between business and personal was causing her trouble; once again she'd got it so, so wrong.

Just then her phone began to vibrate in her bag, which was looped around her ankle in a bid towards theft-prevention. She retrieved her phone and saw that it was Miles calling again. She cancelled the call once more, feeling a twinge of guilt. Why was she putting him off so much, she wondered? A few months ago, she'd have had kittens with excitement over Miles being this attentive. Why was she being so difficult? Was she just an ungrateful person? Her phone buzzed with a text message: 'Daisy, Daisy, give me your answer, do . . . xxx'. Although a part of her was weeping inside at the cheesiness of his text, the new improved Daisy also decided that it was time to start being sensible, and that life was too short to be turning down perfectly good proposals from perfectly good men.

Here was a man who ticked all her boxes. Who was in love with her (allegedly) and who was willing to take care of her (well, he had his parents' money, which was more than he or she might ever end up with in publishing). So what was she waiting for? Not to mention that he really did deserve extra points for that whole gondola/surprise-turning-up-in-Venice business. And so it was, that there in the courtyard of Pizza Express in that particular corner of West London, Daisy decided once and for all that she would accept Miles Metcalfe's offer. She was just planning how to go about breaking this news to him, when Elliot finally returned from the gents.

He sat down and looked nervously at Daisy. He seemed different somehow, she thought as she looked at him. A little less comfortable, and much less self-assured. He opened up his pack of cigarettes and lit one. As he took a long drag, Daisy couldn't help thinking how attractive it made him look. She pushed this thought aside and asked him what was wrong. Instead of shrugging and denying anything was wrong as she'd expected him to, he began to talk.

'So, the thing is,' he said in an almost-whisper. 'I've got to tell you something . . . In case you didn't notice already. I really hope you won't sue me for libel, but it's just that well, some of the material is, well, ever so slightly, if you don't mind . . . a little bit . . . well, a lot . . . inspired by you.'

Daisy was silent again, listening, her breathing on hold. She listened as he explained how most of the sections she'd recognised (and many that she hadn't, too) in his novel were 'kind-of-well borrowed' from her.

'I know. It's OK, Ellie, I picked up on it – well, especially the postcard thing. As if I wouldn't have noticed that! Don't laugh at this, but it actually made me cry. It made me think about my family again – properly this time – and you know what? For the first time, I didn't mind. I actually liked it. It made me remember the good times. There weren't that many, but it made me remember the few that there were … which is better than nothing, I guess!'

'Well, thank you for understanding. I'm sorry that I didn't ask you first.'

'That's OK. I liked it. You can always ask me next time, I guess.'

'Next time?' He looked muddled.

'Well yes, if we sign you up, we won't want just one book. We'll need at least a couple in the future, so we can start' – Daisy made little speech marks with her fingers ironically – 'building you as a brand.'

'Wow. That rocks! I've got heaps of other book ideas, actually.'

Daisy laughed. 'Good! Well, maybe think on them a bit before you meet Belinda, in case she asks. It always helps to have a bit of magic up your sleeve where she's concerned.'

'Sure thing.' Elliot relaxed momentarily and smiled. But then his expression changed again, back to nervous and edgy. Daisy looked at his plate and noticed he'd hardly touched his food.

'Are you OK? You look like someone just walked over your grave. Oh! I've always wanted to say that!' Daisy gave an embarrassed laugh – she'd not meant to say that out loud. 'Anyway, is your food going down all right?'

Elliot smiled. 'The food's great. It's all great. The thing is … there's one other thing … and I've no idea, none at all, how to put this . . .' he stumbled, struggling around for the words. You see, it really is the most awkward, inconvenient thing. I don't want this to mess up our friendship, or our working relationship. And no matter what happens, you have to promise me that.'

'I promise.' Daisy prepared herself for the worst, her heart in her throat.

Elliot stubbed out his cigarette and lit another one immediately. 'The thing is this. I've just got to say something now, to get if off my chest . . .' he was almost shaking now. 'You see, from day one, Dais, I've found your interest in me, and my writing, really, really encouraging. And I'm so grateful . . .'

'It's nothing, really! I've enjoyed it too!' Daisy interrupted.

'Good . . . Um, please just let me get through what I need to say, OK?'

'Sorry. I'll shut up. You won't even know I'm here.' Daisy's stomach tensed up as she waited for him to continue.

'It's just that, well . . . all along the way, I've kind of been using you as my motivation, my inspiration. For want of a better word, my muse.'

Daisy couldn't stop her face from breaking into a smile as he went on.

'The trouble is, the more help you gave me with my writing . . . and the more I got to know you in real life . . . the two things converged to the point where I just couldn't ignore it any longer. And that's why I had to leave, because it was all getting out of hand in my head. So much so, that I couldn't write any more . . . I couldn't stop thinking about you, so I had to get away from you, from the reality that I couldn't have you. Whereas, in the book, in the imaginary world, I *could* have you, which was – well, pretty amazing. But now, sitting here in front of you, I have to tell you, as it's all still going round and round in my head. And if there's any chance – any remote chance – that you felt the same, then I just had to know.'

Daisy was bursting to speak again, but remembering her promise, she kept schtum.

'You see, I tried hard for today to just be about the book. The deal. The important stuff. I've tried to ignore my feelings on this, but it turns out I just can't. And the truth is, fiction aside, I'm nuts about you. Completely and utterly in love with you. There, I've said it. It doesn't matter what you say now – at least it's finally out there.' His face began to regain its usual colour, and he sat back in his seat, mildly, oddly triumphant.

Daisy didn't know what to say. Mentally and emotionally, she'd done so many turns in the road that she felt almost giddy.

Elliot clearly wasn't coping too well with the silence, and began talking again compulsively. 'I couldn't tell you this before, because – well, there were two things. One, I knew that you were in love with Miles – sorry, that you *are* in love with Miles. And two, I couldn't take the risk of you rejecting me and that being the end of the book. You see, I was afraid I couldn't write if you'd broken the spell . . . does that make any sense at all?'

'It makes perfect sense,' Daisy said quietly. Here was a man who, without even trying, was actually fulfilling and verifying even the most naive, idealistic projections from her overactive imagination. Forget Venice. Forget gondolas, and forget fancy engagement rings. Ever since she was a child she'd been daydreaming impossibly romantic scenarios like the one she had with Elliot. But never had anyone, especially a man, ever actually verified any of them the way he just had. To hell with the new, improved, pragmatic Daisy; the old romantic Daisy was back with a vengeance.

Elliot was staring at her expectantly. Another cigarette came out of the packet. Daisy still couldn't speak. She didn't want to get this wrong. Didn't want to rush it. This next sentence had to be perfectly formed, the pinnacle of the romantic climactic moment, beautifully articulate; shockingly poignant. She fought for the words, staring into Elliot's eyes as she did.

'Oh, for the love of Jesus . . .' was what came spewing out. Perfect. Austen would be proud, she thought. She tried earnestly to follow with something less idiotic. She thought hard. She leaned on to the table, and her head fell into her hands. 'Oh, Ellie.'

Suddenly they weren't alone. A waiter was standing by their table, asking if they needed anything else. In harmony they both shook their heads, and the waiter tiptoed away, sensing he'd intruded on to a delicate moment.

'The thing is,' began Daisy, 'your timing sort of sucks. I'm meant to be thinking about a proposal, and whether I'll accept or not. And about ten minutes ago, I'd made the firm decision to say yes.'

The shadow returned to Elliot's cheeks. He nodded. 'Of course. Miles. Stupid old me. But wait. You mean Mr "Can't commit, won't commit" himself has actually proposed? Well that's really something. Good for him.' Elliot broke off, smiled and nodded. Then the sadness returned to his eyes. 'Well, I'm very sorry – it's totally thoughtless of me to pick *now* to say all this. Of course, you're still in love with him. You've never *stopped* being in love with him. Still, I feel better now I've told you. Well, better in an I-feel-like-a-pig-shat-in-my-head kind of way, after seeing the look on your face . . .' he said, self-deprecatingly as ever.

'But, no . . . Elliot, it's really not that simple,' Daisy mumbled, her mind whirring with the strain of her dilemma. Then, after a few moments of indecision-fuelled paralysis, she realised that a) she had no idea what to say and b) this was not a choice she could make in a hurry, and therefore c) she should make the firm, immovable decision to postpone making a decision. She sighed.

'Listen, I should probably be getting back . . . I've got a meeting with Belinda.' It was a lie, and Elliot could tell.

'Sure. Well. Thanks for lunch. It's been great,' he said, attempting joviality. 'Lovely to see you. And Daisy, don't worry. I'll just try and snap out of it, it's fine.' He smiled meekly. 'Oh – and how rude of me – sorry. Congratulations to you both,' he raised his wine glass in the air, somehow pulling it off nobly rather than bitterly, and Daisy wanted to melt. This was all going so very wrong.

She wanted to shout, 'I do feel the same! I do, it's not that simple!' but her lips remained rigidly clamped together. She was scared. Ridiculously, rudely, she said nothing. And then, moments later, she said something that was even worse than nothing.

'So um . . . I've got to get back. I need to think . . . but listen, I'll be in touch.'

She walked away from the restaurant, shock and guilt digging holes in the pit of her stomach. *I'll be in touch*? What in the name of bejeesus was that all about? She felt the echo of the early days with Miles, when he would glibly say the same to her. She was mortified at her choice of Miles-isms, after Elliot had said all those lovely, wonderful things. In fairness, she'd only meant it in the sense that, as his editor, she'd speak to him soon. But she hoped she'd not offended him even more by saying it. Why did she seem so determined to mess this all up?

Everything But Nicotine

The next day was Friday. Marketing meeting day. But this was no ordinary meeting. Instead, it was Daisy's very first launch presentation. Now that a deal had quickly been agreed with Elliot; an agent secured and the book bought at record-breaking speed, it was now down to Daisy to convince the rest of Paddington that it was worth more than the paper it was printed on. The first time an editorial assistant presented a book to the team was always a slightly nerve-racking time – both for the assistant, and the team – (if the assistant turned out to be a Blushing Stutterer, as they occasionally did). Nevertheless, it was a necessary ritual which all editorial assistants had to endure before being allowed on the path towards being a commissioning editor, which one day, give or take five or ten years from now, Daisy hoped eventually to become. As a precaution against Blushing Stutterer-dom, Daisy had taken all of Belle's prescribed herbal potions that morning – Rescue Remedy, Kalms, camomile tea. She'd pretty much O.D.'d on everything but cigarettes. And yet as she sat there in the meeting room, she realised with growing anguish that none of these products were kicking in. Her nerves were already scratching at the ceiling. She bent down to examine her hands under the table. Yep, definite signs of shaking. Watching everyone pile into the room one by one, and noting the unfeasibly high turn out, Daisy had to restrain herself from leaping up and screaming, 'Why are none of you skiving today? Why did you all have to pick today as your day to be conscientious?' Bastards, her inner rage shouted. The only virtue of all this, if it can be called one, was that she'd been so distracted by finalising the book deal that she'd barely had a moment to think about her decision in the case of Metcalfe v. Thornton.

Luckily, Belinda was showing her rare sensitive side today, and wasn't going to make Daisy wait. As soon as everyone was settled, she got going.

'First up is a brand new book by a brand new author, found by none other than my assistant here. I'll let Daisy do the talking but the most exciting thing to say is that it's going to go down in history. It's Mercury's first ever slush-pile publication! Hurrah! Harry Potter eat your heart out.' There was a titter at this – the department was well adjusted to Belinda's inordinate levels of confidence. 'And you will all have heard about the delicious time the Americans have been having, with their own slush-pile baby Rawi Hage's *De Niro's Game*, which has been published to brilliant acclaim and excellent PR. So, over to you, Daisy. No pressure.'

The butterflies in her stomach were having a carnival after hearing Belinda's build-up, but somehow Daisy got it together, ignored the feeling of hotness on her cheeks, and began. 'Thanks. Well, as Belinda says, this is a first novel by a young author whom I've only met very recently.'

Daisy took a deep breath and began a quick summary of the plot, then described the genre and style of writing. She paused for breath. 'So . . . yes, . . . I do think it's a really interesting new voice. Think, a little bit *Instance of the Fingerpost*, and quite a lot *Shadow of the Wind*, and you're getting close. To begin with, it feels like quite a traditional romantic novel, but the novel's really about the mystery of how and why she disappears, and Ed's attempts to track her down. That's the point at which it gets really exciting and gripping . . . so I think there's something in it for a lot of people. Quite a broad target audience, I'd say . . . not just men . . .' Daisy stopped, feeling herself blush, and wishing the spotlight could move away from her just for a bit. 'Amelie's read it too, haven't you?' She stared at Amelie pleadingly.

Amelie sparked up and nodded. 'Oh yes, I really liked it. It's quite a complex idea, but he really pulls it off. Also, I don't know who's read it, but another great comparison is Michael Cox's *The Meaning of Night*.'

Daisy smiled with colossal relief as much of the room began to nod and make noises about wanting a copy of the manuscript to read when it was ready.

'So what's he like?' asked Heidi, looking pointedly at Daisy. 'This Will character. I mean, how promotable is he?'

'Yes – will he do whatever PR we need him to do?' fired Ronald.

'Oh yes. Absolutely,' Daisy shot back quickly. 'He'll be willing to do anything. He's very amenable. And he's really intelligent, lovely . . . and well, really friendly and approachable . . .' she stammered, feeling the heat return to her cheeks.

'But what does he look like?' asked Amelie, staring

meaningfully at Daisy. 'I mean, how old is he? Is he good-looking?'

Daisy narrowed her eyes at Amelie, knowing full well what she was up to.

'Well, like I said, he's a very nice chap. I guess he's about twenty-eight? But I'd say he doesn't look a day older than twenty-four. He's er, reasonable height, dark hair, tanned.' Daisy could feel herself really going red now, and was fast realising that the only way out of this awkward situation would be to use humour as a defence mechanism. 'And, er, he's got blue eyes, freckles, and he has a little dimple on his right cheek. Is that enough information about his looks?' She looked sternly at Heidi and Amelie.

'Yes, that's great. I just needed a picture of just how promotable he is, that's all.' Heidi grinned, pretending to jot down some notes on to her pad. She (and possibly everyone else in the room) could see quite clearly from Daisy's eyes how deep her admiration for the author ran – both on and off the page.

24

One Silly Man

Daisy was well and truly treadmilled. It was Monday now, and for the fifth day in a row, she was dragging her weary and achy bones back from the gym. She hated herself for it, but even though she'd thought of little else all weekend, she still hadn't managed to make a choice between Miles and Elliot, and was instead guilty of drowning out her indecision with obsessive over-exercising and hyperactive Extreme Cleaning sessions. As she walked into the flat and went to collapse on the sofa, mentally preparing herself for a detailed cleaning of the cracks in the kitchen tiles with an old toothbrush, she realised that something was amiss. The flat was empty and calm. This could only mean one thing – no Belle. She began to feel worried – how could there still be no sign of her? It was Monday night, and the music festival had finished yesterday – why had she still not returned from Herefordshire? Keep calm, Daisy chanted to herself. The fact that Belle's mobile was turned off was simply down to the fact that she was out of a) signal, b) battery or c) it had been stolen; and most *definitely* not because she'd been d) kidnapped, e) drugged, f) raped, g) left to die in some ditch covered in luminous body paint.

She was just going through this rationale and toying with the idea of formulating a list to calm herself down, when she turned back to the list she'd started making on the tube home. Having drawn a line down the centre of a page in her newly bought Moleskine notebook, she'd started comparing and contrasting the pros and cons in the case of Metcalfe v. Thornton – her end goal being to finally and wholeheartedly determine which one to choose. She was just reviewing her notes so far when she heard a key in the lock.

'Daisy doll! Are you in?' Belle shrieked at the top of her voice.

'Yes yes! I'm in here! Well, thank God you're OK!'

Belle came bounding into the lounge just in time to see Daisy slam shut the Miles v. Elliot chart and clasp it tightly to her chest.

'Where the hell have you been?!' hollered Daisy, trying to cause a diversion, but it was too late. The chart had been clocked.

'What, in the name of CRAP, is that?' shrieked Belle, horrified. She rugby tackled Daisy for it, won easily, and opened it. Shuddering, and looking at her sister with astonishment, Belle began to read some of the lists aloud.

'Oh my God. This is appalling! Just because you're so *ludicrously organised* in every other sphere of your life, that's no excuse for applying such freakish behaviour to your love life!'

Seeing Daisy's pained expression, Belle sat down on the sofa and draped an arm around her. Suddenly Daisy couldn't help it. Her lip quivered, she looked confusedly at her sister, and burst into convulsive, apologetic sobs.

'Sweetie,' Belle began a little more calmly, 'if you honestly think you can solve your love life by making neatly drawn, pretty lists, then you really do need help. I mean, what were you going to do next? Put the findings into an Excel spreadsheet? Press a few buttons to make it calculate the formula? Hon. Your love life IS NOT AN EXCEL SPREADSHEET! It's in a whole other sphere.' She put her hand on the left-hand side of her chest. 'All you can really do is follow what's in here.'

Daisy nodded defeatedly. 'I know, I know. You're right. I'm just having trouble with hearing what's *in* there.'

'But what's happened to spur all this mental craziness on, anyway?'

Belle curled up on the sofa next to Daisy as she told her all that had happened in her absence, focusing mainly on the lunch with Elliot last Thursday.

'Well, of course!' Belle chuckled at the end of Daisy's story.

'What do you mean, "of course"?' Daisy frowned.

'I mean, of course little Elliot's in love with you! It was soooo obvious.'

'It was?' Daisy moved away from Belle in genuine astonishment.

'Well of course.'

'Stop saying that! Smug witch! Why didn't you *tell* me? Anyway, why's it soooooo obvious?'

'Well. I mean, for one thing, he stopped returning any of my calls and texts.' Belle grinned. 'And, at the risk of sounding like an arsehole, that's never happened to me before.' Daisy groaned and shook her head at Belle's overconfidence.

'Anyway, I knew I smelt a rat then, but I didn't dare say anything, since you were so besotted with arse-face.'

Daisy winced. 'Please don't call him that. He's very romantic. And he's trying hard.'

'In a superficial, obvious way, yes, I suppose he is. Anyway, if you want my money's worth, I know which one you're really in love with. It's obvious from the way you talk about him.'

Daisy looked expectantly at her sister. 'Well then, pray tell me!'

'It's little Elliot.'

'It is?'

'Of course. But I can't tell you that. Only you can really figure that out.'

'Uh! You're no use! And besides, Elliot's not even short! Stop calling him little!'

'Sorry. I just think of him as sweet, and therefore little. Anyway, in my humble opinion, Daisy doze-fest, this is how I see it.' Belle jumped off the bed, then proceeded to narrate her own forecast of things, in the style of a weatherman. Daisy looked on, wide-eyed. 'You see, I think you *think* you're in love with Miles, because you feel sorry for the history of it all. And because you always have been, until now. And because, on paper, I'll bet he looks miles – *sorry* – loads better than wee Elliot. But what use is paper? This is real life, Daisy, not some silly romantic novel.'

Daisy could feel her eyes welling up. 'I know, I know I'm being pathetic. But I just can't decide! Would you like some tea?' she asked, wishing this conversation would end, and getting up off the sofa and heading towards the kitchen. Belle followed her, picking chunks of grass out of her hair with every step she took, leaving a trail all over the floor behind her.

'Hey, I've just realised!' Daisy exclaimed, 'you still haven't told me where you've been! I was starting to think you were dead!' Daisy switched on the kettle.

Belle nodded, and her expression was suddenly serious. 'OK. Now that we've dealt with you – momentarily – I'm going to tell you a story, and you have to promise me that, once I start, you won't interrupt?' she said efficiently, getting to business.

'Of course.'

'It's just too good a story. It's just too good!' she squealed. She jumped up, and began jogging around the room, as she talked. Daisy did as she was told. She busied herself making the tea, and didn't speak until the very end.

'Right. So I'm queuing up for one of the hideous, godforsaken hell-hole Portaloos at the festival, OK? And the queue's massive, so I start going over a song in my head while I'm waiting. One of those new ones that I've written. And there's quite a fit bloke in a silly hat standing near me in the next queue along. Anyway, eventually it's my turn to go into the bog. So I go in, holding my nose, preparing for the worst, and then I see it's not that bad. For once I think some poor bastard's actually cleaned it. So anyway, I'm in the loo, and I start singing. I start right from the beginning, on that new verse I just wrote. And you know what it's like in the loo sometimes, you lose yourself a bit in all the echoes and weird sort of acoustics. And so I carry on singing, getting louder and louder, really put my heart into it like, thinking, I don't sound half bad, do I? And then my time's up in there, and I draw to a close

– on the song, like. I finish off, try and figure out the flush thing and as is always the way in those loos, I can't get it to work, so then I just rinse my hands with that MINGING hand cleanser disinfectant stuff as the tap's buggered as usual – so anyway, that's me done and I shut up the loo, head out, and I don't realise how long I've been in there because when I get out, I'm like face to face with this tall, gorgeous guy with glasses and a funky hat – and I'm thinking, he's rather nice – and he goes to me, "Finally! I was waiting for you!" And I look at him like he's a raving loony, and he goes, "It's OK – I'm not a raving loony, but just come with me a second." So I follow him for a second, just to a nearby tree, away from all the hordes of loo-goers, where we stop, and he turns to me and goes, deadpan, I'm not kidding, like! He goes to me, "Are you signed?" And I sort of have to do a double-take with my ears, until I realise what he's on about. He's like, "Here's my card. You've got just the right sound for what I'm looking for. You've got a beautiful voice. And whose song is that? It was mint." I'm just stood there thinking, "Who says mint in this day and age?", but obviously I don't say that – when the real importance of what he's saying sinks in, and I of course tell him that it was my song, and that yes, I'm seriously in need of a good manager and yeah, let's definitely meet up when we're back in London! Isn't that just the COOLEST thing you ever heard?' Belle finally stopped for breath.

'That really is amazing! Well done! I'm so chuffed for you!' Daisy clapped her hands, did a mini jump up and down, and hugged her sister.

'And that's not all . . .' Belle grinned – 'rather than leave it all vague, we actually arranged it for tomorrow – I'm going there, to his studio, in the morning! And don't worry, I've checked him out, it's all legit. He works at a really reputable label. So we'll see, huh?!'

'Brilliant, Belle! Well done!' Daisy poured out the tea, feeling heartily relieved at all this diversion from the Miles v. Elliot situation.

As though she'd read her mind, Belle spoke. 'So, Little Miss Ludicrous Love Life. Have you made up your mind yet?'

Daisy sighed. Nice while it lasted. 'It's only been a few minutes!'

'Wrong! It's been about twelve days since Miles proposed!'

'Ummmm ... OK ... Well, no, I haven't decided yet. And he's been away, too. So some of those days don't really count. But the good thing to come out of this is that I *have* been to the gym six times this week to take my mind off it, and to help me think.'

'No wonder there's nothing left of you! I can't believe you!' Belle exclaimed, looking around the kitchen in horror. 'And the flat is looking INSANELY clean, what have you been doing to it?' Belle pointed to the recycling box, where there were about five empty bottles of cleaning fluids waiting for collection. She put her hand on Daisy's head condescendingly, 'Daisy dear – I mean, doesn't the fact that you've left Miles's proposal hanging in limbo *all this time* tell you something? That you're not even worried that his offer might expire, and that one day he'll take his offer away? Doesn't the fact that you've not got back to him yet make you see, that you're not that bothered any more?'

Daisy looked frightened at what Belle was implying. 'Mmmmm. Maybe you're right. But maybe I'm not bothered enough about either of them. Maybe I'll just leave them both be. Yes! That's the answer.'

Belle groaned. 'I'm going to have a shower. You're in luck. I've not washed in four days. I stink to high heaven, so I may be some time. But when I re-emerge from said shower, I want a proper answer from you.'

Daisy recoiled in fear. 'No, please don't make me! It's just too hard!' Daisy slumped down at the kitchen table, exasperated and fraught with self-pity.

'No it's not,' Belle stated simply. 'Hard is having to trek three miles through jungle and marshes and then bring back enough clean water for your village to drink. Hard is a big cancerous cyst on your boob. Hard is not being able to see. Try a little perspective, Daisy. They're *just* men. And they're *both* silly. But the fact is, there's only room in there for one silly man,' she said, pointing to the left of Daisy's chest. 'You just need to figure out which.'

I'll Be in Touch

Much to Belle's fury, Daisy still wasn't able to give her an answer, even when two hours later she emerged squeaky clean from the bathroom. Never mind her sister, Daisy was driving herself mad with the dilemma. She couldn't eat, couldn't sleep, couldn't concentrate on anything. In desperation, she tried rolling dice. Spinning her phone around like a wheel. Tossing a coin. But no matter the outcome, she never felt satisfied with the answer. She'd realised – no amount of lists and grids were going to help. In her heart, she just wasn't comfortable leaving such an important decision down to the randomness of chance. No, she needed one more thing to swing the balance.

The next morning she rose from yet another night of manic tossing and turning and maddening, self-perpetuating indecision. As soon as she arrived at work, insomnia personified, she was called into Belinda's office for an emergency meeting.

Returning from there half an hour later, sporting a big smile on her face and much more colour in her cheeks, she went straight to her email. Intending to send out lots of perky, victorious emails to everyone she could think of, she stopped still, seeing an email in her inbox from Elliot. Technically speaking it was from Will, from his fictional Hotmail account. Reading it through in a flash, she saw instantly that it was most unlike his other emails. It was surprisingly short, blunt and formal, unlike his usual style.

Date: Monday 16 October 2006 23.58
Sender: justwilliam26@hotmail.co.uk
To: Daisy.Allen@paddingtonpress.com

D,

Here's the final draft. Worked all weekend on your notes – think you'll find it better now. Thanks.
E/W

She printed off the new draft straight away and began to read, red pen in hand. As far as she could see, she thought, flicking through slowly, everything seemed to be in order. He'd covered all of hers, and Belinda's, points, and all seemed peachy enough. An hour later, she was just about to send the document off to the freelancer to be copy-edited, when the fan on her desk became slightly too enthusiastic, causing some sheets to slide off the pile towards the floor. She bent down to retrieve the few loose pages, and was just returning them to the pile when she noticed something that made her heart grind to a halt.

There, on page five of the prelims, after the biog and the title pages, was something which made her eyes well up with tears. There was, after all, one change that stood out far more than any other. There, on the centre of the page, where previously it had said 'Dedication TBC', it now read in big bold letters, **'FOR DAISY'**.

Exactly one minute earlier, Whilhelmina, workie of the week – who had been sitting reading *Publishing News* for the last three hours, managed to summon up the courage to ask for some work. She took a deep breath, walked quietly up to Daisy's desk and hovered for a moment, while Daisy fussed with some papers on the floor, and sat staring at one of the pages for an unduly long time. Whilhelmina waited patiently for a whole minute more, before finally daring to speak.

'Sorry. Sorry – Hi, it's Whilhelmina?'

Daisy, still crouching on the floor, looked up from the page, and stared vacantly at this young workie. 'Hello . . .?'

'Um . . .' Whilhelmina stammered, 'I just wondered, I've got nothing to do, so – if it's not too much trouble – might you have any jobs that I can help you with? Anything at all?'

'Gosh, sorry. Yes. Bear with me.' Daisy smiled and stood up, almost banging her head on the desk as she did. Putting the papers down, she stood thinking for a moment. Then, repeating the word 'anything?' she opened her handbag and dug around for a few seconds before pulling out a small navy-blue velvet box, about big enough for a ring. She looked at it for a few seconds, invested all her willpower in not opening it for a poignant parting look, and handed it to the girl.

Whilhelmina looked very confused. 'Sorry . . . What is it you want me to do exactly?'

'It's a bit of a strange job but it won't take long,' Daisy said, flapping about, looking for a compliment slip. 'I'd like you to please have this sent, by very special delivery, back to its owner.'

The girl nodded, as Daisy scribbled down the address of Miles's Hoxton loft conversion. Then she paused for a few moments to think.

Dearest Miles,

I'm very sorry. I've thought about this long and hard. I really, really have. I'm sorry. Don't hate me. I hope we can be friends again one day.

I'll be in touch,

Daisy x

In a final display of eccentricity, Daisy blew a nostalgic kiss to the note, she before handing it, the ring and the address, to the befuddled workie.

'Thanks ever so much, Whilhelmina. I'll think of something meatier for you to do this afternoon, OK? I'll come and grab you later . . .'

Whilhelmina smiled, perhaps relieved that her placement was finally getting a little more eventful.

Daisy, meanwhile, leapt back to her PC and bashed out an email, her fingers jittery and jumpy with trying to type at breakneck speed.

Date: Tuesday 17 October 2006 11.46
Sender: Daisy.Allen@paddingtonpress.com
To: justwilliam26@hotmail.co.uk
CC: elliotthornton@yahoo.co.uk

Subject: It's perfect . . .

Dearest Williot,

Thanks very much for your final draft which has now gone off to the copy editor. There are one or two other things I've been thinking about quite a lot. I've had this one idea, too, which I'd really love to run past you. (Both of you.)

Let's meet up soon. Are you free tonight, even? It would be great to see you. Pizza Express, or somewhere more imaginative? Your choice. I'm done with choices.

D xxx

Daisy Allen
Assistant Editor
Paddington Press

p.s. I'll also be celebrating. In case you didn't get the oh-so subtle hint (see above), am being promoted – hurrah! It basically means the word 'assistant' moves from the end of my job title, to the beginning. I know. Check me out. But in real terms it's good. I get a tiny bit more money, a teeny bit more respect from B and H, and a whole lot more fun to be had with non-slushy submissions. Nothing against the slush pile, you understand . . . I mean, occasionally people have struck gold there – but, as you know, that only happens in the rarest cases these days. x

26

Lost and Found

At exactly five twenty-eight, Daisy was standing outside Pizza Express, her stomach wretched with nerves. She was back in her rightful position as early, but she was starting to doubt its virtues. She now saw the attraction of being a lategoer – you never had to experience this, the odd sensation of waiting and feeling like a mug, thinking of all the other jobs you could've squeezed into this window of dead time. Of watch-watching, of going over the time and place arrangements in your head. Of people walking past you and clearly assuming you've been stood up. Of checking the people walking past you aren't the people you're waiting for. Of feeling sick with nerves, and of thinking of how much more make-up and hair tending-to time there could have been had you not left so early. Daisy looked at her watch, and then her mobile, just to be sure. Nope, as far as she could tell, time had stopped.

She looked down at the road, at the leaves on the pavement which were an autumnal mix of burnt oranges and golden browns. She stared back towards the Mercury building, and at the new bridge, which after four months of construction was finally almost built. As she stared in that direction, she saw an Elliot-shaped-figure moving towards her. Her heart in her throat, she stood waiting patiently for him to arrive, wondering at which stage she should be shouting hello, or perhaps giving a casual wave. Instead, she remained still as a rock, her arms frozen by her side, a smile sewn on to her face until suddenly there he was, a few inches away, right there in front of her. Gorgeous, unshaven and smiling apprehensively back at her.

'Hi. So, here we are again,' he said, nervously shifting his feet.

'Yes. Hello.' She wanted to pounce on him then and there, cover him in kisses, tell him that she loved the book, and that she was falling completely in love with him. Instead, she extended a limp, 'Um, it's nice to see you.'

Elliot nodded cautiously. 'Indeed. It's nice to see you too. So . . . what's the big idea?'

He hovered next to her. They were standing beside the brick wall by the restaurant. Neither one of them seemed to want to go in. An awkward silence ensued while in her head, Daisy tested out all the thoughtful things she was going to say, one by one. She stared mutely at Elliot as she rehearsed the clever, witty lines she'd prepared, all of them now sounding silly and forced in the light of day.

'So,' Elliot began, in an effort to fill the silence, and sensing that Daisy was a million miles away, 'the book's gone off to be copy-edited now, has it? That's exciting. Did I mention it's nice to see you? Well, it is. You're looking really well. What have you been up to? By the way, if I forget to tell you later, thanks for everythi—

His last words were lost as Daisy silenced him with a kiss. Closing her eyes, she felt his arms tighten around her as they kissed more deeply. She wrapped her arms around him, feeling his warmth against her. When after some time they pulled apart, Daisy let out a little laugh.

'Um, I'm sorry . . . that was the thing I was trying to tell you about.'

'I'm glad. I like it. A lot.' Elliot smiled back, and leaned towards Daisy, his eyes misty with affection. He kissed her again, this time more urgently. He folded her into his arms and they stood holding each other for a while. Elliot was the first to pull away. He lifted her face to his, and stared into her eyes.

'Daisy, can I ask you a question?'

She nodded expectantly, curiously. He took her hand in his.

'Can we – not go to Pizza Express again? I think I'm kind of bored with it.'

Daisy laughed, relieved that the question wasn't somehow more serious.

'That's a very good point.' Then she looked quizzically at Elliot and thought for a moment. 'Actually, there's a lovely little tapas place down in Westbourne Park – we could give that a whirl?'

Nine Months Later

Daisy put down the Friday edition of the *Independent Arts and Books Review* and smiled. Although there were only a couple of other people in this café on Ladbroke Grove, she was trying to stop herself from running around the room, waving the pages in front of them like a madwoman, shouting, 'Look! That's my first book in print there! See that? I edited that, I did!'

Of course, she didn't. Of course, she sat quietly and remained poised, sipping her cappuccino, dressed in a purple smock dress, brown ballet pumps and matching brown beret. Besides, she reasoned, chances were that none of the people in the café would have understood the significance of having your first commissioned novel finally in print. Nor the incomparable thrill at seeing its author hailed by the *Independent* as 'an assured debut novelist, with more than a light touch of *duende* in his quill'. Instead of running around the room, Daisy contented herself with opening up the paper again to reread the glowing review, and gushing quietly to herself over the exquisite cover design that was pictured next to the column. She studied the stunning illustration of the

Spanish flamenco dancer, with her castanets and luminous ruffled skirt. She smiled with satisfaction at how well *Half A World Away* had turned out.

Daisy stirred her coffee and slurped at the flecks of chocolate on top of the foam. A bell rang. She looked up to see Elliot coming through the café door. Wearing faded blue jeans, a creased Diesel T-shirt and black flip flops, he was carrying a big black rucksack over his shoulder, a thick wad of A4 notes in his arms, and a warm grin on his face.

He waved to Daisy and crossed the room towards her. They kissed hello, and she handed him the review. 'Hurrah – another goodie.' He took the paper and put it to one side. 'Lovely, thank you. I'll take your word for it. So how was work?'

'Oh you know. Same old. Lots of people who can't write and think they can. More importantly – how's the baby?'

Elliot grinned, and held up a big wodge of papers in his hand. 'Great. Made lots of headway today. I think you're really going to like it.'

Acknowledgements

Thanks to all at Random House Publishers . . . although saying that, I should quickly add that 'all characters are purely fictitious and any resemblance purely coincidental', etc . . . especially the food in the canteen . . . Maura's real-life cooking was/is far nicer than the fare served up in this book. A special mention to Sarahs Collett and Morris, Sophie Arnold, Claire Morrison, Louisa Gibbs, Alex Kirby, and all the lovely real-life park dwellers. Big thanks to all at 26 – particularly Rishi Dastidar, Neil Taylor, John Simmons and the Dark Angels of Aracena, for ongoing *duende*. Thanks to Lucy Luck and all at Headline. Thanks to David Lodge, and to Don Hughes. Thanks to Phillipa Ashley, and thanks to Rob Williams. And thanks (for want of a better place) to the following people for help bringing Amelie to the screen . . . the fabulous Sarah Smart, Stephen Pipe, Another Film Company, and Darren Rackham. Cheers to Lee Figueira for helping Amelie find her voice on the tinterweb at myspace.com/steponitcupid. Once again über-thanks to all at AIS . . . especially Steve, Anna, Sarah and Gary, for on-going generosity and Bellinis. Thanks to my lovely Mum, for proofreading prowess and saint-like patience. Hearty thanks to Lauren, Claire and Clare, Hannah, Katie and Charlotte Smith (FFL). Special thanks to the wonderful Camilla, Emil, Danny, Julie, Sarah, Dad and Evie. And last but not least, thank you to the hilarious and hugely talented Guy Lewis, for bringing Elliot to life both on and off the page.

You can buy any of these other **Little Black Dress** titles from your bookshop or *direct from the publisher*.

Step on it, Cupid	Lorelei Mathias	£3.99
The Mens Guide to the Women's Bathroom	Jo Barrett	£3.99
I Take This Man	Valerie Frankel	£3.99
How to Sleep with a Movie Star	Kristin Harmel	£3.99
Pick Me Up	Zoë Rice	£3.99
The Balance Thing	Margaret Dumas	£3.99
The Kept Woman	Susan Donovan	£3.99
I'm in No Mood for Love	Rachel Gibson	£3.99
Sex, Lies and Online Dating	Rachel Gibson	£3.99
Daisy's Back in Town	Rachel Gibson	£3.99
Sprit Willing, Flesh Weak	Julie Cohen	£3.99
Blue Christmas	Mary-Kay Andrews	£3.99
The Bachelorette Party	Karen McCullah Lutz	£3.99
My Three Husbands	Swan Adamson	£3.99
He Loves Lucy	Susan Donovan	£3.99
Mounting Desire	Nina Killham	£3.99
She'll Take It	Mary Carter	£3.99
Decent Exposure	Phillipa Ashley	£3.99